KNOWN THREAT

By the Author

Actual Stop

Worthy of Trust and Confidence

Known Threat

Visit us at www.boldstrokesbooks.com

KNOWN THREAT

by

Kara A. McLeod

2018

KNOWN THREAT

ISBN 13: 978-1-63555-132-7

This Trade Paperback Original Is Published By
Bold Strokes Books, Inc.
P.O. Box 249
Valley Falls, NY 12185

First Edition: January 2018

Credits
Editor: Shelley Thrasher
Production Design: Stacia Seaman
Cover Design by Melody Pond

Acknowledgments

Since I was out of the country when I was supposed to be writing the acknowledgements for the last book, *Worthy of Trust and Confidence*, and clearly couldn't tear myself away from what I was doing long enough to remember that I had responsibilities to attend to, please accept my sincerest apologies and consider the following as intended to include my thoughts and appreciation on that time as well.

In the awards show currently taking place in my head as I type, I would like to award the not-so-coveted Golden Guns and accompanying bulletproof vests to the following superstars, all of whom still have not given in to what I'm sure are nearly insurmountable urges to strangle me…or at least tell me to shut the hell up:

The Golden Gun for Best Publisher: Radclyffe—Sincerest gratitude for everything you've done for me over the years. If I can ever get my hands on an actual Kevlar vest without getting myself arrested, consider it yours.

The Golden Gun for Best Editor and Nicest "What the hell are you doing?" Email: Shelley—You haven't stabbed me with a pen or smacked me with a computer yet, and while I wouldn't blame you for assuming a new identity to avoid future volumes, I hope you stick with me until the end. I can't promise it'll get better, or that you'll want to roll your eyes at me less, but I'd appreciate it all the same.

The Golden Gun for Best Hetero-Soul-Mate: SASD—Congratulations on you-know-what! In celebration, I've included even more derivatives of your favorite words! Yes, this was a good enough reason. Love you to bits!

The Golden Gun for Best UNGA Survivor: Thing One—May this past UNGA truly have been your last. Best of luck in the next chapter of your life.

The Golden Gun for Best Dad: Mine!—What else can I say besides "Thank you"?

The Golden Gun for Most Gracious Alligator: Glocamorra—I apologize that you haven't appeared in the past two books. I'll try to squeeze you in someplace else in future tomes, I promise. Thank you once again for not eating me.

For Riley.

The most amazing champion, fan, and partner
a girl could ever hope for.

Neither words, nor drawings, nor interpretive dances
could ever adequately express what your support truly means to me.

Thank you from the bottom of my overflowing heart!

CHAPTER ONE

*B*ang-bang-bang-bang!
 The insistent pounding on my hotel room door was loud enough that it easily broke through the din of the hairdryer, which I turned off with a frown. A glance at my watch confirmed it was way too early for someone to be looking for me. I sighed and set the hairdryer on the bathroom counter as I moved to answer the summons.

"Coming," my sister Rory called and flashed me a gleeful grin as she breezed by the bathroom and reached for the door. She was already decked out in her running gear, a dark-blue United States Secret Service baseball cap on her head, her perfectly coiffed mane of blond hair tamed into a ponytail sticking out the back. It was a good thing at least one of us was a morning person. My answer to that beckoning would definitely have been less chipper.

Rory opened the door and turned the full force of her cheerful—if not slightly bewildered—smile on the man lurking in the hallway.

Marcus Cressap, tall and lanky with jet-black hair and big, brown eyes, blinked at my sister from behind his rimless glasses and flinched. He fidgeted a bit, fiddling with the zipper on his lightweight windbreaker, and chewed on his lower lip. He appeared wan in the unflattering light of the hotel hallway, and that was saying something, considering he was probably the palest person I'd ever met. And if I'm the one throwing that term around, you know it's true. I'm not exactly infused with color myself.

"Hey, Ryan," Marcus said, almost shyly. He ducked his head and peered at Rory from underneath his thick, dark eyelashes.

"It's Rory, actually." My sister stuck out a hand in greeting.

Marcus blinked at her, obviously lost. I debated leaving him to puzzle the situation out on his own, but that might take a while, which'd prolong his presence in my doorway. Best to help him along, so I could get back to my morning routine. I did have places to be and things to do.

I stepped out of the bathroom and into the cramped little hotel-room hallway behind my sister and watched, thoroughly amused, as Marcus's eyes darted back and forth between the two of us. I could see him mentally connecting the dots.

"Hey, Marcus."

"Ryan?"

"Yup. I see you've met my sister, Rory."

"Uh. Yeah." He blinked again, his eyes continuing to flicker back and forth. "I didn't know you had a twin."

"I try to keep that quiet. Black sheep of the family and all that."

Rory's only reply was a sharp elbow to my ribs.

"So, what can we do for you, Marcus?"

His cheeks flushed, and he dropped his eyes. His body language screamed that he wasn't looking forward to answering my question.

I barely managed to rein in my eye roll and sigh of exasperation. He didn't need to say anything. In that moment, as I took in how uncomfortable he was, I knew why he was there. The rest of the group—an interesting conglomeration of agents out of the New York Field Office—was ready to go and wanted me to hurry the hell up. They'd sent poor Marcus because he had a huge crush on me—a fact everyone in the entire office knew about—and they were banking that I wouldn't tear his head off when he came to rush me along. They were right about one thing at least. If any of the rest of them had been on the other side of that door, my reaction would've been considerably more caustic than the "Tell them I'll be right down" I mumbled at Marcus just now.

Marcus nodded once and smiled, that faint blush still coloring his cheeks as he shoved his hands into his pockets and ambled away. I shut the door to my suite with deliberate gentleness and allowed my eyes free rein to express their frustration as soon as my sister and I were alone. Rory chuckled and moved back into the heart of the room to fetch her iPod. I wrinkled my nose in disgust and went back to the bathroom to pull my still-damp hair into a ponytail and brush my teeth. What a way to start a morning.

When we finally appeared downstairs, all of the guys were standing in the parking lot next to their cars, practically vibrating with barely contained energy. It didn't appear to be your garden-variety anxiety over being late—which we weren't. Nor was it as simple as the desire to get on the road. No, they were up to something. The question was what?

"Hey, guys," I called to the group as we approached, taking in their postures and their facial expressions as I tried to divine what was going on. Some of them appeared uneasy, others secretive, still others almost smug. What the hell?

A chorus of hellos from everyone greeted us as people immediately started breaking into smaller groups and getting into nearby vehicles. I gaped at them before latching onto Rico Corazon's arm as he tried to scoot by me. Another quick glance at him confirmed he was one of the uneasy ones.

"Where's the rest of the girls' team?" I asked him.

"Uh…I think they left already. They said they'd see you there."

"They left without me?"

"Yeah. I guess."

"What's going on, Rico?" This wasn't like him. Normally, he was one of my favorite people to bicker with, and he lunged into that activity with an enthusiasm most people usually reserved for roller coasters or the Super Bowl. Today, however, it was a colossal effort to get him to utter a word.

As if in response to my silent accusation, Rico averted his dark eyes and dug into the pocket of his pullover sweatshirt for the keys to his Volvo. He didn't reply.

"Rico." As I continued to glare at him, something struck me, and I whirled back to where the rest of the guys were mounting up to take off to confirm my suspicions.

The guys all wore identical black running shorts underneath non-matching long-sleeved sweatshirts, windbreakers, or jackets. But what I could see of their shirts underneath their cover-ups indicated they might be wearing matching gray T-shirts as well.

I glanced down at my own outfit of navy-blue lightweight capri pants and a short-sleeved white tee and frowned. It was chilly, sure, but

I didn't think it was *that* cold out. Why were the guys all dressed like it was freezing? And had there been some sort of discussion regarding a team uniform I hadn't been privy to?

I hopped into the front passenger seat of Rico's car and turned the radio off, twisting myself so I was facing him head-on. Rory, who'd jumped into the backseat just behind Rico, wisely busied herself with some mysterious task on her phone.

"Just tell me," I said, feeling a flutter in the pit of my stomach at his facial expression.

Rico Corazon was an old friend. We'd known each other for years and had been partners on countless undercover operations during which our agency had been attempting to take down a nightclub owner who'd been running a counterfeit-currency plant. Rico and I apparently looked good together, so we'd posed as a couple lots of times and had ended up becoming pretty good buddies. It's hard to spend that much time pretending to like someone without it actually happening on some level.

And Rico was a great guy. Typically, I enjoyed his sparkling wit, easy smile, and razor-sharp sense of humor. Rare were the days I'd seen Rico that he didn't have a grin on his handsome face. The fact that today was one of those struck discordant pangs of unease deep inside me.

My heart whizzed inside my chest like a cartoon Tasmanian Devil, and I clamped my hand down on my thigh. "Oh, my God. Is it Paige?" I wanted to know. Paige was Rico's wife. I knew her almost as well as I knew him, and the idea of something happening to her was making me sick to my stomach. "Is she okay?"

Something flickered in Rico's eyes as he finally dared to look at me. Guilt? Regret? It was difficult for me to decipher.

"Paige is fine," he said, letting slip a small sigh and redirecting his attention back out the windshield.

The wave of relief that crashed over me at his words quickly ebbed, replaced by a flood of annoyance and a drop of something not unlike fear. "Rico, what the hell is going on?" He refused to answer me, and I growled in frustration. "I swear to God, if you don't tell me why everyone's acting so weird, I'll get out of this car and scour the side of the road for a stick to beat it out of you with."

Ignoring my sister's guffaw, I folded my arms across my chest and glared at him, rigid with tension. An eternity passed before Rico finally spoke, and when he did, his words made less than no sense to me.

"The backseat," he said, jerking his head in indication.

I glanced over my shoulder and then back at him. "Yup. There it is."

Rico rolled his eyes, and the corners of his mouth twitched. "The bag on the backseat."

I twisted around to look at Rory, who located the parcel he was talking about and handed it up to me. When he didn't say anything further, I opened it and reached inside. It contained a gray tank top and a pair of black running shorts.

"Are these for me?" I asked, unfolding the shirt to reveal the New York Field Office logo screen-printed in black letters on the left breast.

Rico nodded, but his eyes were cloudy, and his grip on the steering wheel was tight enough to make his knuckles white. His jaw was clenched as well, if the subtle cord of muscle standing out on it was any clue.

"Thanks," I said. "That was really nice."

"Turn it around," Rico all but hissed. I'd picked up that he was conflicted about something. This obvious anger was new.

Slowly, I flipped the garment over and held it up so I could get the full effect of the logo on the back. I was struck dumb.

In bold, black script painted low across the shoulder blades were the words, "Faster than a speeding…" Under the words in two spots, one about a hand's width to the right of center and one slightly lower, were what appeared to be realistic-looking ragged, black bullet holes. I stared at the tank top for a moment longer as it suddenly occurred to me my shoulders would be bare if I donned it. The implications of that realization hit me with all the subtlety of a softball to the back of the head.

Dumbly, I glanced at Rico for an explanation, but none appeared to be forthcoming. With a mounting sense of dread, I removed the shorts from the bag and inspected them. Sure enough, on the back right side, approximately two inches below the elastic waistband was a silver "bullet hole."

I heard Rory gasp as I shifted my gaze back and forth from the shorts to the shirt for a second. Then I threw my head back and laughed. Whether I was laughing because I truly found it funny or because the exact opposite was true, I wasn't sure. But laughter seemed like a much more preferable reaction to breaking something, so I went with it.

Confusion colored Rico's eyes and warred with something like relief. "You're not mad?" he asked, his voice small.

"You thought I'd be mad?" I was still chuckling. That explained a lot. No wonder all the guys were acting odd this morning.

"It's a little inappropriate, don't you think?"

I considered that possibility. "Well, it certainly isn't something I'd have thought to do myself."

Rico rushed to defend his friends. "The guys didn't mean anything by it. It's just, you know, everyone kind of thinks of you as a hero—"

My snort of derision interrupted his words, and I clenched the shirt between my fists.

"They're all really proud of you," Rico went on. "They thought you'd like them."

It made sense, in a strange sort of way. Folks in law enforcement tended to have twisted senses of humor and a firm belief that what didn't kill us made us stronger and was therefore fair game for any sort of sick joke that came to mind. Which didn't necessarily mean I was thrilled, but it did make it forgivable. Sort of.

I took a deep breath and let out a slow sigh, keeping my eyes riveted to the outfit in my hands but not really seeing it. "You're all wearing them, aren't you? That's why the sweatshirts? You didn't want me to see."

Rico nodded. "We have T-shirts."

I mulled that over. "And why'd you all feel the need to rush me out this morning and sideswipe me with this while we were in the car on the way to the race? Couldn't you have brought the outfit to my room this morning or even last night?"

Rico cleared his throat and appeared a little embarrassed. "Well, we talked about that, but the consensus was if you had the clothes beforehand, you wouldn't put them on."

"And you all figured I'd be more inclined to wear them if you surprised me with them the day of."

Rico shrugged. "It seemed logical while we were discussing it."

"You were all drunk, weren't you?"

"No! Well, maybe a little." Rico inhaled deeply and then took a moment to really look at me as we waited for the cars to pass, so we could make the turn into the training center. "Are you sure it's okay?"

Was it? Really? No. I'd much rather have tossed the clothes out the window as we cruised down the Baltimore-Washington Parkway than put them on. But the rest of my team was under the impression they'd done something thoughtful, and they were all wearing them, so they'd be seen regardless of what I chose to do. It'd probably be petulant of me to refuse. Check and mate.

"Any chance you guys have an extra T-shirt?" I asked, gazing out the window toward the trees as I held up my commission book for the guard at the gate.

"No. I'm sorry. The girls all have tank tops. The guys thought you'd want them because they were more feminine. Plus, we all know you don't like to be hot and confined when you run, so…"

The car started moving again, and I swallowed hard, thinking about what wearing the tank top would mean for me: my newly acquired shoulder scar would be prominently on display.

Like I said, one hell of a way to start the morning.

CHAPTER TWO

The James J. Rowley Training Center—where the men and women of the United States Secret Service are shaped and molded into the dedicated agents responsible for the physical protection of numerous politicians, heads of state, and foreign dignitaries—is located in Maryland and stretches over almost five hundred acres. Its six miles of roadway make it the perfect place to host the NPC-50.

The National Police Challenge Relay, or the NPC-50, is an annual competition among local, state, and federal law enforcement agencies from all over the world. The race is run by teams of ten, each participant of which runs five kilometers, hence the "50" in the race's name. Each team's entry fee benefits the COPS and HEROES foundations, both of which are very law-enforcement-officer-supportive organizations.

My attitude toward running had never been what one would describe as enthusiastic, and as Rico navigated the car through the hordes of other participants for today's event, I couldn't help but wonder for at least the fifteenth time that week exactly how I'd let myself be talked into this.

The heavy examination of my inner feelings would have to wait until after I killed myself trying to run this stupid race because the rest of the guys were already in the parking lot waiting, and if their facial expressions were any indication, the subject of our uniforms was about to become a hot-button topic. I sighed.

"What do you think?" Allen Cross wanted to know, accosting me with the question before I even had time to set foot out of the car.

The guys all had their jackets and sweatshirts off now and seemed rather proud of their shirts and shorts, but they also all looked as though they wouldn't be able to take a deep breath until I weighed in with my opinion.

I opened my mouth to comment but faltered when I noticed that their T-shirts included an extra "bullet hole" that my tank top, with its missing material, didn't have: the one that represented the shot I'd taken to the shoulder. I snuck a quick glance around to confirm my suspicion that the illustration was accurate and that there were faux shots on both the front and the back of the shirt, high on the shoulder, to show how the bullet had passed through the muscle. It was and there were. Fantastic.

Gathering all my wildly careening emotions together into a tight little ball and pasting what I hoped was a somewhat convincing smile on my face, I got out of the car and held my own outfit aloft.

"These are great, guys. Thanks." The brightness of my tone didn't ring true to my ears, but the guys all breathed a collective sigh of relief, so it must've been credible enough.

"See?" Keith Abelard shouted smugly, snaking one arm around my shoulders and giving me a squeeze. "I told you she wouldn't mind."

Mind? I thought to myself somewhat bitterly. *No, why the hell should I mind? I mean, hey, I got shot five times in the line of duty and almost died, but by all means, let's put my wounds on a T-shirt and parade me around in front of the public like some sort of performing monkey in cross trainers. What's to mind?*

What I actually said was, "Nah. It was sweet. In a fucked-up sort of way." I freed myself from Keith's grasp and headed toward the women's locker room inside the PT building. "See you guys in a minute," I called over my shoulder, ignoring their shouts of protest and suggestions that I could change in the parking lot. Perverts.

Rory followed me silently into the locker room, her face reflecting her unease. She continued to stare at me while I prepared to change clothes, which only enflamed my irritation with life in general. That's why I ignored her and began the ritual of getting undressed without uttering a word.

"You okay?" Rory finally asked.

I paused in the act of placing my now-folded sweatpants into a locker so I could consider the question, glad the locker room was empty, so we could have this discussion in private. I turned back to face her, holding my hand out, wordlessly asking for the black shorts.

"Would it make any sense to you if I said I didn't know?"

At the moment I had focused all my attention on how much of the scar on my thigh might be visible beneath the extremely high hemline of the shorts I was about to don. I slid them up over my legs and settled them as low on my hips as I could get away with without them falling off, frowning as I leaned over to inspect their length. The scar showed a lot, as it turned out. The whole damn thing was clearly on display.

Rory sighed and straddled the bench that was sitting between us, resting her elbows on the tops of her knees. Her sea-foam-green eyes shifted to the tank top she was wringing between her hands, and she stole quick, nervous glances at me from underneath her eyebrows. The sound of the locker room door opening marred the silence and reminded me there were other people in the world besides my sister and me. People I was going to have to face in a few minutes. People who would likely be staring at me in this get-up. My stomach rolled violently.

"Do you think the rest of the girls' team is actually wearing these?" The question was rhetorical. Rory couldn't have possibly known the answer, as she'd come straight to the locker room with me, and we hadn't seen anyone from the girls' team on our way in. I wasn't even sure why I'd bothered to ask, and I winced at the distinct tremor in my voice as I spoke.

"Yes," a familiar voice spat harshly. "They are."

Allison Reynolds stomped into the locker room, her inky black eyes blazing with a righteous fury. I almost felt the click as her gaze locked onto me, and my pulse sped up. It seemed like every single time I saw her, she appeared even more heart-stoppingly beautiful than the time before.

Allison and I hadn't seen one another in weeks. Between her crazy work schedule and my physical-therapy appointments, connecting in person had been difficult, to say the least. I'd missed her terribly. I'd also been under the impression she wouldn't be able to make it back to DC in time for the race, so it hadn't even occurred to me she might make a cameo. To say I was pleasantly surprised didn't begin to cover it.

"Hi. When did you get back?" The trembling in my voice now was due to a completely different reason. I pulled the corners of my mouth up into a genuine smile as my tension ebbed. No matter how many times I lived through it, it never failed to amaze me how just seeing her could make everything in my world all right.

Allison, however, was not experiencing a similar sensation, if her dark facial expression was any indication. In fact, she appeared to be growing more agitated as she took in my shorts and the tank top in Rory's hands.

Rory abruptly stood and handed me the shirt. "I'm gonna go find Joanna," she mumbled, referring to my friend Jamie Dorchester's girlfriend. Jo was running on the team of doctors who worked at St. Elizabeth's, a mental-health facility located in DC. They'd needed an extra body to make a full team, so I'd volunteered my sister, seeing as how she was a doctor herself. Perhaps her hasty departure was payback for that. Traitor!

If Allison noticed her presence or subsequent lightning-quick retreat, she never said. What did come out of her mouth was, "Fucking assholes!"

The venom in her normally honeyed voice took me aback, and I stepped closer so I could rest my hand on her arm.

"It's not that big a deal." I wasn't sure which of us I was trying to convince with that shaky declaration.

Allison glowered at me. "Bullshit!"

"Wanna help me take off my shirt?" I asked, trying to lighten the mood.

Allison set her jaw and drew a deep breath, obviously physically reining in whatever her first response had been. I allowed my hand to slide down her forearm so I could grip her fingers in mine and tugged her a little closer. I then pressed the palm of her hand to my side.

After a long moment, Allison's gaze softened, and she scoured my face with her eyes. What she was searching for, I didn't know, but I remained quiet, content to bask in her attention for the time being. Her fingers started tracing distracting circles on my ribs, and my heart picked up its tempo even more.

"They shouldn't have done that," she whispered, her tone more agonized now than angry.

"It's okay, sweetheart."

"No, it's not!" Her earlier ire flickered back to life briefly before sputtering back out again. "You almost died. That's not something to joke about."

I dropped the tank top onto the bench, forgotten, and lifted my hands to cup her cheeks. Maybe I hadn't been one hundred percent okay with my new attire, but the thought of Allison being distressed about it didn't sit well with me. She was already on edge too much as it was, talking about the events of a few weeks ago and dragging both of us forcibly on guilt trips far too often for my liking, as if I weren't already taking enough solo voyages. For her, I'd pretend this didn't bother me.

Whatever I'd been about to say in an effort to ease Allison's mind slipped my own as her eyes drifted down to rest heavily on my mouth. Her tongue darted out to caress her bottom lip, and I sucked in a startled breath as the familiar heat sparked between us. The expression on her face now as she allowed her gaze to once again meet mine made my heart stop.

Agonizingly slowly, Allison slid her hands down my sides to grasp the hem of my T-shirt and slipped it up over my head. Once it was gone, she shifted her attention to the scar marring the skin halfway between my shoulder and my neck. I couldn't help shivering as she caressed it gently with the pad of her thumb. Goose bumps broke out over my entire body when she ghosted her lips over that scar immediately after.

She closed her lips around it and stroked it lightly with the tip of her tongue, making me moan. I tangled my fingers into her silken ebony locks and pulled her closer. The bench between us made it impossible for us to make full contact, and I cursed it in my head.

"Allison." I sighed as her teeth began lightly grazing the sensitive skin of my neck. My eyes fluttered closed, and I let my head fall back to allow her greater access.

"Oops, sorry!" A voice interrupted us.

Allison and I flew apart, and I flushed hotly, unable to meet the mortified stare of Special Agent Meaghan Bates, who'd apparently entered the locker room silently, like some sort of stealthy, twat-swatting ninja.

"They're asking all the teams to line up so they can get started," Meaghan said, her tone thick with embarrassment.

"Okay," I mumbled, keeping my eyes fixed intently on the tile floor.

The three of us stood there not looking at one another for at least an eon before Meaghan muttered something under her breath I didn't quite catch and fled the scene without looking back. The silence between Allison and me stretched out for another long moment.

"Sorry," Allison finally said, shooting me the barest traces of a grin.

I shrugged and retrieved my T-shirt from the floor so I could stow it in the locker with the rest of my belongings. When I turned back, she was holding the tank top out to me. I accepted it gratefully and slipped it over my head.

"For what?" I strode over to the mirror hanging above the line of sinks so I could study my reflection. The tank top had medium-width straps situated toward the outer edges of my shoulder blades, which meant my shoulder scar was visible in its entirety. Perfect. I frowned.

"For Meaghan walking in on that. I'm sorry. I wasn't paying attention to our surroundings. I guess I got carried away."

I snagged my NYFO hat and my iPod out of the locker and slammed the door shut, relishing the hollow clang in the almost empty room. I set to work arranging my running headphones and my armband so they were perfectly configured. I needed the wires to be tucked out of the way and not flopping around and the iPod within reach, so I could easily indulge my short attention span and change songs as often as necessary.

Allison took over settling the armband around my right bicep, and I was immediately distracted by the feel of her fingertips brushing against my skin. A rush of arousal flooded me, and I fought not to moan. If she wasn't careful, we were going to get a lot more carried away in the not-too-distant future.

"It's fine."

She cleared her throat. "Well, I know neither of us is too keen on being the subject of gossip."

"Meaghan won't say anything to anyone," I assured her, as she strapped the Velcro around my arm tight. "Thanks."

"You're welcome." Allison snatched the baseball cap out of my hand effortlessly and plopped it onto her own head.

"Hey! What am I going to wear?"

Allison grinned at me and handed over her own baseball hat, which she'd had tucked into the back waistband of her running shorts and which was adorned with the logo for the detail she was assigned to. I eyed the symbol for the Presidential Protective Division ornamenting the front of the hat with a certain level of wariness.

"You really expect me to wear this? Like outside? Where people can see me?"

"Yes," Allison stated without looking at me. She was busy adjusting my NYFO hat so none of her hair was sticking out the sides of it.

"I could get kicked off the team for this sort of betrayal. You know that, don't you?"

"Yeah," she drawled sarcastically. "We're a regular Romeo and Juliet."

I rolled my eyes at her. "Always with the dramatics. I'm just saying your PPD buddies aren't going to take too kindly to me wearing their swag, that's all."

She gestured to the hat she was now wearing. "Hey, I'm not going to be winning any popularity points with this thing on, either. But look at it this way. If they kick you off the team, we can have the rest of the morning alone to engage in our own private workout."

My knees almost buckled, and I closed my eyes. "Why wait?"

Allison chuckled throatily, which didn't help my predicament. She leaned in, and her lips brushed the shell of my ear as she spoke. "I'll give you a nice, thorough rubdown *after* the run," she whispered, taking my earlobe into her mouth and sucking on it briefly to punctuate her promise. "How's that?"

I moaned and turned my head to capture her lips in a searing kiss. Every nerve ending in my body was on fire, screaming for her to do something—anything—to douse the flames of passion she'd stoked within me. All I wanted, more than I wanted my next breath, was to take Allison someplace quiet where I could spend several uninterrupted hours mapping the contours of her body and making them mine. At that exact moment, I didn't think I'd ever been so bitterly resentful of an engagement in all my life as I was of the race.

When we finally pulled back, I was dizzy and gasping for air. I studied her expression for a long moment, pleased to note she seemed almost as out of sorts as I felt. I pulled her closer and wrapped my arms around her, inhaling the clean scent of her hair as though it held the key to my sanity, desperate to put off facing the rest of the world for just a little while longer.

The sound of the locker room door opening intruded on the moment, catapulting me back to reality.

"Uh...Ryan?" Meaghan called, presumably from just outside the door. "We have a slight problem."

"I'll be right there."

With a heavy sigh, I reluctantly untangled myself from Allison's embrace. A small, amused smile was adorning her perfect lips.

"What?" I asked as I started toward the door to the locker room.

"Have I ever told you how adorable you are?"

"I don't think so. I've heard beautiful, wonderful, and brilliant from you. As well as the most incredibly sexy woman you've ever laid eyes on. But, no, I don't remember you ever mentioning adorable."

Allison scoffed and gave me a playful slap on the butt as we stepped into the hallway. "Run fast, smart-ass. The sooner we get this over with, the sooner we can go back to my place and cool down."

"The roadrunner has nothing on me. That, I can promise you."

CHAPTER THREE

Allison and I threaded our way through the crowd in the general direction of the starting line. I was searching the throng for Meaghan, but she'd somehow managed to disappear. Well, whatever the problem was, it couldn't have been too important. Otherwise she would've stuck around.

Rory stood chatting easily with Jamie Dorchester and Joanna Sheahan, and I made my way over, noticing some stares and whispers aimed in my general direction as I went—some covert, others not so much. I clenched my fists and my jaw against my rising discomfort.

Allison's hand sketched a light line across the small of my back, and I turned to shoot her a grateful smile. The grin I received in return went a long way toward distracting me from my anxiety.

"Oh, get a room, you two," Jamie said loudly, rolling her eyes as I spun to scowl at her.

Out of the corner of my eye, I noticed that the man standing closest to her—though not exactly part of the group—blinked, obviously startled, and favored me with a cool, appraising look. He looked somewhat familiar, but I couldn't place him.

Joanna elbowed her girlfriend hard enough to elicit a grunt and leaned in to give me a brief, welcoming hug. "How are you, Ryan?"

"Good, thanks. How are you?"

"Fine, fine." Her eyes dropped to examine both of my visible scars briefly. "You've healed up well. Any lingering soreness or stiffness?"

I rolled my injured shoulder a little, as though her words had either brought on or perhaps made me more aware of the ever-present ache that stubbornly refused to abate completely. "Some. But it could always be worse."

"Yeah, you could be dead," Rory muttered. Clearly, my sister hadn't yet worked through all her issues surrounding what'd happened. She and I should probably talk about that at some point, but this was neither the time nor the place.

"Ryan!" Meaghan shouted behind me. When I pivoted to face her, she was weaving in and out of the horde of runners and appeared out of breath. "There you are. Listen, Shannon's son was in a car accident late last night—"

A veritable chorus of exclamations on the theme of, "Oh, my God! Is he okay?" interrupted her.

Meaghan appeared simultaneously worried and lost. "I don't know. He was in surgery when she called me to let me know she had to go. She promised to hit me up as soon as she heard anything."

"That's awful," I said, wishing I could do something for Shannon and her family.

"I know," Meaghan said. "It is terrible. And it also leaves us a man down for the run today. Without Shannon, we don't have a full team."

"Oh." I considered that fact. "I wonder where we can find a replacement on such short notice."

Allison shrugged. "I'll run with you guys."

I stared at her, puzzled. I was curious to see how she planned to get away with running for the PPD team and our team at the same time. I opened my mouth to ask her but didn't even get a word in before the man who'd been lurking around the edges of our group interjected.

"No," he barked, his voice harsh and authoritative.

It was my turn to blink, taken aback. I couldn't pinpoint what had me immediately bristling and ready for a fight. It might've been his tone or the rigidity of his posture. Or maybe it was his expression as he eyed Allison. I wasn't sure, but he'd rubbed me the wrong way right off the bat.

"Excuse me?" He couldn't possibly have been talking to us.

He sneered at me, his derision plain. "Stay out of this," he ordered me before refocusing on Allison. "Absolutely not."

"I'm sorry." I was both baffled by and annoyed that this unknown man had inserted himself into our private conversation. "Have we met?"

"Beau," Allison said softly, her tone thick with warning.

At the sound of the name, his identity clicked. This was Allison's boss, Beau Byers, the one who'd been giving her such a hard time lately. Well, that certainly explained why I'd instantly disliked him.

Byers ignored my question. Instead, he ran his eyes slowly down my body and back up again. The inspection made my skin crawl, and I had to fight not to snarl at him to keep his fucking leers to himself. However, I was more pissed that he'd been making my girlfriend miserable for months.

Byers's attentions finally wandered up to the top of my head, and he took in my hat. For some inexplicable reason, he faltered, and then his eyes darted over to Allison's hat. When he noticed the logo on her ball cap, his expression became stony.

"You're not running for their team." Byers's voice was a low growl. "It's out of the question."

"I was unaware you had the authority to decide that for me," Allison replied, her words laced with disdain. "Oh, wait. That's right. You don't." She glared at him.

"Allison," I murmured so only she could hear me, gripping her wrist lightly. I didn't disagree with either her take on the subject or the fact that this guy clearly deserved to be reminded of his place in her life—or lack thereof—but I wasn't positive that getting into a pointless argument with him in front of all these people wouldn't adversely affect her career somewhere down the line. This wasn't worth it.

Allison turned the full force of her glare on me. "No. He doesn't get to make that call. If I want to run with you guys, I will."

"But won't the PPD team be down a man then?" I asked.

Allison shook her head. "No. I was never on the roster because I wasn't supposed to be back until tomorrow. I'm not actually running at all."

"Then why are you here? For that matter, why are you back so early? I forgot to ask you before."

"Because I wanted to see you, smart-ass." The smile she favored me with and her affectionate tone took any sting out of those words. "Are you complaining?"

I grinned back and brushed my thumb over the skin of her arm where I was still holding it. "Nope. Definitely not."

"Well, then, stop asking so many questions."

"Your wish is my command."

"Awww," Jamie gushed. "You guys are so sickeningly adorable it makes me want to vomit." She made several dramatic retching sounds, and I stuck my tongue out.

"You're on PPD," Byers stated loudly enough to draw our attention back to him, as well as capture the interest of several bystanders, who looked at him, then at us, then at each other uncomfortably. "So you can't run for the NYFO team."

"I used to be in NYFO," Allison snapped back. "And I'm going back there as soon as my time on the detail is up."

"You are?" I couldn't help but interrupt. We hadn't discussed any of our future plans. It'd seemed way too soon. But hearing that she'd obviously thought about it, that she wanted to come back, made me giddy. I beamed.

Allison shot me a fondly exasperated glance that told me she thought I was an idiot for even asking, and I grinned wider. She shook her head and went back to glaring at Byers.

"I'm a former New Yorker," Allison pointed out again. "I don't see why I can't run for the NYFO team if they need me."

"It doesn't matter that you're a former New Yorker." Byers's countenance had darkened considerably since the start of this conversation. "You can only run for them if none of the other teams objects. And one does."

"Why?" Allison demanded. "This is a charity run. What difference does it make who I run for?"

"I said no!"

"Jesus fucking Christ." Allison shot him one last furious glare before she stomped off.

"Allison," I called after her. I shot Byers a vengeful look of my own, barely besting the urge to punch him in the face, before starting after her. Meaghan's hand on my arm stopped my getaway.

"That still doesn't solve our problem," Meaghan said. She appeared to be truly sorry that she couldn't allow me to go after Allison just yet.

"I know it doesn't. I just don't have any other solution. Not if *someone* is going to stop Allison from running." I favored Byers with another pointed glance, making my voice loud enough so the bystanders could hear me as well. "I can't think of another option. Everyone here is already on a team."

"Well, since we don't have a viable replacement, one of us will have to run two legs if we still want to compete." Meaghan was peering at me intently.

"Ah," I said. "I see where this is going."

Meaghan's expression was an interesting mix of apologetic and sympathetic. "You're the only one with any hope of being able to run that far in a competitive time."

I sighed heavily and glanced away, only to meet the concerned eyes of Joanna and Jamie. Was I up to six miles today? I hadn't done more than four since "the incident" but once and had cursed whoever had invented any pace faster than a meander the entire time, even though I'd run both extra miles as slowly and leisurely as possible.

I was just about to express my reservations and apologize to the team when I caught sight of Byers's smug face. He was definitely gloating, and seeing his beady little eyes glimmering with satisfaction made my blood boil.

"Fine." I stared directly at him as I assented. "I'll do it."

"Ryan?" Rory said softly. I didn't look at her, but she was clearly worried.

Byers's expression morphed from one of self-righteous jubilation to shock to disbelief in the space of about three seconds. "You can't be serious."

"Oh, I'm always serious."

"No, you're not." Jamie laughed as though the very idea were uproariously funny.

I rounded on her and gave her a warning glance. "Well, I am about this."

"You really think you can run six miles?" Byers asked incredulously. "In a time fast enough to be competitive? You're crazy." He let out a grating laugh that set my teeth on edge.

"Absolutely."

The crowd around us had gradually started taking more interest in our little showdown until a circle of people surrounded us, all watching the exchange with a sort of sick fascination. It reminded me of a schoolyard brawl. I wouldn't have been surprised if people had started chanting, "Fight, fight, fight."

Byers seemed to notice our audience about the same time, and he stood up straighter and puffed his chest out. He clearly thought he had something to prove to someone, though I couldn't imagine it was me.

"Care to wager?" The words were a definite taunt.

I rested my hands on my hips. "This is a charity run. Doesn't adding a side bet seem rather gauche?"

"Gauche?"

"Yeah. Do you need me to define it? It means tacky, uncouth, tasteless. I'm surprised you're not more familiar with the term."

I heard an "Ooooh" and a faint chuckle from different parts of the crowd. Byers's jaw clenched, and his left eye twitched. He took a step closer and stared down at me. If his proximity coupled with our height differences was supposed to intimidate me, he was about to be disappointed.

Prolonging this altercation was a spectacularly terrible idea. Beau Byers wasn't just a boss; he was Allison's boss. The consequences for insulting him the way I just had could be nearly catastrophic for her, to say nothing of what could happen to either of us if I did something even worse. Like kick him in the balls. But something inside me wouldn't let me walk away anymore. This man was an absolute douche bag, in a way the definition of the term doesn't quite prepare you for. I wanted so badly to humiliate him at this point I could almost taste it.

Byers took a deep breath. He was clearly attempting to save face and appear unaffected by my careless quip, but I could tell he was fuming. "What's the matter? Afraid to put your money where your mouth is?"

I grinned at him. "Not at all. What'd you have in mind?"

"Five thousand. And I'll even make it sporting. Your team doesn't have to win, but the combined time for both your legs does have to be faster than our two fastest girls' times put together."

The bystanders gasped and exclaimed, everybody appearing to balk at the amount. I tried hard not to gape at him myself, but it was tough. Five thousand dollars was a lot of money to spend on anything, let alone a pointless wager. I wasn't sure saving face in front of him was worth that much.

I stared at him for a long moment, and as I did, some of the comments of the people lingering nearby drifted through the angry haze I'd been floating in and penetrated my awareness. In addition to the opinion that the terms of the bet might be a little steep and the questions regarding what each of us was trying to prove, a lot of people were speculating whether I was actually up to the challenge. Whether I'd be up to any other kind of challenge ever again. Or whether I should just accept complete disability and call it a day.

Something unidentifiable inside of me burst and then curdled. My heart shriveled, broken because Rico's claim that everyone thought I was a hero had been a wild exaggeration, because I'd just found out some of my colleagues now doubted my ability to perform my job. But something else resonated within me on a deep and primal and urgent level. And it fractured some unknown part at the very core of me.

I tried not to let any of that agony show on my face, relying on my fury in the face of Byers's arrogance and my disappointment in the rest of my coworkers' reservations to see me through. I tilted my chin up in defiance as I held my hand out.

"Five thousand," I repeated. "You're on."

Again, Byers appeared shocked, but he covered quickly and took my hand, effectively sealing the deal. I dropped it like a hot rock and wiped my palm on the front of my shirt as I turned to walk away, determined to find Allison and talk to her before this debacle started. The announcer was already on the PA explaining the heat system to everyone, so we didn't have too many people running at any one time lest the going be unbelievably slow. I needed to be quick.

Byers roughly grabbed my arm. I fixed the offending appendage with a dark glare before shifting it so I included him in my extreme displeasure.

"Wait."

"What?" I shook him off.

"How do I know you're not going to cheat?"

I goggled at him. "Excuse me?"

"How do I know you're not going to cheat?" he repeated with exaggerated slowness, as though I were a moron.

I folded my arms across my chest and fumed, shaking. Who the hell did he think he was? "And just how do you think I'm going to cheat?"

Byers inclined his head in my sister's direction. "Get her to run for you."

"What?" He had to be the stupidest man alive.

"I'm just saying, it'd be pretty easy for her to run in your place."

I rolled my eyes so hard I wouldn't have been surprised if they'd gotten stuck in the back of my head. "You have *got* to be kidding me."

"Beau, come on." One of the guys in the crowd tried to intervene. "Let's just go get the team lined up."

Byers and I never broke eye contact. "I need some assurances that you won't pull some sort of switcheroo on us, that's all."

I breathed in so long and so deep that my lungs should have exploded. I counted the beats of both my inhale and my exhale, attempting to calm my boiling temper. It didn't work.

"First of all," I said, my voice low, my words careful and deliberate, as though that would help me keep my tenuous grip on my slippery disposition. "I don't know in what universe you think it's appropriate to impugn someone's honor with absolutely no facts or evidence to back the accusation up—especially someone you work with—but seeing as how you obviously missed the memo, let me clue you in on something: that's not how we roll here in the Secret Service."

Byers's brow pulled down in a scowl, but he didn't reply.

"Secondly," I said, when it became clear he had no comeback. "In case you haven't noticed, Rory's running for another team. She won't be able to run for me, as she'll be busy with her own race.

"Thirdly, Rory would never in a million years be able to get away with pretending to be me, as there are a few surefire ways to tell us apart. Starting with our outfits."

"You could always duck off the path into the woods and switch clothes."

"Oh, my God. Do you even hear yourself? What is the matter with you?"

"Stranger things have happened. And desperate people have done more for less." Byers appeared devoted to his argument, although I wasn't positive he really believed it. I suspected he was simply sticking to it to disagree with me. If I'd said the sky was blue, I'm sure he would've challenged that assertion.

"Yeah," I said, allowing the sarcasm to bleed through and taint the word. "I can see that."

Byers's face contorted, and he clenched his hands into fists. If I were a smarter woman, it might've occurred to me to tread lightly, as he appeared to be considering whether to take a swing at me. But I was on a roll.

"And while we're out in the woods changing clothes so she can run my extra leg of the *charity* race that has no real impact on our lives outside of today, we'll be sure to put in colored contacts to change the color of our eyes. Oh, and I'll have to get out the professional makeup kit. You know, to cover up the *very* visible scars I'm sporting and give her matching ones."

The surety in Byers's gaze flickered a little, and I used the opportunity to go in for the kill. I stepped even closer to him so our toes were almost touching. My head was swimming, and my ire was making it difficult for me to see straight.

"But lastly, and probably most importantly of all…" I all but whispered, so both he and our ever-present crowd of voyeurs would have to lean in and hold their breath to hear me. I paused to ensure I had everyone's attention. I wanted them all to hear this last declaration. "I don't need to cheat. Not to beat you, at any rate."

Byers looked as though I'd slapped him. Hard. He even reeled and took half a step back before his jaw dropped. His eyes bulged and his lips started moving, but nothing even remotely coherent came out of this mouth.

And with that, I turned and stalked away from the crowd and in the direction I'd last seen Allison headed, leaving a din of voices behind me.

CHAPTER FOUR

As I stomped away from the scene with all the grace and dignity of a pouting four-year-old just informed she couldn't have a cookie before dinner, I tried to calm myself. I searched the crowd as I went but didn't see Allison. Dejected and resigned to give her the space she obviously needed right now, I gripped the back of my neck with the palms of my hands so hard it hurt.

I paced back and forth, back and forth, turning the scenario over in my mind again and again, analyzing everything I'd said, everything I hadn't said, and everything I felt like I should've. Furious, both with Byers for getting me all riled up and with myself for allowing him to push my buttons like that, I kicked at the ground. A huge wad of dirt flew through the air, and I watched the remaining dust float slowly back to the ground.

"*Ay-vo!*" Rory called angrily, causing me to freeze. She didn't often slip back into addressing me by her nickname for me from when we were kids, but when she did, she was almost always serious.

"What?" I couldn't restrain my annoyance.

"Are you crazy?" Rory demanded once she'd caught up with me.

Without taking my hands off my neck or lifting my head, I raised an eyebrow at her and glanced around to see whether anyone was paying any attention to us, but they didn't appear to be. I still took a few steps closer to the tree line. You could never be too careful.

"Not now, Rory."

"Yes, now. What the hell is the matter with you?"

"That guy's a fucking prick," I practically shouted, wincing when

I heard how loud I'd been. I took a deep breath and tried again at a more reasonable volume. "He's a complete and total asshole, Rory."

"That may very well be, but he's also a boss." At my pointed look of disbelief, she went on. "Jamie told me who he was after you left."

"So what?" I shoved my hands deep into the pockets of my shorts. "That doesn't give him the right to be a dick."

Rory's lips twitched, and I could tell she was trying not to smile. Instead, she rested her hand on my shoulder. "No, you're right. It doesn't. But you don't have to make it clear you feel that way about him, either."

"It doesn't matter."

"Oh, really? And why's that?"

"Because what's done is done. And my time machine is on the fritz, so I guess I'll just have to live with the consequences. Speaking of which, I need you to pace me."

"Huh?"

"For the race. I need you to pace me."

Rory had run track all through middle school, high school, and college. Somewhere along the line, she'd developed an uncanny ability to divine at exactly what speed she was running without the use of a watch or any sort of electronic tracking device. Even though she'd more or less cajoled me into training with her for most of that time, I'd never managed to pick up that particular skill. I found it more than a little eerie, actually. But today it seemed her odd superpower would come in handy.

"I didn't want you running at all." Rory regarded me with a dark look. "I still don't think you're healed enough. No way in hell will I condone you running twice the original distance."

"I don't need you to condone it. I just need you to help me do it."

She narrowed her eyes. "Why's it so important to you that you do this? You could really hurt yourself, you know."

"I'll be fine," I said automatically.

Rory scoffed. "You're not invincible, Ryan."

"I know that."

"And you don't have anything to prove to that asshole."

"I know that, too," I said quietly, though that wasn't strictly true.

"So why the hell are you letting him push you into this?"

"It isn't him. Not entirely, anyway."

"Well, then what is it?"

I let out a long breath as I considered how to explain it to her so she'd truly understand. "Rory, you work in a male-dominated field. You have to know what it's like trying to get along as a woman in a man's world."

"I do. Believe me, I do. But that's no reason to risk your health just to prove some sort of sadistic point to a bunch of jerk-offs."

"They're like sharks, and I'm bleeding in the water. It's sink or swim now, and none of them will throw me a life preserver." I was mixing my metaphors and, judging by her puzzled expression, not making a whole lot of sense.

"Ryan, I—"

"Look. My entire job rests heavily on my reputation, earned or unearned. It doesn't really matter which. Popular opinion can make or break you, and word travels faster than the speed of sound in this agency. If I back out now, that's all anyone will remember. If I fail now, that's all anyone will remember. From what I just heard back there, a lot of the guys already doubt my ability to recover from what happened. If I were a man, they probably wouldn't focus on it as much. But I'm a woman, which means they're all watching me, holding their breath, just waiting for me to crack."

I paused and stepped closer, resting my hand on her upper arm to ensure she'd be looking at me when I explained. I needed her to understand. I needed her to get it, not just intellectually but on a gut level. I needed her to help me, and if I couldn't make her see why I had to do this, I had no hope of pulling it off.

"One tiny slip is all it'll take, Rory. One wrong word. One tear welling up in my eye that I don't wipe away fast enough. One grimace of pain that the wrong person sees. One reaction deemed just a tad too sensitive for the situation." I waved my free hand in the direction of the rest of the rest of the runners and spared them a quick glance. "One mistake, and I'll end up branded an overly emotional woman. The guys won't even see me as an agent anymore. They'll just define me by my gender. Everyone will treat me with kid gloves to my face and talk shit about me behind my back."

"Ryan, you were shot. Your ex-girlfriend basically died in your arms. *You* almost died. Surely they'll cut you a little slack."

I shook my head, saddened. "It doesn't work that way. And I think deep down you know that. As long as I stay strong, the guys will think I'm a hero. But if I show even the barest hint of weakness— of humanness—suddenly everything I've ever done to secure my reputation as a competent agent no longer matters, and they'll look at me as someone who isn't up to snuff."

"So you're saying that everyone you work with is an asshole?"

I laughed. "No. I'm saying despite the fact that we're more than a decade into the twenty-first century, this is still very much a good-old-boys club. And if I expect them to accept me and let me play—really let me play—I have to prove that I'm tougher and more stubborn and better than they are, over and over again, every single day."

Rory studied me for a long moment. I regarded her back, nervously. Clearly she was still torn on the issue. I didn't think it was because she didn't believe me. She was apparently still just worried about how physically taxing this run would be for me.

I waited as patiently as I could, which just about killed me. Patience may be a virtue, but it'd never been one of mine. Yet I also knew my sister well enough to realize when to keep quiet and not push. Now was definitely one of those times.

She narrowed her eyes at me and cocked her head to one side. Strands of blond hair that'd escaped her ponytail peeked out from under her hat and created a sort of wispy halo. She exhaled forcefully.

"That's fucked up, Ryan."

I shrugged. "I know. But what else can I do except vastly exceed their expectations and look fabulous doing it?"

"This is really that important to you, what these guys think?"

I nodded.

"How fast do you want to run this in?" she asked finally, resignation seeping into her voice.

I smiled and tried not to appear too relieved. "Uh…I'd be happy if I could keep it under forty."

Rory's countenance relaxed. "Oh, good. I was afraid you'd push yourself too hard. That's a nice, easy pace for—"

"For both legs."

My sister froze and gaped at me like I'd just told her I was the result of a virgin birth. "What?"

"I want to run the entire 10K in under forty minutes."

"That's a sub-seven-minute mile."

"See? That's why I need you. It would've taken me forever to do that math." I flashed her a grin.

"You couldn't have done that before you were shot! You expect to be able to do that now when you're still recovering from a serious injury and have barely gotten back into running?"

"Yup."

"How?"

"I'm counting on adrenaline."

"You're out of your damn mind."

"That may very well be, but I fail to see how that impacts this situation."

"No."

"No, what?"

"I'm not going to help you."

"What? Why not?"

"I'm not going to help you run yourself into the ground. I refuse. Absolutely not."

"*Asha.*" I was hoping my use of her old nickname would sway her opinion.

"*Ná. Ná gída ma korá.* It won't work."

I sighed, defeated. She'd lapsed into full sentences of our special twin language—which was an interesting combination of what Gaelic obviously sounded like to toddlers blended with made-up words—and told me not to bother. When she was in this frame of mind, nothing I could say would get through to her. Perhaps I needed to consider a compromise. Maybe if I agreed to a slower pace she'd capitulate. But then I wasn't sure I'd be able to win. What to do?

"I'll do it," a soft voice said behind me.

I turned, startled to find Allison standing a few feet away. Her face was an impassive mask, and my heart dropped into my stomach with a spectacular splat. I hadn't seen her this closed off in a while.

Unfortunately, Rory was much less adept at reading the subtle nuances of my girlfriend's facial expressions and found it a perfectly good time to berate her. "You absolutely will not."

Allison raised one eyebrow and pursed her lips. "Excuse me?"

"Allison, you didn't hear what she just asked. She'll hurt herself if she tries to do this."

"*I* can hear you," I said, annoyed that she was talking about me like I wasn't standing right there.

Allison waved one hand dismissively. "She'll be fine. I'm sure her body will give out long before she does any major, lasting damage to it."

"See?" I chimed in. "Wait. What?"

"And if she does fall out, it's not like there aren't a veritable slew of EMTs and paramedics wandering around all over the damn place. Ryan will get the best care available."

I frowned. I wasn't thrilled with the specific points she was making, but they did appear to be silencing my sister's objections.

"Look, Rory, I know you're worried about her. But she's a big girl, and she's stubborn as hell. She's like a junkyard dog with a bone."

"Hey!"

Allison ignored me. "We both know she's going to do this whether we help her or not. At least this way, I can keep an eye on her and make sure she gets immediate medical care if it comes to that."

Rory scowled at both of us and hesitated for a long moment, clearly debating whether she wanted to argue with us, but she must've thought better of it. She gave Allison a curt nod, spun around, and stalked away, muttering something under her breath. She and I were going to have to have a come-to-Jesus about that habit. It was grating, to say the least.

Once my sister had left, I refocused on Allison. She was staring off in the general direction of the starting line, refusing to look at me. Seeing her expression and how it didn't thaw even slightly increased my anxiety.

"Thanks. You know, for standing up for me with my sister. Sort of."

"Oh, make no mistake, it's a stupid idea. You had a collapsed lung, for crying out loud."

"It isn't collapsed anymore, I don't think. I mean, it's probably not."

"Very good, Ryan," Allison said, her tone acerbic. "By all means, let's joke about it some more. Because the entire situation was absolutely hilarious."

Allison's dark eyes were flashing, but beneath that, I caught fleeting glimpses of fear and guilt. I was a moron. I should've realized what she was doing sooner. She was picking a fight in an attempt to avoid talking about whatever was really bothering her. Old habits die hard, it would seem. But that didn't mean I had to let her get away with it.

I smiled at her and took a step closer. I brushed the tips of my fingers across her upper arm. "Hey. Come on."

Allison blinked, obviously surprised, and slowly dragged her eyes over to meet mine. I saw no warmth there, no sparkle. None of the usual light and life I associated with those rich, brown orbs. Only the barest hint of a cold, burgeoning fury that chilled me.

I took another step closer and caressed her biceps with both of my hands. They were trembling as a result of my wildly vacillating emotions, but I couldn't do much about that. Instead, I chose to focus on how to get Allison to reconnect with me.

"You promised," I reminded her. "You promised you'd talk to me about the things that were bothering you. Really talk. Not just pick a fight with me to push me away."

At my words, Allison's cold expression started to melt. Not a lot, but enough to loosen the knot that'd taken up residence in the hollow of my chest so I could breathe. More or less.

"You're right. I owe you an apology. I'm sorry."

"Funny. I was just thinking the same thing."

Her eyes narrowed into slits, and her anger threatened to return. "You were thinking that I owed you an apology?"

I laughed. "No. I was thinking I owed you one."

"Oh. For what?"

I chewed on my lower lip and averted my gaze. "I…uh…may've accidentally made things worse with your boss."

"How? What'd you do?"

"I may've insulted him. A little. Or kind of a lot. In front of a whole bunch of people."

Both of Allison's perfectly arched eyebrows went up, and she stared at me. "Really?"

"Maybe."

"Well, he probably deserved it."

"You're not mad?"

"Of course not. Why would I be mad?"

"I was afraid you'd think I was trying to fight your battles for you. And that really isn't my place."

"That's right. I don't need you to defend me. I can handle him."

"I know you can."

"Is that what you were doing?"

I shook my head. "No. I wasn't. My initial dislike of him may've hinged on his recent treatment of you, but believe me, when he and I were getting into it just now, it was all for me."

"What'd you say, exactly?"

I fidgeted, adjusting my borrowed ball cap unnecessarily. "I might've implied that he was stupid."

"Fair point."

"Then, when he all but accused me of being a cheater, I asked him what the hell was wrong with him."

"Valid question."

"And it's entirely possible I made a bet with him that I could beat both him and your two fastest female runners. Hence me needing someone to pace me. Who's your fastest female runner, anyway?"

Allison shook her head, a look of disbelief scored with undertones of smug satisfaction painting her features. "Me."

"Well, lucky for me you aren't running, or I might have a serious problem. Who's the next fastest after you? Who do I need to be concentrating on?"

"Jamie."

"Oh. That'll be fine, then. She's easily distracted. All I have to do is smack her on the ass or pull up my shirt as I run by, and she'll trip and fall on her face." When Allison looked confused, I went on with a shrug. "Jamie's a boob girl."

Allison's countenance became sinister. "I don't suppose you'd care to explain how you could possibly know that?"

"It's come up in conversation," I lied, cursing myself for my slip. Allison didn't appear to believe me, so I hastened to drag the conversation back on topic before she could pursue that line of questioning any further. "Anyway, the bet was five thousand dollars, and I plan to use it on those five dates I owe you to woo you like you've never been wooed before, thus securing my chance at getting into your pants and bestowing upon you the most mind-blowing orgasm in the history of orgasms. So it's really in your best interest to help me win."

"Do you even have five thousand dollars?"

"Not yet. But I hope to by the end of the day."

"Ryan!" Her tone was pure exasperation. "What if you lose?"

"Haven't you been listening? That's why I need you."

"You're a mess, you know that?"

"I do. So, you're okay with helping me further humiliate your boss, then?"

"Absolutely. I'm looking forward to it."

I hesitated. "Is it going to get you into more trouble with him?"

"Don't worry about it. I told you I can handle him. The question is, can you?"

"Oh, I've got this."

The announcer got back on the PA and asked everyone running in the first heat to line up. I looked around and caught sight of Meaghan waving at me frantically. I nodded and held up one finger, silently asking her to wait a second.

Allison grinned at me. "Good. I like a girl who isn't afraid to stand up for herself, and I'd hate to think I was dating a pushover."

"You most definitely aren't. You may be dating an idiot, but not a pushover. I really feel terrible about this, Allison. Baiting your boss like that was akin to poking a hornet's nest with a stick. In a garage. Whose door is nailed shut. While covered entirely in liquid sugar. Not my best plan. And while I'm not too worried about me, it's possible he's going to hammer you for this. Which should've been enough to give me pause and shut me the hell up. So, I apologize in advance for whatever the fallout is."

Allison scowled. "Fuck him."

I wrinkled my nose and made a face. "Gross. No, thank you."

Allison froze and pinned me with an odd look. I smiled and leaned in so I could whisper in her ear. "Not really my type. Although someone else has managed to pique my interest."

"Is it Jamie?" Allison demanded. "I'll kill her."

"It's not Jamie," I murmured, grazing her lips a little with my ear as I hummed, enjoying the resulting shiver. "I have a very specific type, and Jamie definitely doesn't fit the bill."

"She'd better not." Allison stepped back out of my reach and took my chin between her thumb and forefinger so she could look at me. I relished the furious glint in her eyes.

"Why, Agent Reynolds." I gasped in mock surprise. "Are you jealous?"

"Do I have any reason to be?" Uncertainty flickered across her face.

I pretended to consider the question, which earned me another glare and a playful smack on the arm. "Absolutely not."

"Good." She surprised me by giving me a quick, sweet peck on the lips and taking my hand in hers to swing it between us as we ambled toward the starting line. It was a far cry from the way we used to interact when we were out together, and I was still adjusting.

"Ryan." Meaghan panted as she emerged from the thundering horde.

I took my place among the starters and started fiddling with the settings on my iPod, searching for a good, fast song to run to. "What?"

"You're all set. You sure you're good to run two legs? Really? Because I could do it if you're not up to it. It's not a big deal. I just won't be as fast."

Allison and I exchanged a meaningful glance. "I'm good," I assured her. Or maybe I was trying to assure me. Hopefully one of us believed me, at any rate.

"Okay. Well, you have the option of doing the legs back-to-back or resting in between. Your choice. Just let me know, so I can tell the guys recording the times."

"I'll do them in succession. I'm afraid if I rest, I won't be able to make myself start running again."

"All right," Meaghan said, clapping me on the back. "Good luck."

"Thanks. I'm gonna need it," I mumbled to myself as she strode away.

CHAPTER FIVE

Okay, it was official. This had been, hands down, without a doubt, the worst idea in the history of ideas. And I wasn't just talking about my ideas, either, but all bad ideas that'd ever gone on record since the beginning of time. I don't know what the hell I'd been thinking when I'd agreed to this insanity, but I was now resolved that, in the future, I was no longer permitted to make decisions on my own behalf without consulting a quorum or convening a conclave. Maybe then I'd be able to avoid finding myself smack-dab in the middle of situations like this with no foreseeable escape. Maybe.

My entire body was buzzing, but unfortunately, it wasn't with adrenaline or the excitement of a race to be won. No, over the past mile or so, I'd become convinced it was humming as a warning, a precursor alarm of sorts to let me know it was preparing to revolt. Like how a microphone emits a piercing squeal of feedback when it gets too close to the speaker. Or the way a rattlesnake shakes its tail as a sign of danger.

My legs felt rubbery and heavy, and at the same time, my entire frame—including all of my extremities—was shot through with dizziness and nausea. Except for my lungs. They were just burning as they strained to take in and then release each ragged, shallow breath. Oh, and I tasted blood in the back of my throat, which I didn't think could ever be taken as a good omen.

I glanced toward Allison to see how she was faring, both pleased and annoyed to see she was stunningly flawless, as usual. She ran next to me with an easy grace I don't think I could ever have hoped to emulate. If this run was stressful or difficult for her, she wasn't showing it. Her olive skin glistened with a light sheen of sweat, and the play of muscles working together in tandem under smooth flesh mesmerized me. Or it would've if I weren't concentrating so hard on remaining conscious.

My breath was coming in wheezing gasps, and I turned my head to the other side so I could spit. Even swallowing was too difficult for me. I was afraid to interrupt the painstakingly crafted *puff-puff-pant-pant* rhythm I'd adopted at some point near the start of my second 5K, lest I run out of air in the space between labored breaths and fail to reestablish the cadence.

I flailed one arm clumsily in Allison's direction in a desperate attempt to get her attention. I ended up smacking her hand hard, and though I tried to apologize for my awkwardness, no words came out. I settled, instead, for shooting her a rueful smile.

"You okay?" she asked.

I shook my head. No. I definitely was *not* okay. I was very far from okay. I'd dedicated what little energy I had left that wasn't devoted to propelling my unwilling body forward to refraining from throwing up. The world around me seemed fuzzier and much farther away than I remembered it being, and something about that realization made my stomach heavy with dread.

I tapped the top of my left wrist with the first two fingers of my right hand, asking a silent question. I hoped she could read my unspoken clues, because if she couldn't, I had a problem. Talking and running had become mutually exclusive propositions.

Allison appeared concerned, but she refrained from engaging in any more stupid inquiries. Instead, she consulted the fancy GPS watch she wore for running for what felt like an eternity before she finally answered. "We're running at about an eight-minute pace, give or take."

Fuck. That was a lot slower than I'd wanted. I ducked my head, thinking hard. I was undecided whether I should simply accept the fact that I likely wouldn't win this stupid bet and take the rest of this race nice and easy or whether I should strive to make up lost time and push harder. After a moment, I determined that there were still too many unknown variables for me to make an informed decision on the subject.

I grabbed inelegantly at Allison's pistoning hand again and then slapped my right thigh with the palm of my right hand. I followed that up with a wild wave in the direction of the road in front of us. I licked my dry lips with what felt like an equally arid tongue and tried not to think about how thirsty I was. My eyes became unfocused until the road and the people stretched out in front of me lost all detail and became indistinct blurs.

"Hey, relax," Allison was saying. It took me a second to realize she was talking to me and about five seconds to remember I'd asked her a wordless question. "Just breathe. You're doing great."

Easy for her to say. She wasn't the one of us who felt like she was chasing death, practically begging for it to take her. Anything to bring this hell on earth to an end. I hadn't realized just how quickly my running skills could deteriorate. I promised myself right then that I'd never give Rory shit about pushing me to run ever again. I also vowed to never land myself in this sort of situation, either.

I whacked my leg and pointed again, this time more insistently. When Allison frowned at me, obviously puzzled, I attempted to speak. "How...far?" I managed to croak out.

"Oh! Sorry. A little less than a mile. Keep it up, Ryan. We're almost there."

I shook my head as tears of frustration and fatigue sprang to my eyes. I sniffled once, swallowing hard, and lifted the hem of my tank top so I could swipe at the rivulets of sweat dripping down my face, lamenting for the second time that day my outfit's lack of sleeves. That's what I normally used to dry my face. Although there was something to be said for not having to turn my head into my bicep to dry off. With the state I was in, even that quick move would likely make me lose my balance, and I so didn't need even one more thing to focus on.

I heard a curse and then a loud, drawn-out sort of scuffling sound accompanied by some shouts off to my left and a little behind me that suggested that someone had tripped, but I couldn't afford even the split-second break in concentration that turning around to check would cost me. I probably would've followed suit. And if I went down, I was certain I wouldn't get back up.

Allison did chance a glimpse, however, and she made sort of an unsophisticated snort. I spared her a passing glance but could divine nothing of her facial expression.

"You were right," she said.

"'Bout...what?" Did tongues swell when they dried out? Mine had certainly seemed to. It felt like it was sticking to the inside of my mouth, which was starting to impede my breathing. Psychologically, of course.

"Jamie being a boob girl, apparently."

I frowned at her and lifted my hands in what I hoped was a questioning gesture. I had no idea what the hell she was talking about.

"When you raised your shirt to wipe off your face just now, she tripped." Her tone held an interesting mixture of amusement and ire, and I was grateful for my perfectly legitimate excuse not to engage in this conversation.

"Sports bra." I thumped my fist twice against the hollow of my chest over my heart to emphasize my ineloquently illustrated point. I didn't know why anyone would've balked at my lifting my shirt. It wasn't like they'd see anything. Several women were running in only sports bras. In fact, somewhere between miles three and four, I'd debated removing my own offensive tank top altogether and tucking it into the waistband of my shorts so I'd have a sweat rag handy, but I was a still self-conscious about the small surgery scars on my back.

Allison shrugged. "Guess that was enough for her."

"Good." I huffed. "I might...still...win...then." I sucked in a few huge, greedy gulps of air. "She...okay?"

"Yeah." I thought she might've sounded a bit petulant, but it was difficult to tell through the ringing in my ears. I didn't bother to reply.

We ran in silence for what felt like another few days before she spoke again. "You ready?"

"For...what?" I asked warily.

Allison pointed up the road a little ways and just off to her right. I followed the line of her hand to a small pack of men tooling along ahead of us at a pretty good clip.

I favored her with another curious glance. I doubted I would've known who she was pointing out to me even if I had been able to see straight. I squinted again in the direction she'd indicated, but it didn't help.

"Byers is up there," Allison said. "He switched to this heat on purpose so he could run against you."

Ah. I narrowed my eyes and looked again. I could maybe make out the side of his head, but it was hard to say for sure through the press of unfamiliar bodies. I'd just have to take her word for it.

"Listen to me," Allison went on, resting her hand on my forearm as we ran. "We have just over half a mile to go. You can do this. All you have to do is match me stride for stride. Got it?"

I nodded. Or I tried to anyway. My entire body felt like it was beyond my control and all over the place at that point, so I wasn't sure if she caught the gesture.

"Okay. You ready?"

I shook my head vigorously and held up a hand, wordlessly asking her to wait. Then I fast-forwarded through my iPod play list until I found a song I thought might motivate me enough to do as she'd asked. I gave her a thumbs-up as the first strains of the track filtered to my ears and waved my hand, indicating that she should go ahead.

Allison flashed me a feral grin and lengthened her stride a bit. Not a ton. Certainly not drastically. But as exhausted as I was, I still struggled with it. I let out a little huff of annoyance, and it took me a few seconds to catch up with her.

"Come on, Ryan," Allison called encouragingly. "Keep up. You've got this. Let's go." She cranked it up another notch and started swinging her arms as she got into the new pace.

The taste of blood on the back of my tongue intensified, and I was positive my lungs were on the verge of bursting. With each desperate exhale that escaped my lips, I was half afraid I might vomit. I wasn't certain what was going on with the rest of my internal organs—I'd have to remember to ask Rory later if she could explain it to me—but I did know that they were in cahoots with one another and organizing some kind of coup. Not that I blamed them. If they'd managed to successfully mutiny, I doubted I'd have put up much of a fight.

Left, right, left, right, left, right, I told myself, swinging my own arms as I struggled to match Allison's pace, right down to which foot hit the ground at what time. The music blaring in my ears was mere background noise and wasn't helping me much at all. I wasn't paying any attention to it, at any rate.

Without warning, Allison increased her tempo once again. I let out a frustrated puff and hurried to keep up. I was staring daggers into the back of Byers's head. He was bobbing in front of me like a beacon, and just beyond him—the way a target floats out of focus just ahead of the front sights of a gun—I could make out the finish line. I narrowed my eyes as a low growl escaped my throat, and a new swell of anger rose within me. Fuck him. No way in hell was I just going to give up and let him have this.

Also, no way in hell was I going to prolong this any more than

I had to. I wanted this race to be over, and I wanted it to be over now. It was time to turn up the heat.

I didn't even spare so much as a glance for Allison. I ducked my head for an instant as I struggled to increase my pace even more. My lungs screamed at me as my arms and legs pumped furiously. Closer. Closer. Every step I took brought me infinitesimally nearer to Byers. My heart had been running at a continuous roar for some time now, but the thought of actually beating him made it jump and then kick into overdrive.

I was locked into an all-out sprint. I closed my eyes for a second as I bolted, determined, desperate to reach that finish line before he did. I couldn't hear anything. Even with my eyes opened, I could barely see. My entire body was one giant longing. For me to win. For this to end. Whichever came first. A part of me was halfway to not caring.

When I was about eight or ten steps behind Byers, I took my eyes off him so I could shift my focus to the finish line. Tons of people stood there, cheering and clapping and shouting encouragement at those of us unlucky enough to still be running, but I hardly noticed them outside of the fact that they were marking my goal.

I frowned, and my mouth stretched wide as I grimaced. I dug down deep, reaching as far as I could into the recesses of my soul, searching for any sorts of reserves I could dredge up that would help me win this thing. Not that it mattered. I mean, honestly, I didn't think I even needed to win at this point. Not to save face anyway. Even if Byers managed to cross the finish line ahead of me, I would still have come close to beating him, and I'd run twice as far as he had. The implication that I'd have won if we'd run against one another in the first heat would be clear enough to embarrass him, our five-thousand-dollar wager notwithstanding.

In my mind's eye, I saw the look on Allison's face as Byers had forbidden her to run. I remembered the sound of her voice all the times we'd spoken on the phone in the weeks since he'd started being an asshole to her—how frustrated and angry and, at rare times, damn near broken she'd sounded. Something in my chest cracked at the recollection. It might've been a rib, but I doubted it. No, there it was. That was the fuel I'd been looking for.

I opened my mouth and let out a roar born of equal parts fury and anguish. My arms and legs were swinging wildly as I dashed toward the end. I didn't think I'd ever run so fast. I'd certainly never tried this hard. One hundred steps. Sixty. Closer. I was getting closer.

"Go, Ryan, go," Allison screamed as she ran next to me.

Somehow, I managed to pick up the pace even more, although where this burst of speed was coming from, I couldn't have said. Forty-five steps. Thirty. The burning sensation in my lungs faded to the back of my awareness until it barely registered at all. Twenty steps. Fifteen. My leaden legs suddenly felt light as they moved. Ten steps. Five. My upper body pitched forward dangerously as I overbalanced. My legs struggled to keep up, but it was much too late for that now.

"Move, move, move," I shouted at the people milling around the finish line.

I flew past the marker and barreled through the crowd, intent on getting off to the side and out of the way, bouncing off a few spectators and tripping and falling headfirst onto the pavement. I felt a jolt of pain as flesh met blacktop, but it broke through my consciousness only dimly. I pushed it aside and crawled on my hands and knees the rest of the way to the grass lining the roadway, where I retched violently.

There's no telling how long I knelt there on the side of the road just steps past the finish line, throwing up the entire contents of my stomach. If the ache in my abdomen when I was finally done was anything to go by, it had to have been at least a millennium, but someone probably would've tried to bring me in out of the snow when the seasons changed, so that couldn't have been accurate.

I sensed someone settling down into the grass next to me and felt a gentle hand resting on my back. I allowed my head to hang as I waited to see whether I was actually done vomiting. The hand started making small circles, and I wanted to say thank you but was afraid to turn my head to make eye contact lest the heaving start again.

"That's it, Ryan," Allison murmured as she removed the baseball hat from my head. "Let it out."

The cool air on my overheated head felt fantastic, and I let out a contented sigh. I closed my eyes and sank down so that my weight rested mostly on my heels. I raised a shaky hand to run the back of it across my mouth and smacked my lips a couple of times, wrinkling my nose at the horrid taste coating my tongue.

Like some sort of angel, Allison produced a bottle of water. I accepted it with a muttered "Thanks" and set to rinsing my mouth out.

After a few rounds of swish and spit, I felt sufficiently comfortable to take an actual drink. The cold water felt heavenly cascading down my throat, and, unable to help myself, I tipped my head back for a long, greedy gulp.

"Whoa." Allison chided me, taking the bottle away.

"Hey."

"Slow down. You're going to make yourself sick. Again."

I chuckled and sagged bodily against her. The heat radiating between our sweat-slicked bodies was surprisingly pleasant. I was happy to sit there as long as it took for the dizziness and nausea to abate.

Allison raised my ponytail, giving the cool air access to the back of my neck. It helped. I was still weak and unsteady, but I was slowly regaining my strength.

"You have vomit on your shirt," Allison pointed out.

I wrinkled my nose and looked down, disgusted. "Ew."

"Do you need help taking it off?" Her tone was innocent, but the expression on her face as I turned to look at her and the darkening of her eyes definitely was not.

"Maybe when we get inside the locker room. I'm not too keen on stripping down out here." I held my hand out. "Help me up?"

Allison stood gracefully and pulled me to my feet. She had a huge smile on her face as she handed me back the hat she'd taken off my head. I accepted it and snagged the bottle of water from her while she was distracted, managing to force myself to take only a modest sip.

"You're bleeding," Allison said, her voice an interesting blend of concern and exasperation.

"Where?"

"Everywhere."

Allison frowned, presumably at my disheveled state, but who could really tell? She took my right hand in hers and turned it over to graze her fingertips over the road rash marring my palm. Then she took my other arm and lifted it so I could see the giant scrape decorating the underside of my forearm. I followed her eyes when she glanced down and noticed that my knees and shins were pretty banged up, too. But what surprised me the most was when she caressed the hollow of my left cheek with a feather-light touch, which sparked an unexpected stab of pain.

"So, I guess I look like kind of a mess, huh?"

"You look beautiful."

"Oh." I blushed hotly at her words, as well as the sincerity in her eyes. My insides fluttered, and I suddenly felt uncharacteristically shy. "Thanks."

Allison smiled and tucked a wayward lock of hair behind my ear. She allowed her fingers to linger, tracing my jaw almost reverently.

"I'm so proud of you," she whispered.

"I couldn't have done it without you," I whispered back.

"Guess we make a pretty good team."

"Looks like. We should collaborate more often."

"I'm sure if we put our heads together we could come up with a project or two that could benefit."

Allison's eyes dropped to my lips, and I could see she was thinking about kissing me. I inhaled sharply as a fissure of excitement skittered down my spine to ignite fireworks in places decidedly lower. I licked my lips and had just resolved to kiss her senseless when someone bumped into me, reminding me that we weren't alone. The unexpected impact knocked me off balance and shattered the intimacy of the moment.

I blushed again, embarrassed that I'd been caught so off guard, and hastened to reestablish my footing so I wouldn't literally fall into Allison's arms. I cleared my throat and brushed a few more stray wisps of hair back off my forehead and out of my eyes.

"You need to stretch," Allison reminded me. "Or else you'll be really sore later."

"If I recall correctly, someone promised me a thorough rubdown after this fiasco." I was flirting shamelessly as I started in the general direction of the locker room, pleased when she fell in step beside me. "I don't like to brag, but I think I've earned it."

"Oh, you do, do you?" Allison asked, a playful lilt to her tone.

"Yup. I do."

"We'll see." But the curve of her lips and the twinkle in her eye left no doubt I'd be reaping my reward.

"Great job, Ryan," Jamie said as she intercepted Allison and me on our way back to the PT building. She clapped me on the back. "I didn't even have to throw the race. Although I was absolutely prepared to do that just to see the look on Byers's face when he has to hand over five thousand dollars."

"Thanks." Even now, I was as wobbly as a newborn fawn trying to walk for the first time, and my body was still buzzing more than I was comfortable with. I looked to Allison hopefully. "So, it's official? I really beat him?"

"Yeah, you did." Jamie's expression shone with triumph. "I was right behind you guys. I saw the whole thing. You won by at least four or five paces, easy. There wasn't even a question."

Allison's smile widened into a full-fledged, shit-eating grin. She inclined her head to where Byers was standing next to the timekeeper, peering over his shoulder to look at the clipboard with a dark scowl marring his features. "Looks like he's still trying to wrap his mind around it."

"He's so pissed right now." Jamie chortled.

I grinned as I let out a whoop of pure joy and launched myself at Allison, crushing her in a jubilant embrace. I was so happy, my chest felt like it was about to burst. I hugged her tight for a long moment, burying my face into her neck and breathing deeply. As quickly as I'd bounded into her arms, I leapt back out again. I put a hand over my mouth, horrified at what I'd just done.

"Allison, I am so sorry. I got carried away. I didn't mean to do that."

"Hey. It's okay." Allison took a step closer to me and stared into my eyes. "I've told you a dozen times now that I don't care who knows we're together. You don't have to worry about casually touching me in public."

Her reassurances pleased me, but, for once, that hadn't been my concern. "Uh, no. That wasn't it. I accidentally just got blood and throw-up all over your shirt." I pointed at the evidence and winced. "Sorry."

"Oh! Gross!"

"Want me to help you take it off?" I asked, not bothering to attempt to make my tone even half as innocent as hers had been when she'd made the same inquiry a few minutes ago.

"Come on." Jamie groaned theatrically. "You two have got to give it a rest. It's too much. I'm going to go find Jo. Hit us up later if you want to grab a drink or something before you head back north."

I met Allison's eyes. "Thanks, Jamie. But I think I'll be otherwise engaged later."

Jamie laughed. "Yeah. I figured. But it doesn't hurt to ask."

As Jamie took off to locate her partner, Allison and I resumed our slow mosey back toward the locker room. I was eager to get out of this outfit and take a hot shower. Once I was back in regular clothes, with my scars safely hidden beneath layers of cotton, maybe the sheer number of stares and whispers I garnered would decrease.

"So," I said, as a nervous flutter tickled my insides. "Are you free tonight?"

"Why, Agent O'Connor. Are you asking me out?" Allison batted her long eyelashes at me.

"Maybe. You interested?"

"Perhaps. What'd you have in mind?"

"It's a surprise." I didn't have anything specific in mind at all, but I didn't want her to know that. I'd always been good at operating under pressure. I assumed I'd be able to pull something out of thin air, and she'd be none the wiser.

"Oh, yeah? You know, I'm not normally a huge fan of surprises."

"I know. But I thought that—" Someone else bumped my shoulder hard, knocking me off balance and almost causing me to fall. Allison caught me as I stumbled into her, and I shot an irritated glance toward the offender.

Beau Byers was glaring at me, his lips twisted into a cruel grimace. "Oops."

Allison was immediately livid. "You did that on purpose."

I put a restraining hand on her arm. "Allison, it's fine. Let's just go."

"What the hell is the matter with you?" Allison demanded, ignoring me in favor of engaging Byers.

"Allison, come on. It doesn't matter."

Allison still refused to look at me. She was glowering at Byers, her hands clenching and unclenching at her sides, looking like she was considering decking him.

"Did you want something, Beau?" Allison's voice was a low, warning rumble.

Byers cast a sidelong glance at me before he returned to sneering right back at her. His expression was angry and defiant as he stared at her, but something else lurked beneath his eyes. I tried to put a name to it and failed.

"There was, actually. I need to talk to you."

"Well, it's going to have to wait. I'm busy." Allison attempted to breeze by him, but he roughly grabbed her elbow.

A powerful wave of rage washed over me at the sight of him manhandling her like that, but I gritted my teeth and tamped it down as best I could. Allison would not have appreciated any comment I might've made on the subject, so I opted not to say anything.

"No, Agent Reynolds. We need to talk now," Byers stated, his intonation positively dripping with meaning and innuendo. Couple that with his expression, and it was evident that he was less than happy with his subordinate at present. That knowledge didn't help my peace of mind any.

Allison studied him for a long moment, the fury pouring off her lithe frame in heavy waves. Whatever Byers had demanded to talk to her about, she clearly wanted no part of.

"Fine." She took a deep breath and then turned to me. I was relieved to note her countenance soften. "Why don't you go on ahead? I'll be there in a minute."

I frowned, equal parts puzzled and suspicious. I doubted Byers would retaliate for both my and Allison's attitude toward him today, right here in the middle of the road at JJRTC, but I couldn't be certain. The notion that he might made me reluctant to leave Allison here alone with him.

"I don't mind waiting," I told her, pushing against the niggling feeling of anxiety swirling around my guts.

"No, it's okay." Allison tried to dismiss me again. "This won't take long. Trust me." She shot Byers another look meant to wither.

Something about this situation didn't sit right and was nagging at me. I couldn't put my finger on why, though. I hesitated, and my mind whirled as I attempted to come up with some sort of appropriate rejoinder. I was drawing a complete blank.

"Jesus, Ryan. Just go." Allison's voice was sharp, and the razor edge to the command cut me deeply.

I started at the venom in her tone and recoiled as if she'd slapped me. The thought that it might've hurt less if she'd actually struck me flitted through the haze left in the wake of her anger, but upon seeing Byers's smugly triumphant expression, the idea shattered like a water balloon hurled at a brick wall. Only a dripping, unsalvageable mess remained.

A scalding embarrassment bubbled up inside me, but the rising tide of my own fury quickly drowned it. I loved Allison to death, but I couldn't come up with any acceptable scenario for her to address me in such a fashion, certainly not in front of a coworker, especially one who'd sought to humiliate me himself. I didn't appreciate her taking it upon herself to finish the job he'd started.

I drew myself up to my full height and set my shoulders. I lifted my chin almost defiantly and pinned Allison with a cold glare. I nodded once, curtly, and clenched my jaw to rein in all the biting comments clamoring over one another, fighting for the chance to be the first to escape my lips. Without a word, I spun around and stalked away. That she didn't even bother to call after me as I left hurt almost as badly as her snapping at me. But I was determined not to let her or anyone else see how much her attitude had upset me, so I deliberately maintained my pace as I strode toward the locker room.

CHAPTER SIX

The warm water from the shower felt divine as it cascaded off my head and down my soap-slicked skin, washing away suds and sweat alike. My muscles were still a tad rubbery from exertion, and I could feel little pinpricks of pain wherever the water ran over the new scrapes I'd acquired during my spectacular tumble at the finish line, but it was a small price to pay in exchange for such bliss.

I'd been grateful that the locker room had been empty when I'd stormed in, partly because I hadn't wanted to rush through this heavenly shower experience, but mostly because I'd been seething, and I'd wanted to give in to my rage and let it bubble and boil. I hadn't wanted to have to explain my fit of temper away or, worse yet, pretend I was fine when I definitely wasn't.

So, I'd fumed for a bit, enjoying being able to give in to my childish urge to slam the locker doors as hard as I wanted. I'd banged the heel of my unscraped hand violently against the wall to one of the toilet stalls a couple of times, and I'd punted my duffel bag across the entire length of the room. The physical release of my mental anguish helped a little, but I was still a long way from feeling mollified.

Now, in addition to the indignation I was experiencing, I was also tired and drained. The emotional and physical tolls of the day had finally caught up with me and demanded a hefty payment. All I wanted at the moment was to stand in the scalding-hot spray of the shower until the water cooled and then go back to my hotel and sleep for a year.

The sound of the shower stall door opening behind me and a gust of cool air broke into my reverie, and I froze. I could think of only one person who'd have the gall to encroach upon my bathing time like that. A surge of renewed anger rushed through me, and I knitted my eyebrows together and set my jaw again before I turned around.

Allison was leaning with her hip against the opened doorframe, an apologetic expression on her face. She was gloriously naked, but I refused to be distracted. In fact, I viewed her current state of undress as a deliberate attempt to redirect my fury, and I didn't appreciate that ploy. The notion that she might be calculating enough to intentionally try to avoid answering for her earlier behavior in this fashion only served to fan the already ardent flames of my ire.

"This stall is occupied."

"I know. That's why I chose it."

"Well, choose another one. I don't want you in here."

"No." She continued to stare at me, which only made me more angry.

"What?" I demanded, eager to hurry this pointless discussion along. I rested my hands on my hips as the spray from the shower pounded against my shoulder blades.

Allison's eyes were liquid, her expression remorseful. "Ryan, I'm really sorry."

"Yeah? Good for you. You should be." I turned my back to her and bought myself some time by sticking my face in the streaming water and rubbing my skin vigorously with my palms, wincing a little as they skittered over the newly acquired scrape decorating my cheek.

"Ryan."

I childishly ignored her, preferring instead to continue to cling to all the reasons I had a right to be furious with her the way a koala bear hugs a tree.

"Ryan, please look at me."

I tipped my head back and allowed the water to tumble across my brow and back over my crown as I ran my hands through my hair. I didn't want to look at her. I didn't want to talk to her. I definitely didn't want her to know how badly she'd hurt my feelings.

"Please." Her voice was almost a whisper, barely audible over the sound of the shower, her tone pleading.

I sighed and capitulated, unable to not give in to her every whim and desire for very long, despite myself. I took my time turning around, trying to harden my heart against what I imagined her expression to be before I actually saw it. I wanted to retain at least a modicum of pride, and crumbling instantly in the face of her distress wouldn't help me.

As I'd expected, when I finally met Allison's eyes, they were miserable and brimming with sadness and regret. The walls I'd so painstakingly erected around my heart started to crack. In an attempt to combat that weakness, I put my hands on my hips again and waited, somewhat impatiently.

"I am so, so sorry." She reached out toward me as though she longed to touch me but thought better of it and pulled back at the last second.

"You're saying that a lot today," I shot back, still not quite ready to forgive her. "And as I've previously stated, you should be."

Allison wrung her hands in a gesture I recognized as nervousness and took a tentative step closer. I took one step back. Hurt cut a wide swath across her features, but I didn't care. She'd hurt me when she'd dismissed me like an errant child to have a throw-down with Byers. She'd embarrassed me, too. I'd just spent the better part of fifteen minutes nursing that pique. I wasn't quite ready to loosen my grip on my righteous indignation. Not just yet.

The door to the shower stall swung shut behind Allison, and she took yet another small step toward me. My next move left me pressed bodily against the tiled wall directly underneath the showerhead. The only thing standing between us now—the only thing helping me continue this standoff—was the water cascading from the nozzle above my head.

Allison wasted no time closing the remaining distance between us. She strode through the scalding spray and stopped scant inches from me. We were standing close enough to one another that if either of us took too deep a breath, our breasts would touch. The little droplets of water now clinging to her eyelashes mesmerized me. The compulsion to tenderly kiss them off welled up.

"No. You stay over there. You know I can't think when you touch me."

Allison didn't reply. Not verbally, anyway. Instead of complying with my halfhearted request, she continued to stare into my eyes, her own awash with guilt and trepidation. Which, naturally, made me feel remorseful. I sighed and massaged my temples with the thumb and middle finger of my right hand. Goose bumps broke out across my skin when I felt the light caress of her fingertips skate over my left shoulder.

"Please forgive me," Allison said softly, breaching that last bit of space that separated us by stepping closer. The feel of her pressed up against me scrambled my brain, making it damn near impossible to complete a train of thought.

I dropped my hand from my brow so it rested against the side of her neck. My other hand snaked loosely around her hip, and I tilted my head so my forehead was resting against hers.

"You hurt my feelings," I said. "And you embarrassed me."

"I know."

"It's probably stupid of me to feel either of those things, but that doesn't change the fact that I do."

"I shouldn't have spoken to you like that. Definitely not in front of someone we work with. Especially not in front of him. I'm sorry."

"No, you shouldn't have."

"I said I was sorry."

"I know." I took a long, deep breath and closed my eyes again, content to bask in the glow of our connection.

"So...where does that leave us, then?"

I mulled that question over for a long moment. "I don't know."

"I'm not very good at this," Allison admitted. She sounded damn near heartbroken, and the rest of my anger evaporated.

"Me, either." I sighed, suddenly exhausted again. "Well, I guess we haven't had a lot of practice interacting as an 'us' in front of our peers. We're bound to have a learning curve."

Allison pulled back, her expression hopeful. "Does that mean you forgive me?"

I nodded. "Don't let it happen again." I wasn't kidding or trying to be cute. She'd had her one mistake, and I was willing to let it go, but I wouldn't tolerate that sort of behavior becoming a habit. I was nobody's punching bag. Not anymore.

"I won't. I promise."

"Okay."

We stood quietly, holding one another for a while. Allison started tracing absent patterns on the wet skin of my back that made me shiver. I squeezed my thighs together to subtly relieve the ache building there.

"So, um...Do you want to tell me what's going on with you and your boss?" I asked, barely managing to bite back a low moan when Allison's hands skirted down over my ass. I was trying to stay on topic, and she was making that extremely difficult.

"No," Allison murmured, shaking her head. Her eyes dropped to zero in on my lips, and I gasped at the stab of arousal that pierced me.

"You…promised." I faltered as Allison slid her hand up my side and brushed it across the outer swell of my breast, barely glancing off one already-stiff nipple with her thumb. The contact was enough to make me scream for more. But, stubborn as I was, I refused to give in to my desires. "You said you'd tell me what happened with you two. You've been stalling for weeks."

"I know," Allison replied, her lips gliding over my jaw as she spoke. "And I intend to keep that promise. Just not right this second."

As she finished, she closed her lips over mine in a slow, languid kiss. I lost track of…well, just about everything as I allowed myself to become lost in the sensation. She kissed me deliberately, her pace unhurried, as though we weren't standing in a shower stall in the locker room of the training center, and we had all the time in the world.

I slid my hands into her silky black hair and twined it around my fingers as I pulled her even closer. I felt her smile against my lips, and I matched the gesture with a tiny grin of my own. Without breaking contact, I pushed off the wall and walked us a step or two so we were fully immersed in the spray.

I sketched light, random patterns across her slick skin, enjoying both the feel of her beneath my fingers as well as the tiny gasps and moans she made under my touch. Allison tipped her head back, and I set to work licking the droplets of water off the delectable flesh of her neck.

Allison fisted my hair and clutched me tighter to her. I wrapped my arms around her waist. As I palmed one perfect ass cheek, Allison gasped and rolled her hips into me. I bit down lightly on the tendon in her neck and inserted my thigh between both of hers, bracing the ball of my foot against the tiled wall for leverage. When she undulated her hips again, I pulled her even closer, gasping a little under my breath at the feeling of her warmth against my leg.

"Oh, my God, Ryan." Allison's voice was a low, throaty moan that did wicked things to my already aching sex.

Allison used the hand she'd threaded through my hair to guide my head down to a pebbled nipple and used the other to press my fingers to the apex between her thighs. It was my turn to moan as I felt just how ready she was.

I took her nipple into my mouth and sucked on it gently as I slowly toyed with her slick folds. Allison hissed and tried to angle her hips so I was touching her where she wanted me to. I smiled against her breast and moved my hand away. Not enough to completely deprive her of my touch, but enough so she got the message that we were going to do this according to my whims, not hers.

Allison groaned and dropped her head so her lips were pressed into the crown of my head, but she stilled her hips and waited. I moved my mouth over to her other nipple. As a reward for her compliance, I stroked her more firmly and ran the middle finger of my other hand lightly down the crack of her ass.

Allison's hips bucked, and she turned her head and rested the hollow of her cheek against my hair. When I repeated my motions, she squeezed me tighter and let out a whimper.

"You're driving me insane," she whispered.

"Mmm. Good," I mumbled around the mouthful of flesh I was busy enjoying. I bit down hard enough to make her gasp and then soothed the ache with a gentle caress of my tongue.

"Christ, I've missed you."

I dipped the tips of two of my fingers into her opening, awed by the moisture collecting there. I took my time spreading it over her swollen lips. "I can see that."

Her grip in my hair tightened until it was painful. "Stop teasing me."

I chuckled lightly. "Never."

I slowly slid my fingers inside her, reveling in her groan. I ran my free hand down the back of her leg until I'd almost reached her knee pit, at which time I tugged. Allison immediately obeyed my unspoken request and hitched that leg up so it was wrapped around my waist. The new position provided the perfect angle for me to grind the heel of my hand against her as I thrust in and out.

"Mmm, yes," Allison mumbled into my hair. I could feel her rolling her head from side to side. "Oh, God. Just like that."

The loud bang of the locker-room door being thrown open interrupted our carnal activities, and Allison and I both froze. Our heads shot up, and we stared at one another. Had the new arrival heard anything incriminating? I couldn't tell. All I caught were the faint rustling sounds of someone rifling through their belongings, underscored by a low, almost absent whistling.

The *thwap-thwap-thwap* of flip-flops steadily became louder as they got closer and then softer again once they'd passed by. After another moment, I heard the sound of a shower-stall door being opened and water turning on. Then the door closed, and the soft whistling resumed.

Allison and I stared at one another for what felt like an epoch. "What now?" she mouthed silently.

I shrugged, not considering the consequences of the action before I performed it. The motion jostled the hand I still had buried knuckle-deep inside her, causing her to gasp. I grinned as a thought occurred to me.

"No," Allison growled as loudly as she dared.

In response, I wiggled my fingers and used the pad of my thumb to make light circles around her clit. Allison's eyes fluttered, and she bit down on her lower lip.

"We can't," she murmured in my ear, but her tone wasn't convincing.

I smiled as I noted the flood of moisture that coated my hand as well as the way her inner walls were starting to clench around my fingers. I drew my fingers out and pushed them back inside her, making sure to drive the palm of my hand against her as I did.

"Oh."

I pressed my lips to hers for a long moment, enjoying the sensation of kissing her just as much now as I had the very first time I'd done it. When we finally parted for air, I nuzzled her chin and made my way slowly over to her ear.

"Want me to stop?" I punctuated the question by rolling one of her nipples between the finger and thumb of my free hand.

"I will literally kill you if you do."

"Be very, very quiet," I whispered, emphasizing the command by taking her earlobe between my teeth and biting down on it gently.

Allison nodded and buried her face into the crook of my neck. She latched onto the sensitive skin there, presumably in an attempt to muffle her groans. Her leg tightened around my hip as her hands dug into my back.

I wrapped my free arm around her waist and clutched her to me, as much in an effort to still her hips as to forge a physical connection. I enjoyed nothing in the whole world as much as I enjoyed holding her. Except maybe causing her to come undone with my fingers. Or my mouth. Or possibly—

Allison's teeth sank hard into the juncture where my shoulder met my neck and pulled me out of my musings and back on task. Her breathing had become shallow and ragged, and those uneven puffs against my skin were making me dizzy. Her hips were bucking frantically now, and occasional grunts escaped her lips as she drove herself closer and closer to release on my hand.

I smiled into the flesh of her upper chest and continued to match her motions thrust for thrust. She was on the edge of losing it, I could tell. Her fingers dug into the flesh of my back hard enough to bruise, and the muscles in her body became rigid. The one leg I was using to support her weight trembled, so I sought purchase against the shower wall with the heel of the other.

I slid the hand not buried inside her up her back and tangled my fingers in her hair. I made a fist and pulled, forcing her to release the skin of my neck with a loud pop. I winced at the slight ache I felt there and made a mental note to talk to her later about her propensity toward marking me.

I tilted her head back so I could meet her eyes. The passion I saw swirling in those inky depths left me breathless. Having caught her attention, I released my hold on her hair and cupped her cheek in my palm, caressing the soaked flesh of the hollow there.

Allison's inner walls were fluttering now, and her hips were slamming into my hand. I decided to forsake my hold on her cheek in favor of wrapping my other hand around her hips. I had a feeling she would need the extra support very soon.

Allison's lower lip started trembling, and her eyes glazed over right before they shuttered closed. A low groan bubbled up in the back of her throat as she chased her orgasm, and I surged forward, pressing my lips to hers to swallow the sound.

Her pleasure seemed to go on forever, yet it wasn't nearly long enough. All too soon, her hips stilled and her breathing slowed, until eventually she sagged against me.

I continued to kiss her for a long moment as she set her leg back down and slid her hands up to rest against the sides of my neck. She broke the kiss to press her lips lightly to my nose, my cheeks, my eyes before pulling me in for a long hug. I felt more than heard her sigh and closed my eyes.

"I love you so much," she whispered softly into my ear.

"That's only because I give you the best orgasms you've ever had," I whispered back, trying not to laugh.

Allison pinched my ass hard, and I yelped. She slapped her hand over my mouth and glared at me. The water in the other shower stall turned off, and a long, drawn-out silence followed. I was afraid to even breathe. We stayed huddled, intertwined with one another like that until whoever had just finished washing off had wandered past us and back toward the front of the locker room.

Allison shot me a warning look and slowly removed her hand from my mouth.

"Love you, too," I mouthed, grinning like an idiot.

She smiled brightly and rewarded me with a soft kiss. Her countenance turned thoughtful, and she tilted her head as the faint sounds of a locker being opened and someone rustling around drifted to my ears. A mischievous gleam shone in her eyes.

I gulped, simultaneously titillated and wary. "What?"

"Looks like we still have some time to kill until we can get out of here without being seen." She slid her hand purposefully down my chest as she pinned me with a meaningful stare.

I swallowed hard again and bit my lower lips as her hands slipped between my legs. "If we must, we must," I said with great difficulty.

"Oh, we must."

CHAPTER SEVEN

The last thing I wanted to do with my remaining time in DC was sit in a doctor's office taking round after round of intense psychological tests. If a person hadn't been disturbed before, they sure would be after having to slog through all that. It was like high school all over again with all the dots I had to fill in. After about forty-five minutes, I wanted to poke my eyes out with one of my number-two pencils.

Of course, after I'd finished taking the tests, I had to wait until they'd been scored and the doctor had a chance to go over them before this tableau could proceed. It gave me plenty of time to reflect on how wrong I'd been earlier, that *this* was the last thing I wanted to do with my remaining time in DC. At least Allison was working while I was stuck here, so it wasn't like I was really missing anything on that score. I wouldn't have been able to see her anyway. Small consolation, but it was better than nothing.

"So, Ryan," the doctor said as, a very long while later, he entered the room I'd been holed up in, perusing the contents of the folder in his hands. Based on the context, I assumed it was my file. He never once lifted his eyes from the page he was reading, not even when he moved to sit, and for some reason, that absorption grated on my nerves.

"Yes." I bounced my feet a little. This interview was mandatory if I wanted to go back to work and get on with my life, but I really didn't want to be there.

"It says here you were shot." The doctor spoke again, still keeping his face buried in my file.

Is he kidding me? I mentally snorted even though I shouldn't have been surprised. Not with the nonchalance that'd been the agency's response to the entire incident. "Yes."

Something about my tone—or perhaps lack thereof—made him pause. He finally settled his attention on me and took his time studying me. "I see."

The urge to fire back with a snarky retort bubbled up inside me, but I managed to tamp it down, reminding myself that the ultimate goal here was to tell this man whatever he wanted to hear in order for him to feel comfortable clearing me for full duty. I bested the compulsion to fold my arms across my chest, too, knowing the posture would be seen as defensive. I watched him warily.

"Normally I'd ask how you feel about that, but I imagine the answer would be 'not good,' so we'll skip that line of questioning for the time being."

"Much obliged."

The corners of the doctors mouth lifted in a small smile, but he didn't comment. Instead, he refocused on the file in his hands. "It also says here that your doctors feel you're ready to go back to full duty." He paused and glanced at me from underneath his eyebrows. "Physically."

"Yes." I hesitated, unsure how much to expose. "I'd like to go back to work."

The doctor took his time closing the folder and placing it on the edge of his desk. His left hand rested on top of it, and he toyed with a ballpoint pen. "You haven't really been out of work, though, have you?"

"What do you mean?"

"You've been reporting to the office. You've been doing casework."

"Only what was absolutely necessary. And it was just paperwork stuff." How the hell did he know that? I opened my mouth to ask but decided that'd seem too much like I was ashamed of those actions. I wasn't, and I didn't want him to get the wrong idea.

"How often?"

"I'm sorry?"

"How often did you report to the office?"

"I'm not sure I understand what you're asking me." That wasn't strictly true. I was just trying to gauge his feelings on whatever my answer was likely to be.

"Was it every day? Every other day? Once a week? How much time did you actually take off to recover?"

I averted my eyes, uncomfortable with the direction of this conversation. My idea of appropriate recovery time and his were most likely two completely different things. And unfortunately for me, in this scenario, his carried far more weight.

"That's what I thought," he said.

I met his gaze again, determined not to be intimidated or shamed into feeling guilty. I'd done what I'd had to in order to cope with the situation as best I could. And no amount of forced embarrassment would undo that, so why bother?

He appraised me for a time. "How have you been sleeping?"

I tried not to cringe but was afraid I didn't manage it very well. "Okay."

He took a deep breath and let it out slowly. He sat back in his chair and allowed it to tilt a little bit. He clicked the pen a couple of times as he watched me. "You know, I've been doing this for quite a long time."

I cleared my throat, attempting to ignore the feeling of unease building inside me, but said nothing.

"Long enough to tell when someone is lying to me."

"I'm not lying. I am sleeping okay. Not great, but okay." I paused, considering whether to say what was probably the key word. "Now."

"So, you admit you had some trouble sleeping before."

I sagged, defeated, and broke eye contact. "Yes. I did. For a while."

"And now?"

"It's better. For the most part."

"Did you dream?" The doctor sat back up, clicked his pen back open, and poised it over the paper.

I felt an unwelcome twinge inside my chest and swallowed hard. I didn't want to talk about this. But it appeared we were going to. "I did."

"Often?"

"More often than I wanted to, yes." That didn't even begin to paint an accurate picture of what'd happened every single time I'd closed my eyes, but it wasn't exactly a lie, either. Briefly, I wondered whether I should put aside my natural instinct to play the semantics game and just lay all my cards on the table. This might go faster if I did. Of course, it might get me benched for an indeterminate amount of time, as well.

"Do you still?"

"Sometimes."

"What do you dream about?"

"Different things."

"The incident?"

"I really wish people would stop calling it that." My response was immediate, my tone sharp.

"Why is that?"

"Because I think that moniker minimizes the entire experience, don't you?"

"I'm much more interested to hear what you think."

"And I just told you."

The doctor paused and allowed the metaphorical dust to settle before trying again. "Do you think headquarters is deliberately trying to minimize it?"

"I don't know what they're trying to do. I only know that they haven't formally acknowledged it."

"And you want them to."

"It'd be nice."

"What part would you like them to acknowledge, exactly?"

"All of it. Any of it." I knew what the doctor was trying to do with this line of questioning, but that didn't make me any less frustrated.

"And how would you like them to express this acknowledgment?"

"I don't know! I just think someone should say something about the fact that Lucia died, and one of our agents was responsible for it."

The doctor brought his hands together, and the fingers of his right played with the wedding band adorning his left. I was curious whether that was a conscious or unconscious action.

"I find it interesting that you want them to acknowledge that part," he said after a long moment. "Not your getting shot but hers."

"I lived," I said simply. And that was the crux of it. I was the only one of us left alive to be angry. It only made sense that I exercise that privilege on her behalf.

"Do you wish you hadn't?"

"Of course not." My answer, though instantaneous, wasn't accurate. Some days, very occasionally, I wished more than anything that I'd died instead of her. But I knew that was the guilt talking.

"Do you feel like it was your fault that she died?"

My heart stopped, and a distinct coldness washed over me. I'd voiced that sentiment aloud only twice since it'd happened; once to my sister and once to Allison. I didn't generally enjoy talking about it, for obvious reasons.

I clutched the arms of the chair and tried to force myself to feel calm. Or at the very least, to appear not so visibly upset. "It *was* my fault she died."

He sat back up and made a brief notation on my file. "Let me ask you something. Are you at all familiar with the phenomenon of survivor's guilt?"

"I have a master's degree in psychology." I blushed when I realized how condescending I sounded. I hadn't meant to come across that way. I'd just resented his inference. I worked to deliberately soften my tone. "Yes. I know what survivor's guilt is."

If my attitude put him off, he didn't show it. Instead, he said, "Good. Then I won't need to waste either of our time explaining it to you. Is it safe to assume, then, that you have a valid reason for rejecting that theory?"

"I do. I reject it because it really was my fault that she died."

"How so?"

My stomach tried to physically force its way up into my rib cage. The pressure against my heart was maddening. I clasped my hands together in my lap and ran my thumbnails against one another.

The quiet that settled between us was heavy and oppressive. It reminded me of the sensation that humid summer air created, like it was actually sitting on your shoulders, weighing you down, which was an odd notion. Air tends to be weightless.

"She wouldn't have been in the line of fire if it weren't for me," I said finally.

"I see." He resumed watching me then, as though he knew there was more to the story than what that one sentence revealed.

"She was mad at me for something I'd done. Something that hurt her. She'd come to yell at me for it. And if she hadn't, if she'd stayed at the front of the motorcade with her car, she'd still be alive."

"Ah."

I hesitated again as I tried to determine how or even whether to explain the rest. I fidgeted in my seat. "And when she decided to take her anger out on me in a more physical way, she ended up saving my life. And losing hers in the process."

The doctor appeared to mull that statement for a time, during which I glanced around the room, looking at anything except him. Tears prickled at the backs of my eyes, scalding and sharp, and I tried to blink them away. The last thing I wanted to do was cry in front of a complete stranger. Especially one who was evaluating my emotional state.

"Rationally, I know it wasn't my fault. I didn't hire the person who pulled the trigger. I get that in a perfect world she would've come to the PI car, yelled at me, and been on her merry way. When I consider just the facts, when I examine the situation on a purely intellectual level, I recognize that I had nothing to do with her death. But I *can't* see the situation purely intellectually. And on a gut level, I can't help but feel guilty."

A small smile stole over the doctor's lips. "I'd be worried about you if you didn't."

A sliver of a smile touched my lips as well. "No need to worry. I have enough guilt to last a lifetime."

"Tell me something. When you dream of the incident, what do you dream about? I mean, specifically."

I took mental note of the fact that he'd phrased his question in the present tense despite my having deliberately avoided confirming that I did still dream about what'd happened that day. I sighed as I considered how best to respond.

"I dream about gunshots I can't tell the origins of. A hotel I can't navigate. And Lucia. Dying. Always."

"I see. Anything else?"

"Yeah. Different things. Sometimes other people are there with me. Only one or two, but I'm not always alone. They never hear the gunshots, though. And they never take my desire to discover their origins seriously."

"And Lucia? You said she's always there. Does she speak to you?"

"Yes."

"In every dream?"

"Yes."

"What does she say?"

"In the beginning, she kept telling me I was missing something that she needed me to see."

"Interesting. And what do you think she needed you to see?"

I'd thought a lot about that question the past few weeks and had managed to form a loose working theory. "I think she needed me to see that something was off about the shooting. I think my subconscious was trying to call attention to the little details that pointed to me being the intended target. Details I should've noticed right off the bat but that got lost under the landslide of emotions I'd ended up buried under."

"That's extremely likely. And now that you have it all worked out, what does she say to you?"

I tucked a stray lock of hair back behind my ear as I stalled. My feelings on the subject of Lucia and her death were layered, at best. They were also very personal and very private. I hadn't taken anyone's advice to go seek counseling voluntarily so I could work through them. I definitely wasn't keen on getting into the weeds on this because I was being forced to.

The doctor sat and watched me patiently, his face impassive with the barest hint of sympathetic undertones. He seemed content to let me get wherever I was going on my own. I appreciated his consideration.

"She says different things to me," I said finally, my voice so soft that if there'd been any other ambient noise in the room whatsoever he might've missed it. "None of them nice."

"I see. So, in your dreams she's still mad at you?"

I nodded miserably and cleared my throat in an attempt to dislodge the lump that'd settled there. It didn't work. "Yes."

"Do you think that has something to do with the guilt you feel over her death?"

"I'm sure it does. But knowing that doesn't make it go away. I still feel guilty, and in my dreams, she's still angry with me."

"Is there any chance you're angry with her?"

I tensed. We were wading into some dangerous waters, waters I'd rather we left uncharted. "Is this relevant to my being declared fit for duty? Because if it's not, I'd really rather just skip it."

He studied me for a moment before making a notation in my file. "No. It isn't relevant per se. But I do think it's something you need to work through at some point. These feelings you're having won't simply vanish because you're good at pretending they aren't there."

I stopped myself from laughing out loud, but only just. The mere idea that I was even remotely skilled at pretending my feelings didn't exist was hilarious, especially considering when I felt like all I did lately was wallow. But instead of answering him, I nodded as though I were taking what he'd just told me under advisement.

"I'd like it if you'd go talk to someone in New York."

"Is that an order?"

"It's a strongly worded suggestion."

"Okay. I'll consider it. Anything else?"

"If I prescribed you something to help you sleep, would you take it?"

"Probably not."

He smiled a little. "I figured as much. So I'll just say this: you need to remember that you carry a gun. As a result, the consequences of sleep deprivation have the potential to be that much more catastrophic. I can see you're taking Lucia's death to heart, so I'm sure I don't need to point out to you that you don't want anyone else's demise on your conscience because you had a lapse in judgment due to those consequences. If you won't take something, then you need to find some other way to ensure you get the proper amount of rest."

I couldn't argue with him there. I nodded, relieved that he seemed to be okay with wrapping this up. "You got it."

He fixed me with a very deliberate look. "I'm not kidding, Ryan. The last thing you need is to get into a shooting and have it come out that you're sleep-deprived. Any attorney worth their salt would crucify you for that. And the press would have a field day. And while we're on the subject, how do you feel about the way this situation has played out publicly? It's garnered a great deal of media attention."

Damn. So close. I scowled. "Don't remind me."

"I take it you're not too thrilled with being in the spotlight."

I shook my head. "No. I hate being the center of attention. It's worse that it's because of something like this."

"Do members of the general public recognize you on the street?"

"Sometimes. But it's pretty rare. And I don't go out much."

"What do people say to you?"

I narrowed my eyes and gazed at the ceiling. "Not many people say things *to* me. More often, they say things *about* me and just assume I can't hear them."

"What do they say?"

"Pretty much what you'd expect. 'There's that Secret Service chick.'" I presented the statement in the kind of exaggerated whisper I'd heard many times.

"Does that bother you?"

I shrugged. "Not overly. Not in the way you'd think. I'm used to it. People tended to talk about me like that before I was shot. They do it with all of us. During almost every protection assignment I've ever been on, someone has nudged whoever they were with, gestured to me, and whispered, 'There's Secret Service.' They either think we can't hear them or we're not paying attention."

The doctor appeared amused. "And what about your coworkers? Do they treat you any differently?"

I tensed before I was able to stop myself, which I'm sure instantly clued him in on the fact that he'd just broached a very sore subject. I tried for an air of nonchalance. "Some of them. Not all."

"That bothers you." It wasn't a question.

"Wouldn't it bother you?"

"We're not talking about me."

I rolled my eyes. "Yes, it bothers me."

"What about it bothers you?"

I paused for a moment as I reflected on the conversation I'd had with Rory less than twenty-four hours ago about reputation and perception and how both could be altered in less time than it took to blink and mar your career forever.

"I don't like the idea of the guys thinking I can't do my job."

"And you're afraid they do."

"I know some of them do. And the longer I'm on light duty, the more their suspicions are confirmed."

"Reputation means a lot to you, does it?"

"In this line of work, it's all you have."

"I see." He scribbled for a bit before he asked his next question. "Since we're on the subject of your coworkers, let's change direction for a moment. How do you feel about Mark Jennings?"

I raised my eyebrows at him. "Seriously?"

"Yes. I'm curious to hear what you think about him. You haven't mentioned him."

"Yeah, well, that's because I don't really think there's much to say."

"Humor me."

I wrinkled my nose in distaste. "My feelings about Mark are... complex."

"Mmm-hmm."

"What do you want me to say?" My tone clearly evinced my irritation and frustration. I tried hard to tamp down on my anger, recognizing that it definitely wouldn't help me achieve my current goal, but it was a lost cause. "He got into some shit he had no business being into, and because of his selfishness, Lucia died."

"You see his motivations for what he did as selfish?"

"Maybe that's not exactly the right word. He thought he was protecting his family, which I can understand, but the way he went about it was unconscionable. He decided my life was an acceptable trade for theirs." When I thought about that, it made me furious, so I tried to avoid that line of thinking as best I could. I had nothing to gain by being angry. It wouldn't change anything.

"Do you think you could ever forgive him?"

"Not as long as I have breath in my body," I answered without missing a beat. "I'm simply not that good."

CHAPTER EIGHT

No one was more surprised than I when, despite my outbursts, the doctor cleared me for full duty. Needless to say, I tried to keep a lid on my shock, and I didn't ask a whole lot of questions. I simply thanked him and got out of there as fast as my little legs would carry me. Which, after that hellish race, wasn't very.

I sat at my desk my first day back to work drumming my fingers against my blotter as I waited for my sister to call to let me know she was waiting for me down in the lobby. Since I'd basically ditched her two nights ago in favor of accepting Allison's offer of a thorough rub-down, we'd decided to have lunch together today to properly celebrate my reinstatement.

Unfortunately, she was running late, and I was getting hungry and restless. We'd agreed to meet for lunch well over ninety minutes ago, and I still hadn't heard from her. If she'd gotten caught up in some crazy surgery and forgotten to call, she was going to get it. I hated it when she did that. I didn't care that stuff came up and life got in the way—no one understood that better than me—but I at least wanted to be granted the common courtesy of a phone call.

I eyed my cell phone cagily as I attempted to decide whether I should just call her or give up and grab something to eat on my own. Hmm. I'd better call her. The way my luck was running, she'd show up the second I'd finished whatever I'd picked up for myself, and she'd expect me to eat lunch twice.

I'd just started scrolling through my phone's contact list looking for her number when I was unceremoniously sidelined.

"There she is," Rico exclaimed from the hallway just outside my door, loudly enough to draw the attention of every hearing person within a hundred-mile radius. "All hail the conquering hero."

I snapped my head up to stare at him. "Something's seriously wrong with you, you know that?"

Rico ignored the jibe and made himself at home in my office. He settled himself in the chair opposite my desk and started chaining my paperclips together one by one.

"So?" he prompted after a long moment. He glanced up from his arts-and-crafts project expectantly.

"So, what?"

"Is it true?"

"Is what true? That I'm finally off light duty? Yes, it's true." I patted the bulge my newly reacquired weapon made under my suit jacket for emphasis.

"Don't play coy with me. You're all anybody's been talking about. I just want to separate the myth from the legend, so to speak."

"I have no idea what you're talking about, Rico."

"I heard that you told the SAIC of PPD to go fuck himself at the race the other day. True or false?"

I laughed at what I assumed had to be some kind of a joke, but the good humor died in my throat when his expression never changed. I gaped at him. "You're kidding."

Rico shook his head. "Afraid not. And if the rumors are to be believed, your language was extremely graphic and colorfully descriptive when you instructed him on exactly how to do the deed." He regarded me for a moment. "That part I could believe. You always did have a mouth like a sailor."

"Wait. Slow down. People are seriously saying that I told off the SAIC of PPD?"

"In front of the entire eighth floor, from what I heard. Although I had my doubts the director was actually present. I can't imagine even you would be that foolish."

I rolled my eyes. "I'm concerned about the state of the information-sharing network of this agency. If our rumor mill is that far off base, I don't even want to know what the majority of our investigations look like."

Rico appeared disappointed. "So, it isn't true."

"No, it isn't true!" I cried. "Of course it isn't true. Do you really think I'd do something like that?"

Rico shrugged. "If it was warranted, sure."

"Good heavens," I muttered under my breath, aghast.

"What did happen?"

"I had a little chat with one of the ATs from PPD. That's all."

"And knowing you and your tendency to downplay everything, it was less of a little chat and more of a downright nuclear explosion."

I hesitated. "Well, I may've asked him what the hell was wrong with him."

"That was just stupidity on your part. You never ask a question like that when you're pressed for time. You have no way of knowing how long the answer may be."

"Where were you with this wisdom yesterday? I could've used your expert advice. Maybe then I wouldn't have ended up making that stupid bet."

"Aha! So, the part about the bet was true."

"That depends. What'd you hear? We had a bet. Whether the terms were accurately reported to the masses remains to be seen."

"Ten thousand dollars, a favor to be named later, and the loser had to tattoo the winner's name somewhere on their body."

I stared at him. Was he joking? It was impossible to tell. "No. None of that is even close."

"Oh." He seemed let down. "At least tell me this. Was a tattoo involved at any stage of the game?"

"No! There were no tattoos. Listen, it—"

"Hey, Ryan?" PJ Clarke barreled into my office, half out of breath and looking thoroughly tickled about something. "Oh, good. You're here. Hey, Rico."

"Hey, PJ," I drawled, raising one eyebrow. "What's up?"

"You're never in a million years going to guess who I just got off the phone with."

Rico and I exchanged a glance. "You're probably right. Who?"

"Adam Royce Walker."

"What?" Huh. Would you look at that. He'd been right. Even if I'd been given an infinite number of guesses, I still don't think I'd have come up with that.

Adam Royce Walker was one of our more persistent and dangerous threat subjects. I'd managed his case a couple years ago before he'd decided to relocate himself to DC, but life in our nation's capital must not've been exciting enough for him because he was back now. He and I'd had a brief run-in a few weeks ago, but as far as I knew he'd been relatively quiet since then. Although I had to admit, it was probably tougher for him to communicate with us than usual, considering I'd had him involuntarily committed to the psych ward at Bellevue. Tougher but not impossible.

"I know," PJ went on, clearly pleased with my obvious surprise. "Crazy, right?"

"Well, I guess it was only a matter of time," I mused. "He was bound to be released sometime. They never keep him in for long."

"But that's not the best part," PJ said. "Wait until you hear what he wanted."

"You mean he didn't call to demand that we let him see Hurricane?"

Hurricane was the code name for Zoey Carmichael, the president's only daughter and youngest child. She maintained a residence here in the city. Walker was obsessed with Hurricane and entertained any number of varying delusions about his relationship with her. I'd originally been surprised when he'd left New York for DC because Hurricane herself didn't spend much time there, but as soon as I'd learned he'd gone intending to ask President Anderson Carmichael to grant him his daughter's hand in marriage, it'd made a whole lot more sense.

"Oh, no, he demanded to see Hurricane," PJ said with a snort. "But you'll never believe what he tried to use as a bargaining chip to force the meeting."

"What?"

PJ paused for dramatic effect, and Rico rolled his eyes. "He said he had you."

I frowned. "He said what?"

"He said he had you."

"I don't get it. Had me? What do you mean he had me?"

PJ laughed. "He said he'd kidnapped you, and he was going to kill you if we didn't set up a meeting with Hurricane."

While Walker's claim amused PJ, a dark feeling of foreboding overwhelmed me. I rubbed my bottom lip with my thumb. Walker was delusional on a frighteningly spectacular level, but he was also eerily smart about some things. Making false claims of this nature—the kind that could be easily verified to then ruin whatever angle he was working—wasn't his style.

"And you're sure that's what he said?" I asked. "You're sure he said he had me?"

"Oh, I'm sure. He was going on and on about how you were going to pay for what you did to him a few weeks ago, and how he'd show you suffering like you'd never dreamed of. How Hurricane would see this as a display of his dedication and undying devotion to her. I even heard some muffled whimpering in the background. He really went all out."

"Wait a minute! You just took a call from a dangerous paranoid schizophrenic who's likely off his medication *again*, you heard sounds of someone in distress on his end of the line, and you think it's funny? Where the hell was he calling from?"

PJ's good humor evaporated in an instant, replaced by uncertainty and dread. He ran the palm of his hand through his hair. "I don't know. I just thought what I'd heard was from the TV or something."

Rico let out a long, noisy breath as I closed my eyes and massaged my temples with my thumb and middle finger. I was caught somewhere between being aghast and furious that he and I were even having this conversation. "Okay. Did you at least write down the number he called from?"

"I'm sure it's on my caller ID."

It was my turn to take a deep breath. "Go look for me, please." I may've configured the words in the form of a request, but my tone left no doubt that it was a command.

PJ hustled out of my office, and I lowered my hand from my forehead, trying to ignore the fact that it was trembling. My insides felt like so much Jell-O, and I couldn't shake the gnawing sense of trepidation worming through all that gelatinous goodness.

"What do you think is going on with Walker?" Rico asked.

"I have no idea. This isn't like him at all." I mulled over the situation as I understood it, attempting to figure out what to do next.

"Do you really think Walker has someone?"

I ripped out my hair tie in a fit of pique and ran my fingers through my hair in frustration. "He has to. But who? And where is he keeping her? How did he get her there in the first place?"

"And why is he insisting it's you?" Rico wondered.

"That's the million-dollar question, isn't it? I don't know."

"I mean, you were his case agent for what? A year? A year and a half? How many times during that period did you meet with him? He knows damn well what you look like."

"Exactly. I think he must—" Something hit me just then with all the subtlety of an Acela train at the peak of a DC to New York run. The unexpected force of the realization knocked me back, and I leaned heavily against the backrest of my chair. I couldn't believe how long it'd taken me to reach the most obvious conclusion. My bile rose, thick and cloying, to coat the back of my tongue. "Oh, my God."

Rico's brow wrinkled with worry. "What? What's the matter?"

"Rory." No, that was crazy. Wasn't it? No way could some lunatic manage to snag my sister off a busy New York street. I mean, those sorts of things didn't happen in real life. Right?

"What about her?" Rico eyed me with confusion for a long moment before comprehension settled in. "Oh, shit. You think Walker has Rory?"

I nodded as the unease roiling in the pit of my stomach alchemized into full-blown panic. I'd really wanted him to tell me how ridiculous that theory was, but judging by his expression, I suspected I was about to be on the receiving end of yet another painful lesson on how we can't always get what we want.

"That would explain why he told PJ he has you," Rico said, the words falling from his lips with great reluctance. "He thinks he does."

"Fuck," I muttered, my heart stopped.

I scratched my neck and then ran my palms across my thighs. Okay. I needed to think. I couldn't let fear distract me. Hell, I wasn't even one hundred percent positive Walker actually had Rory, so there was no sense in getting all fired up until that theory was confirmed one way or the other. As my dad would say, I shouldn't invent things to worry about.

I pushed back from my desk and stood so I could prowl the room as I mentally sketched out a plan. My insides felt ice cold, and a vague dizziness tickled the back of my awareness. Possibilities and options swirled in a chaotic mass in my mind, fogs of anxiety I tried to dispel occasionally obscuring them.

"Okay," I said aloud, only half talking to Rico at that point. "Obviously, *something* is making Walker think he has me. It's probably best for whoever he may have to let him go on thinking that, which means I can't talk to him. Until we have him in custody or until we have whoever might be with him safe with us, you all need to play along. Act as if you can't find me, and you're worried."

"Ryan, I am worried." His voice was soft, his tone anguished.

Hearing the concern and angst coloring his words generated some huge cracks in my carefully constructed veneer of calm. I swallowed and cleared my throat, buying myself some time in order to repair them sufficiently so I wouldn't completely crumble.

PJ scuttled back in, his eyes wide. His face indicated he was halfway toward having his own panic attack. If the situation weren't so potentially dire, I'd have felt bad for him. As it was, I could barely refrain from screaming at him to get the hell out of my sight.

"Please tell me you have a number for me," I all but begged him.

PJ wordlessly handed over a piece of paper. The number scrawled on it was written in a shaky hand and was nearly illegible. It was yet another physical testament to just how upset PJ was about the metaphorical ball he'd just dropped.

"Thanks, PJ," I said, taking care to keep my intonation deliberately bland. "We'll take it from here."

"Ryan, I—"

I glanced up from the paper to fix him with a dark glare, cutting him off. He was staring at me with sad puppy-dog eyes. Okay, that made me feel a little bad. I sighed, rueful he felt so distressed and aggrieved that I needed to worry about his feelings at all in the middle of this nightmare.

"PJ, just go. Please. Rico and I will take care of this."

"What can I do?" PJ pleaded.

"Can you go ask Jim who's been handling Walker's case since he got back to town? I'd like to know how long he's been out and see how he's been cycling lately."

The logical choice for that honor would've been me, seeing as how I'd handled the case when Walker was in New York before. But I'd been on light duty because of "the incident" and was therefore technically not supposed to be working any cases. Plus, I was on the Joint Terrorism Task Force, and none of the JTTF reps carried any Secret Service cases. They were too time-sensitive, and the bosses had never wanted to chance that we wouldn't be available to devote the necessary attention to them. Better to leave that to the guys who didn't have outside-agency responsibilities to worry about.

On the bright side, that system had left me free to concentrate on my terrorism-related investigations. On the down side, it meant I knew next to nothing about what'd been going on with Walker since his return. That left me at a severe disadvantage. I wanted to rectify that and level the playing field as quickly as possible.

PJ nodded and left without another word, and Rico and I sat in silence for a while, each lost in our own thoughts. My mind was racing, considering and then discarding a multitude of courses of actions. Taking care of this situation with Walker—I still refused to actually think the words "getting Rory back," as though the thought alone might have the power to make that necessary—was going to be a lot like playing chess. Before I directed each move I wanted my guys to take, I'd need to consider all the possible reactions Walker could have. Just like when playing the game, I'd have to make allowances for each move after that in succession, on and on until neither of us had any moves left. To say that it wouldn't be easy would be a colossal understatement.

Anxiety hit me hard, and I struggled to tamp it down just enough so I'd be able to function. Nothing good could come from me completely losing my shit. I'd figure this out. I had to.

"Ryan." Rico gently broke into my thoughts.

"Hmm?"

"Do you want to call one of the other guys in the squad over to talk about this?"

"No. Not yet. I'll brief them as soon as we're completely committed to our next move, but I don't want them here yet. Not until I've had a minute to process this situation."

"Are you sure you want me here?"

I favored him with a look I hoped expressed how ridiculous I found that question. "Of course. Why wouldn't I?"

Rico's brows knitted, and he fiddled with the paperclip chain in his hands. He paused, obviously tussling with his next words. "I've never been in PI. I'm not sure I even remember what to do with a PI subject. Especially not one like Walker. What if…What if I do something wrong? What if…?"

My heart melted. I understood his apprehension. This situation could go pear-shaped in at least a million different ways, none of them pleasant. It entailed a lot of responsibility, having someone's life in your hands like this. The fear of fucking up, knowing the consequences of even the smallest of mistakes, was daunting.

"Rico, look at me." I had to wait a few seconds for him to comply, but I was patient. I needed him to see the sincerity in my eyes when I spoke. "You're going to be fine. *We* are going to be fine. I know Walker better than anyone in the Service. And I'm going to help direct you every step of the way." I hoped my bravado was enough to convince him. It wasn't quite enough to convince me.

"Okay," he said, almost resignedly.

"Rico, you're like a brother to me. There's no one I'd rather have here with me. You know that, right?"

Rico nodded solemnly, and for the first time in the history of our relationship, I regretted all the times I'd jokingly told him to be serious about something. I could've used a double shot of his wry humor right about then. I'd have to remember to be careful what I wished for.

CHAPTER NINE

Rico and I spent the next hour or so discussing the pros and cons of various courses of action and trying to prioritize our goals in order of importance. It wasn't easy, seeing as how we didn't agree on those points.

That we needed to pinpoint Walker's exact location, well, that was a given. But we were divided on whether we thought that took precedence over determining if Walker even had someone at his mercy and whether that someone was Rory. I'm sure you can guess where my priorities were.

"I still say we need to run a trace on both phones," I told Rico for what felt like the tenth time.

"That might not give us what we want," he insisted. "There are too many variables for that to be a viable option. Rory's phone needs to still be on, and it needs to still be on her person. Same thing with the phone for the number PJ gave us. If it's a burner phone and he ditched it, it does us no good."

"I disagree. Even if it is a burner phone and he dumped it, we can glean valuable information from that. We can track it to where it is now and pull video surveillance from any surrounding cameras to see what direction Walker went after it was dumped. We might even be able to track him via camera to his current location. Same with Rory's phone. We can figure out where the phone is now. If he does have her"—I was still clinging to the extremely unlikely chance that we'd run this trace and discover she was safe and sound at her apartment or the hospital where she worked—"and even if the phone is off now, we can figure out where it was pinging when he took her. That's something."

"Ryan, even if what you're saying is true, and we can track the phones and they do give us some place to start, it's going to take too long to run the trace. Rory hasn't been missing long enough for anyone to commit to that sort of measure. We need to call the number PJ gave us and see if he answers."

I'd thought of that, actually. His point about Rory not having been missing long enough and the reluctance of anyone to initiate a trace on her phone without proof that she was, indeed, in some kind of peril was valid. But I thought I had a solution for that. I'd just been reticent to discuss it with him.

Hurricane's soon-to-be-ex detail leader, SAIC Claudia Quinn, had several high-level contacts in the Counterterrorism Division of the Department of Homeland Security. One phone call from her to the chief of the Counterterrorism Division of the Assistant United States Attorney's Office for the Southern District of New York was all it took to get that particular ball rolling. She'd assisted me with something similar a few weeks ago when I'd been attempting to get to the bottom of who'd shot me. All I had to do was ask, and I'd have the information I needed within the hour.

But this wasn't exactly a terrorism matter. The last time I'd solicited Claudia's assistance with an issue like this, it'd been after what had, on the surface, looked like an assassination attempt on the president of Iran. Even if what she'd done for me had come out in the media, no one would've been able to argue that she was within her rights to exercise that power to get to the bottom of the plot in order to verify no one else was in danger. Now, however, the waters were a little murkier.

That Walker insisted on a face-to-face audience with Zoey Carmichael as a condition of Rory's safe return was a point in our favor. No one could blame Claudia for pulling out all the stops to ensure the safety of the president's daughter. On the other hand, Hurricane wasn't in any real jeopardy at the moment, and therefore taking such drastic measures was unnecessary. I sighed, torn with indecision.

"Okay, how about this?" I attempted to compromise. "I'll call Rory's phone from my work cell, which has a blocked number. We'll see if it's at least on. If it's not, then we can wait about fifteen or twenty minutes and do the same with the number PJ pulled from the caller ID. We'll put it on speaker so I can hear the voice to see if it's him, but pretend to be a telemarketer or something. Hopefully that won't get him too hinked up."

I didn't have the guts to say aloud what I knew we were both thinking: that things could go very badly for Rory very quickly if Walker became the least bit suspicious. But I couldn't see any way around it at this point. I was out of ideas.

"And then what?"

"And then, once we've determined as best we can whether the phones are on and if someone actually has physical possession of them, I'll get us the traces we need. We can go from there."

Rico thought about that plan for a moment. He nodded once. "Okay. It's probably the best we're going to do."

I inhaled shakily and held my breath as I dialed my sister's number with trembling fingers. My heart was pounding, pumping pure anxiety through my veins at an unprecedented rate. I felt ill.

It took an eternity for the phone company to establish the connection, but eventually, after several long, tense heartbeats, the room was filled with the sound of a tinny ringing.

I sagged, flooded with the smallest measure of relief. I still wasn't sure whether Rory was safe, but at least her phone was on. Even if it got turned off now, we could still trace this call and get at least that much closer to where she was right this second.

I had slid my thumb over to the "end call" button to disconnect when the ringing stopped as someone answered. No one spoke, and I froze, uncertain what to do in the face of an open line.

Several long seconds dragged by, and the longer we sat there, the more panicked I became. Shit! If it really was Walker on the other end, he could react very badly to this deviation from his carefully planned script. I needed to hang up now.

"Ryan?" Rico asked suddenly, taking the decision out of my hands.

A ragged gasp sounded on the other end of the line, and I cringed and shot him a look equal parts terrified and annoyed. Hadn't we already established that we couldn't let Walker know he didn't have me? What the actual fuck? I didn't even want to think about what Walker would do when he realized he'd made a mistake. Hopefully he'd see Rory as a bargaining chip of equal or greater value.

Rico leaned closer to the phone, making it clear in that instant that he wasn't actually talking to me but rather pretending to talk to me on the phone. That'd been a genius move on his part and made me glad at least one of us was sort of thinking clearly. If Walker thought I was his captive, then he wouldn't have been surprised that someone would call "my" phone looking for me. I let out the breath I'd been holding.

"Ryan, stop fuckin' around," Rico said into the speaker, adopting a passable imitation of an Irish brogue, which I assumed was an attempt to disguise his voice. "I know you know it's me. Why you always have to be such a goddamn smart-ass whenever family calls is beyond me. Ma told me to ask if you were going to be able to make it to Aunt Mary's surprise party this weekend. So, call her and let her know, all right? And if you leave me alone to deal with Uncle Seamus again, I swear to God and all the saints, I'll drown you in a barrel of Michael Collins and then drink to your passing."

Rico and I both held our breaths as we waited to see whether someone would reply. All we got for our efforts was the click of the call being disconnected. We exchanged an uneasy glance.

Rico and I knew one another well enough to realize that neither of us wanted to give voice to the obvious: it was looking more and more likely that Rory was in Walker's clutches. My stomach fluttered and writhed, and I tried to ignore the rising panic gnawing away at the inside of my chest, clawing its way up the back of my throat.

Half dazed, as if in a dream, I picked up the handset to my desk phone and started punching buttons.

"What are you doing?" Rico wanted to know.

I finished my task and replaced the receiver in its cradle. "Rolling all the calls for the squad line directly to my extension. If Walker phones back, I want to be the one fielding that call."

What I didn't say out loud was I was afraid of what might slip through the cracks if someone else answered. I was also terrified of what could happen if someone handled Walker the wrong way. I didn't like the idea of leaving my sister's fate in anyone else's hands.

For lack of anything better to do, I rose from my chair and walked over to the filing cabinet standing sentinel in one corner of the office I shared with Meaghan, who must've been out on something because I hadn't seen her all day. A nice-sized dry-erase board was clinging to the side of it. I plucked it from its rightful place and snagged the cup of markers that always sat on top of the cabinet.

Then I carefully laid the board on my desktop and took more time and care than necessary cleaning it off, erasing all traces of the notes from another case. Once it was clear, I went over it again with a paper towel soaked with nail-polish remover to ensure no unwanted marker remained. Then I dried it with a fresh towel.

Rico broke the silence. "So, now I guess we wait, huh?"

"Guess so."

"We'll get her back, Ryan."

"Yeah, but in what condition?" I murmured, allowing a sliver of my terror to bleed through to my words.

"You can't think like that. You'll drive yourself crazy."

"I can't help it."

"No," Rico said miserably. "I guess you can't."

We sat there in silence, but it wasn't long before I became restless. I couldn't breathe. I needed to get up, to do something, to burn off a bit of the nervous energy collecting in my gut. My movements were jerky and quick as I stood, knocking my chair back with a clatter that sounded loud and harsh in the muffled quiet of my office.

"Where are you going?" Rico looked wary and concerned.

I palmed my personal cell phone and moved toward the door. "I need to make a call."

"Ryan, you can make it here."

I shook my head, holding out one hand, bidding him to keep his seat. "No. I'll just be a minute. Stay. Please. And answer the phone if it rings."

Rico nodded, but I barely noticed. My mind was already consumed with the call I was about to make. I shut the door behind me as I left and wandered down the hall toward the window and relative privacy.

With trembling fingers, I dialed Allison's number and held my breath as I waited for the call to connect. Tilting my head so I could hold the phone between my ear and my shoulder, I pressed my palms flat against the wide windowsill and leaned my weight on them. My forehead rested against the glass, and I peered onto the street below.

I took in the people and cars I saw beneath me in a kind of dismal wonder. Life was going on, progressing without a hitch for all of them while my world had been thrown into chaos. It didn't seem fair to me on any level, and I begrudged them their seemingly easy existences.

"Hey, baby." Allison's voice floated across the line to my waiting ears like a cool, gentle rain on a scorching-hot summer day. I closed my eyes and squeezed them shut against the tears that'd gathered.

I opened my mouth to speak, but nothing came out. I cleared my throat and tried again, but all I managed was a hoarse, strangled whimper.

"Ryan?" Allison sounded confused.

"Yeah," I forced out. "Allison?"

"Is everything okay?"

Her immediate concern was touching and somehow made it that much harder for me not to completely break down. I shifted my position so I could hold the phone with one hand and rolled my head so one cheek pressed against the window pane.

"No," I choked out, fighting back tears. "Everything's definitely not okay."

"What happened?"

The lump in my throat made it tough to formulate a response. I swallowed thickly and sniffled. "It's Rory."

"Okay, Ryan. Take a deep breath. Tell me what happened." Allison's tone was both tender and firm.

I did as she commanded and closed my eyes again so I could try to pretend she was there with me, that she was wrapping me in the safety of her arms. I attempted to conjure up the intoxicating scent of her perfume in order to make the fantasy more realistic. It didn't work, but it did give me something else to concentrate on.

"Ryan?"

"Yeah?"

"What happened? Is Rory okay?"

"I don't know," I whispered, as the truth of that statement finally hit me. "I just don't know."

"Where is she?"

"I don't know, Allison. I think…I think maybe one of my PI subjects has her."

"Wait. What do you mean someone has her?"

"PJ took a call. I wasn't there. I didn't hear it." I was borderline rambling now, and my sentences weren't flowing coherently. "Supposedly it was Walker, but he said he had me."

"So, you don't know for sure that he has Rory?"

I shook my head but then realized she couldn't see me. "No. Not for sure. But it's the only thing that makes sense. He knows what I look like, and she looks exactly like me."

A long pause on Allison's end of the line. "I don't have any valid argument for that."

The sick feeling returned to my stomach, and I rested one hand across my abdomen. "Damn. I was kinda hoping you would."

I heard Allison sigh. "Ryan, I'm really sorry. What can I—" A PA announcement declaring that US Airways shuttle 2184 to New York LaGuardia was now boarding drowned out her words.

"Where are you?" I asked stupidly.

"I'm at the airport. I'm sorry, Ryan. Can I call you back in a few minutes?"

"Sure thing. Where are they sending you? Anywhere good?" The question rolled out of my mouth reflexively, but I was sure Allison could hear my heart wasn't in it.

Allison hesitated so long I thought I'd lost her. I pulled the phone away from my ear to check. Nope. Still connected.

"I'm coming to New York."

"You are?" Relief overwhelmed me. While I never would've even considered asking her to come up, I couldn't deny how much I needed her here with me.

"Not to see you," she said.

Ouch! That hurt like a punch to the gut. "Oh."

"I mean, obviously, I would've come to see you. I *am* coming to see you. It was supposed to be a surprise, actually. I just meant that's not the underlying reason for my trip."

"Okay."

"Sweetheart, I have to go. Don't read too much into it. I'll explain everything when I get there."

I was only half listening to her. Rico was gesturing to me from the doorway to my office, waving his arms and making exaggerated motions that either indicated we had a phone call or something was wrong with his ear and he wanted to lie down on my desk. I was betting on the former.

A shiver racked me, and I took a shaky breath. "Yeah. Okay," I said to Allison, much more concerned with the problem at hand than whatever she was up to. "I'll see you later. Safe trip up."

I hung up with unsteady fingers and took one last glance out the window to the untouched world below, wishing I could fall into it and disappear. And then I took a deep breath, set my shoulders, and strode briskly back down the hall to my office.

Showtime.

CHAPTER TEN

I slid around the corner, skidded into my office, and saw Rico had poised his hand to press the speakerphone button to answer the call. He looked at me expectantly, and I nodded as I threw myself into my chair. I motioned for him to come around to my side of the desk and set about unlocking my laptop so I could type.

"Secret Service," Rico said as the call connected.

"I know this is the fucking Secret Service," Walker shot back, derision poisoning every syllable. "I called you."

Rico and I exchanged a worried glance. I wasn't positive what he was so concerned about, but my apprehension stemmed from Walker's inflection. In all my many months of dealing with him, I couldn't recall a time when I'd ever heard him sound quite this angry. At least not so early on in a conversation. Normally we worked our way up to that. I'd need to tread very lightly in the next few minutes. Lord only knew what would happen to Rory if I messed this up.

"So you did," Rico replied, his tone one of forced cheer. "What can I do for you, sir?"

"Don't play games with me, asshole. I know you know I have her."

My fingers flew over the keyboard as I attempted to capture the conversation as it played out for future reference as well as interject the direction in which I thought Rico should steer the dialogue. Rico leaned in to read over my shoulder.

"Ah, Adam," Rico said, dropping some of his earlier good humor. "Nice of you to call back. I trust Agent O'Connor is fine?"

"She's not gonna be if you don't let me see my wife."

"And by your wife, I assume you mean Zoey Carmichael."

"Of course! What are you, stupid? I know she's talked to you about me. And I know you know that Zoey and I are happily married."

Interesting. That was the third time Walker had referred to me since the exchange had started, and all three times he'd refrained from using my name. Was that deliberate on his part? And if so, how could I use that to my advantage? I typed again.

"You're talking about Agent O'Connor," Rico read.

"Yes," Walker said venomously. "Her."

That was four. So, definitely deliberate, then. I typed some more.

"Well, now here's the thing, Adam. I need to be certain you have Agent O'Connor first before I can even think about addressing anything else. And I need to verify that she's okay."

"Are you trying to put pressure on me?" Walker sounded incredulous. I scowled and shifted closer to the phone in a vain attempt to pick up on some background noise that would give me even the vaguest clue where Walker might be. "Because you don't have any leverage in this situation. I hold all the cards."

"Well, that's not strictly true, now, is it?"

"What do you mean?"

"Well, if you held all the cards, you wouldn't have needed to kidnap Agent O'Connor in order to force us to facilitate a meeting with Miss Carmichael, would you?"

I held my breath anxiously as I waited to see how he'd respond. A lone bead of sweat made a slow trail between my shoulder blades and down the center of my back. I wiped at the droplets dotting my upper lip as I tried to control the trembling of my fingers.

The silence stretched on and on until I was positive I'd go mad. I inhaled so long and slowly I thought my lungs would burst, and still Walker didn't speak. Terrified now that I'd managed to irrevocably screw up already, I turned to Rico for reassurance. He placed a comforting hand on my shoulder.

While I waited, I retrieved Rico's earlier-constructed paperclip chain from the other side of my desk and removed one of the makeshift links. I took my time straightening it out until I had one long piece, and then I proceeded to press the tip of my thumb against one end. Hard.

"If I let you talk to her, you'll let me see my wife?" Walker asked out of nowhere, startling us both.

"It's not as simple as that, Adam."

"Stop trying to confuse me! She does that. She always tries to confuse me." Walker's voice had gotten softer and louder in turn as he'd spoken, suggesting he was fidgeting as he spoke.

"I'm not trying to confuse you, Adam. I just want you to know where I stand on things. I don't want you getting upset with me later and saying I tried to trick you. Is that fair?"

"What do you want?"

"Well, right now, I want to talk to Agent O'Connor. I want to hear for myself that she's okay."

"Okay," Walker said slowly, drawing out the word in obvious consideration. "And then what?"

"Then I'm going to need you to promise me you won't hurt her. Because I swear on whatever deity you believe in and all the ones you don't that if you so much as pluck a single hair out of her head, there will be no place on earth you can hide from me. And what I'll do to you when I find you will make whatever your sick, twisted mind can dream up look like something out of a children's show. Of that, you can be sure."

I blinked, taken aback by Rico's ad lib. His dark eyes were blazing, his jaw set in a hard line. He was glaring at the phone with fury, and if it were physically possible for him to have reached through the handset and throttled Walker with his bare hands, I think he'd have done it.

Walker must've been surprised, too, because he didn't say anything for a long moment. And then, "Okay, so I let you talk to her, and I promise not to hurt her. And in return, you let me see my wife."

"Hang on. There's one more thing."

"I'm tired of talking to you."

"Well, if you don't talk to me, you don't see Miss Carmichael, so I suggest you suck it up just a little while longer."

"I could just kill her now," Walker said, his intonation sly.

"You could. And then you can spend the rest of your days knowing you *almost* got to see Miss Carmichael, had you only not lost your temper. Because if Agent O'Connor dies, Miss Carmichael will never see you. She won't even be able to look at you."

"That's not true. Zoey loves me." The words were shaky, uncertain.

"That may or may not be the case, Adam. And I'm not here to debate with you about what Miss Carmichael does or doesn't feel. It's not my place. But I can say with a fair amount of certainty that she'd never be able to trust you if you killed one of her agents. Is that what you want?"

"No." The reply was soft, barely a whisper. I wasn't even sure Walker was aware he'd spoken aloud.

"Okay. So, back to that other thing I need from you."

"What?" Walker sounded like he was pouting now.

"I'm going to need you to let Agent O'Connor go."

"Do you think I'm an idiot? The second I set her free, it's over for me. I'll never get to see my wife."

"Adam. Let's not play games. You know as well as I do that you're going to have to let her go at some point. Why not save yourself a whole mess of trouble and make it sooner rather than later?"

I heard a faint rustling sound that was likely Walker scratching the stubble on his chin. He did that a lot when he was thinking. "I'll let her go the minute you let me see my wife."

"I'm going to need some sort of assurances."

"Don't trust me at my word?"

"Not as far as I can throw you."

"Hmm. Well, it seems we're at a standstill."

Rico looked at me helplessly, silently pleading with me to tell him what to do. I huffed quietly in frustration as I scanned the transcript of the conversation as it'd already played out, searching for the places where it'd failed to traverse the path I'd wanted. Conversing with Walker was tough enough when I was the one actually speaking. I was finding it a million times harder to try to tell somebody else how to handle him. I pursed my lips and started typing again.

"Tell you what," Rico read. "How about you comply with my first two requests as a show of good faith, and you can think about the pros and cons of complying with number three?"

Silence reigned as Walker presumably considered that suggestion. "I let you talk to her now, and I promise not to hurt her, and you'll let me see my wife?"

"I'll let you have a moment to consider just how much time with Miss Carmichael means to you and whether you think it's worth Agent O'Connor's freedom. It's the best I can do."

Walker didn't reply for the longest time, and I tapped my fingertips together in a rapid-fire rhythm. My heart was thudding painfully, and my mouth was dry. Was it possible that was because I was sweating so profusely? And how could I feel so cold? My skin was clammy to the touch, which I didn't think was a good sign.

"So, do we have a deal?" Rico had finally grown weary of waiting.

Walker sighed noisily. "Yes, yes. Fine," he spat, sounding impatient. "I'll let you talk to her."

I heard the muffled sound of cloth against the phone, which could've meant any number of things. He could've thrown the phone onto a couch or a bed. He might've pressed it against his body or slipped it into a pocket. I couldn't be sure. And none of those possibilities gave me any clue where he was keeping Rory. Again, I struggled to make out any ambient noise in the background but came up empty.

The seconds seemed to tick by with all the speed and urgency of molasses in winter, each instant taking a near eternity to pass into the next. I chewed on my lower lip and fiddled with my paperclip spear for lack of anything better to do. Another drop of sweat trickled down my back to join the first in soaking the waistband of my pants.

Just when I didn't think I could take the suspense any more, I detected a faint movement on the other end of the line. Someone picked up the phone or took it out of a pocket, and I heard a soft, scratchy, "Hello?"

Rico and I looked at one another. His face exhibited equal parts relief, disappointment, and fear. I could sympathize. I was thrilled Rory was alive but shattered to confirm that Walker actually had her. The fear, of course, stemmed from the uncertainty about how the rest of this scenario would play out.

"Ryan?" Rico said into the phone. "Is that you?"

A pause, the clearing of a throat, then a slightly stronger, "Yeah. It's me."

I let out a breath, thankful Rory had realized she should pretend to be me. Now, I needed to figure out a way to convey to her the correct responses to some of the statements he was bound to make to her so she could continue with the ruse.

"Are you okay?" Rico asked her.

Another beat. "I'm fine."

Rico shot me a meaningful look that said he thought Rory was just as stubborn as I was. I made a face and went back to my laptop.

"Are you really?" Rico asked at my direction.

Rory hesitated. It was brief, but I caught it. "More or less."

My fingers flew over the keys as I typed, attempting the hail-Mary pass to end all passes. Because if this didn't work, we were all about to regret it. I'd thought I'd figured out a way to deliver the information I wanted Rory to have. I assumed Walker was listening in. I needed to impart this without making him *too* suspicious. I hoped I was right.

"You're not giving Adam any trouble, are you?" Rico emphasized Walker's first name exactly the way I'd intended him to when I'd typed it, and he looked at me like I was a lunatic after he read that. I ignored him. I didn't have time to explain my reasoning.

Rory sighed. "Not anymore," she whispered.

I closed my eyes against the tears welling there and swallowed hard despite the tightness in my throat and chest. My lower lip quivered, and I tensed. If I could trade places with her, I'd do it in less than the fraction of a second it took my heart to beat. I pleaded with God and the universe at large to please just let her be okay.

Rico made a soft noise in the back of his throat and tapped my knuckles to recapture my attention. I glanced at him, simultaneously warmed and devastated by the sympathy coloring his handsome features. I swallowed again and started to type.

"Good girl," Rico read over my shoulder. "How would your big sister tell you to keep it up in Gaelic? *Dearg choíche?*"

He shot me a puzzled glance as he stumbled a bit over the phonetic pronunciation I'd typed out, but I just nodded. *Come on, Rory,* I whispered silently to myself. *Please pick up on what I'm trying to do. Please, please, please.*

After a pause, Rory sniffled and said, "You remembered. Nicely done. I didn't think you paid attention when I tried to teach you Gaelic."

I let out a shaky sigh of relief. She'd at least realized I was trying to tell her something. Whether she knew exactly what remained to be seen. I'd have spelled it out for her if I could've, but I was afraid if I had Rico say too much more, Walker would become suspicious at best and enraged at worst.

"Of course I pay attention to you," Rico read aloud. "Listen to this: *éigin, muinín, socair.* I came, I saw, I conquered, right?" Rico frowned at me, obviously puzzled.

"Very good," Rory choked out, her voice strangled. "We'll make a right fine Irishman of you yet."

"Can't wait. Listen, Ryan, can you let me talk to Adam again, please?"

"S-sure." Rory's voice was laced with panic and desperation. My heart shattered, like so much fine crystal being hurled to the floor.

"*Laval, Asha,*" I had Rico say. "Just do whatever Adam says, and we'll get this resolved as soon as we can, okay?"

Walker must've wrenched the phone out of her hands before Rory could reply. I heard her exclaim softly.

"Well?" Walker demanded. "Are you satisfied? She's alive. And she's okay. Mostly."

"Yeah, it's the 'mostly' part I'm worried about," Rico shot back. "Does she need a doctor?"

"No."

"Ask her that."

"What?"

"I want to hear her say she doesn't need a doctor." Rico frowned at me and pushed my hands out of the way so he could type. "*Would you be able to tell?*"

I nodded. I trusted Rory to be honest with me. If she needed medical attention, she'd say it.

"Do you need a doctor?" Walker asked her.

"No." Rory's voice floated back over the line from far away. "I'm okay."

"See?" I could hear Walker's sneer in just that one word, and my blood boiled.

"Thank you," Rico said. "I appreciate your cooperation, Adam."

"Now you'll let me see my wife?"

I deliberately had Rico pause as I considered my next move. The silence went on a little longer than I'd intended, but I honestly wasn't sure how to proceed. I mean, no way in hell was Walker going to get to see Hurricane. But I was afraid if I told him that, he'd never let Rory go. And I wasn't prepared to live with that outcome.

"Adam, you know as well as I do that I don't have the authority to make that kind of promise. But I can tell you this: I'll go talk to the head of her detail and see what we can get worked out. Is that fair?"

Out of the corner of my eye, I could see Rico staring at me like I'd lost my mind. As I waited for Walker's response, it occurred to me that my grasp on reality might be slipping, but I couldn't afford to dwell on that notion. Not now.

I prayed that Walker would agree to this scenario. I just needed to buy us some time. With time I'd be able to think and breathe; I'd be able to figure out how to get Rory out of this. All I needed was time.

"You have one hour" was Walker's curt reply.

My heart free-fell. It wasn't nearly enough.

"I need more, Adam," I had Rico plead. "I'm not even sure where Miss Carmichael is right now."

"Do you think I'm stupid?" Walker screamed at the top of his lungs. I flinched at the rage in his voice. "Do you think I don't know what you're trying to do?"

"Adam, I promise, I'm not trying to do anything. But you have to know an hour is unreasonable. It could take me an hour just to get to Miss Carmichael's apartment." Rico sounded beseeching now, and I closed my eyes against the terror threatening to choke me.

The seconds ticked by with agonizing slowness as my heart raced. I kept my hands curled into fists on my blotter, and every nerve ending in my body felt like it was almost fried.

"I'll give you three," Walker said finally. "But if I suspect you might be thinking about double-crossing me in some way, Agent O'Connor dies."

The silence after Walker disconnected was ominous. I let out a shaky breath and turned so I could look Rico in the eye. His face displayed every emotion I felt, which didn't reassure me. I'd been assuming that one of us needed to be strong, but from what I could see, it didn't look like either of us wanted to take up that mantle. Perhaps we should've discussed those roles prior to our conversation with Walker.

"Well," Rico said after a long moment. He perched himself on the edge of my desk and looked at me expectantly.

I cleared my throat and wiped my sweaty palms against my pant legs. "Yes. Well."

"That went…" He lifted his hands in a helpless gesture.

"Yes, it certainly did."

"So, now what?"

I sat back in my chair, and some of the tension drained out of me. My entire body sagged. I tipped my head back and ran my palms roughly over my cheeks. That was the million-dollar question, wasn't it? Now what? I wished like hell I knew.

"I guess now I start calling in the cavalry." My words were hollow, flat, my mind running through a million different scenarios and options, and I didn't have the energy for more than one task at a time.

"Do you have some sort of a plan?"

I'd heard his words, but only dimly. "Huh? Oh. Sort of." I lapsed back into my own thoughts.

The list of things I had to do was daunting, and I was having a lot of trouble trying to decide exactly what order to tackle those tasks in. I wanted to talk to whoever Walker's case agent was. Whatever info we had available regarding his mind-set and his whereabouts of late would be invaluable. I definitely needed to call Claudia. Not only did I need her help with obtaining the necessary cell-phone data, but she also needed to be aware of this situation on a personal level. She was still technically Hurricane's DL, after all. At least for a few more days. She deserved to know how off the deep end this guy had gone. Then I had to talk to my dad.

Shit! How the hell was I supposed to tell him something like this? I tried not to feel the stab of pain that accompanied the mental image of his face when I broke this news to him, but it didn't work nearly as well as I'd hoped. He'd be devastated. Tears welled in my eyes, and the muscles in my jaw quivered.

Rico rested a gentle hand on my arm. "Do you want to let me in on it?"

I blinked. It wasn't that I didn't understand the question. But I was fixated on something else and determined to follow my thought through to its obvious conclusion.

I had to drop the bombshell on my father that his oldest child was in the hands of some lunatic who thought he'd taken me. I couldn't imagine how I'd even begin that conversation. Fuck.

"Ryan?"

"What? Oh. Yeah. The plan. Uh, I guess I should start by talking to the SAIC." My heart thudded wildly, and I ran my tongue across dry lips.

Rico nodded, completely unaware of the problem's subtle nuances. "Need me to do anything?"

"Yeah. Can you find Jim or Austin and brief them for me? I'm going to the file room real quick to see if I can put my hands on Walker's case file. I need to get up to speed on what's been happening with him the past few weeks. Maybe that will have some clues for me, since apparently PJ can't tell me who his case agent is."

"You got it. I'll make the proper notifications and see if I can get that information. I'll have it by the time you get back."

"Thanks." The word was soft, barely a whisper. I might not have even said it at all. Rico was now the furthest thing from my mind as I turned to leave the office.

"Ryan?"

I paused in the opened doorway with my back to my friend. I didn't bother to face him. I was barely holding it together as it was. The last thing I needed was to look into his eyes.

"This isn't your fault."

I sighed, too spent to even play at a veneer of strength. "Yes, Rico. It is."

CHAPTER ELEVEN

After taking a few minutes to locate and then peruse Walker's case file, I took the long, scenic route around the office up to what the agents had dubbed Mahogany Row, where all the big bosses sat. I'd desperately needed the extra minute that side trip bought me to scrape my game face into a pile and sloppily slather it on. I'd debated taking a detour down through the lower floors as well but had decided that would just have been stalling. And I really couldn't afford to waste that kind of time.

The nausea plaguing me for the past hour or so had increased exponentially as I lingered outside my father's office, unable to make myself go in. The longer I dawdled, the longer the inevitable was delayed, but that sound logic did nothing to light a fire under my ass. This would likely be one of the most difficult conversations I'd had to date, and I wasn't eager to begin.

I took a deep breath and slowly counted down from ten, putting a specific time limit on my procrastinating. When I finally reached one, I squared my shoulders and rapped sharply against the closed door before I could come up with yet another reason to put it off.

My father's muffled voice floated out to me. "Come in."

With trembling fingers, I turned the handle and let myself in. Dad was on the phone when I entered, and he grinned at me, gesturing for me to sit in front of his desk. As I obeyed, the nest of scorpions inhabiting my stomach twisted, writhed, and stung. I perched on the very edge of the chair and tapped my hands against my knees while I waited for his full attention.

My dad took a few more minutes to wrap up his phone call before turning his focus to me. "What's wrong?"

I'd put a great deal of thought and consideration into how I would break the news. I doubted I could find any good way to inform him, but I'd at least ease into the bad news rather than blurting it out.

"We just received a phone call on the main squad line."

Dad's expression was impassive. He appeared content to let me get this out in my own time without pushing.

"It was from Adam Royce Walker." The wild fluttering in my belly appeared to have spread to my extremities. Hundreds of fireflies seemed to be flitting around just beneath the surface of my skin. "He indicated that he'd kidnapped someone and would kill them if we didn't let him see Hurricane."

My dad's expression now was one of mild surprise mingled with curiosity. "Well, that's new."

I felt like I might be sick. Not just nauseous, but as though I were actually teetering on the edge of throwing up. I cast my eyes around the room for a trash can, just in case. "He has Rory."

"What?"

So much for not blurting out the bad news. I tried to swallow the lump rising in the back of my throat, but it refused to be dislodged. The leaden ball growing steadily in my gut probably held it there. "He thinks he has me."

After a long moment of silence, he spoke. "Are you sure?"

"I'm sure. Rico spoke to her briefly. I was listening in. It's her."

"I see." Dad sat back in his chair and steepled his index fingers beneath his lower lip. His eyes glazed over.

I endured the silence for as long as possible, which was about ten seconds. "We're working on it. I just wanted you to know."

"How?"

"How, what? How are we working on it?"

He nodded and sat back up, resting his forearms on his desk. "Yes. Did you call NYPD?"

"Not yet. I wanted to inform you and the detail first before I brought in any outside agencies."

"Probably a good idea."

I didn't reply.

"So, what's your plan of action?" he asked.

"As of about five minutes ago, both Rory's and Walker's phones were still on. I was going to have Claudia—I mean SAIC Quinn—get us a ping order for both numbers and then use the cell-tracking team to locate the phones. Once we had that, I figured we could ask ESU to do an extraction."

It was a shaky plan at best and contingent upon a number of variables, any of which could shift at a moment's notice. But I hadn't been able to come up with anything better. I'd sort of hoped someone else would have another proposal. This wasn't my area of expertise. Not that it would've mattered much if it had been. My thought processes weren't exactly what one would call clear.

"That plan is going to take a while to implement."

"I know. But I don't have any better ideas."

Dad ruminated for a bit. "No, you're right. That's likely the best course of action, given what we know and the assets available to us. How much time do we have? Are we on a schedule?"

"Yes. And not nearly enough."

"Of course not. How long?"

I consulted my watch. "Two hours and forty-nine minutes."

"And then what happens?"

"I have no idea. He indicated he was going to kill her. I'd like to say he doesn't have it in him, but before today I'd have sworn he didn't have *this* in him so…" I cleared my throat and tried not to dwell on my failure in assessing his level of dangerousness as I twirled a few stray tresses of my hair around my finger. "What he wants above all else is to meet with Hurricane. At the very least we have that in our favor. He's probably more likely to attempt to use Rory as a bargaining chip than he is to…do anything else."

"But you don't know that for sure."

"No." I gave up on my twirling in favor of clenching my hands on my knees. "I don't. Hence my plan to contact Claudia and see what she can push through for us."

"It's a long shot."

"I know."

"I don't like relying on long shots."

"Neither do I. But what choice do we have?"

Neither of us spoke for a long time after that. I didn't know about being able to hear a pin drop, but I could definitely hear the soft *tick-tick-tick-tick* of the small gold desk clock that sat next to my dad's monitor. Once I took note of it, it only made me that much more aware of the passage of time. As if I weren't already conscious of it enough.

"How did this happen?" The question was whisper-soft and most likely rhetorical, but I felt the need to answer anyway, if only to dispel the suffocating silence.

"I haven't figured that out yet. I won't be able to until I can see historical cell-site data for the phones to determine where they met up so I can pull footage from any security cameras in the area. That's going to take some time. It might not even be worth it to pursue that avenue. Not until after we get Rory back."

"That isn't what I meant. I meant *how*."

He didn't elaborate, but I didn't need him to. I knew what he was asking. He wanted to know how someone we were supposed to have been monitoring could've pulled something like this off. How he could've taken us so completely by surprise. How we could possibly have dropped a ball this big. How I could have failed to see this coming. Unfortunately, I didn't have any answers. Not concrete ones, at any rate. All I had were theories and gut feelings. And voicing them wouldn't undo what'd already been done. It would've been pointless to dwell on that line of thinking. Not that I wasn't already doing exactly that. But I did recognize the fruitlessness of my self-flagellation.

"Adam Royce Walker is extremely intriguing in that he's intelligent on a level you wouldn't think him capable of, which is a large part of what makes him so dangerous. He's a paranoid schizophrenic who's off his meds more often than he's on them, and you'd think that would make it impossible for him to function effectively outside his persistent delusions about his relationship with Hurricane. But he's smart enough to recognize that at certain times he needs to play the part to get what he wants."

"Play the part how?"

I gathered my hair into a bunch and pulled it down over one shoulder so I could play with the ends. "Cleaning himself up. Fixing his hair, shaving, wearing cologne. Donning the appropriate clothing for the environment. Walking with confidence, acting as if he belongs.

Little things. It's not necessarily enough to get past us—especially not those of us who've seen him and know what he looks like—but it's enough for him to not stand out as crazy to the general populace. Depending on the situation, sometimes that can be sufficient." I didn't have to say that it sounded like it'd been sufficient today.

"You're telling me he can turn it off."

"That isn't the term I'd use. You can't turn off mental illness, obviously."

"So what term would you use?"

"I guess I'd say he can rise above it in order to further his delusions when he needs to. He can't keep it up long-term. But he can certainly do it long enough to effectively cause us a whole mess of trouble when it suits him."

"Good God." Dad ran a weary hand across his eyes.

"That about sums it up."

"So how do you think he got Rory?"

"I don't know."

"I'm not asking you to etch your theories in stone. I realize you're not certain. I just need some idea what we're up against. Paint a picture for me. Tell me how you think he could've done it."

I tilted my head back and cast my eyes toward the ceiling. "It's tough for me to say. I don't have any idea how long he's been out of the hospital or where he is in his cycle. His periods of lucidity fluctuate, especially when he isn't compliant with his prescribed medication schedule, which will directly impact how comprehensive a plan he could put together. Even with all that information, I'd be guessing. Without it…"

"Then guess. I need to know what this guy is capable of."

"Dad, I can't—"

"Do you think he hurt her?" My father's voice was small, and I'd have sworn I heard a tremor. The sound caused the already-deep furrows in my heart to tear even wider.

"I had Rico ask her if she needed a doctor. She said she was fine."

Dad pinned me with a pointed look. "That's not what I asked you."

I sighed heavily and sagged in my chair. "I know it isn't."

"Oh."

We sat in silence for a few long moments, each floundering in our own worries and fears. Dad was too much of a professional to allow any of his to show on his face, but, try as I might, I was afraid my own attempts at appearing strong weren't cutting it. I was feeling too many things inside every single moment. I didn't think I could handle keeping all of them under wraps. Not completely, anyway. Some of them were bound to bleed through.

I glanced at my watch again and stood.

Dad blinked. "Where are you going?"

"The clock's ticking. Literally. I need to reach out to Claudia and get this ball rolling sooner rather than later."

Dad stood, too. "I'll come with you."

I held up one hand. "No. I think maybe you should stay here."

Dad looked pained, incredulous, and irritated. "You don't seriously think I'm going to sit here and do nothing while my daughter is in the hands of a lunatic."

I opened my mouth to point out all the reasons why he shouldn't be involved in this situation but thought better of it. For one thing, someone could apply whatever case I'd been about to make to my continuing presence in this investigation, and I was not at all eager to have that person point it out to me. For another, I knew how he felt. No way in hell would I let anyone bench me. I could understand why he'd feel the same way.

"Of course not. It's just that I have some paperwork to pick up from the squad and a few phone calls to make. Maybe you'd like to meet me over at the Sin Bin after you talk to the guys down in the cell-tracking unit? Get them set to move when I have something for them to go on?"

"Okay."

As I moved toward the door, Dad moved to retrieve his suit jacket. I was just about out of his office when something occurred to me, and I stopped. Slowly, I turned back around.

"Dad?"

"Yes?" His tone was absent. He was busy gathering up his phone, wallet, and keys and stuffing everything into his pockets or clipping it onto his belt.

"*Dad*," I said again, louder, trying to make him look at me.

He did. "What?"

"You need to call Mom," I said softly.

Dad's walls visibly cracked then, and his eyes widened just a tad. We stared at one another for a minute before he nodded. "Of course."

I gazed at him sympathetically. "I'll see you over there."

I turned to leave then, not envying the task I'd just set him to. I heard him take a seat and closed the door on the telltale clacking of phone buttons being hastily yet deliberately punched.

CHAPTER TWELVE

The ride over to the Sin Bin seemed to take damn near forever, and I was a wreck the entire trip. My heart raced. My stomach felt as twisted and knotted as a loaf of braided bread. And my thoughts bounced around with all the grace and subtlety of a wine bottle tossed down a trash chute. My insides practically clanged as ideas banged back and forth in my overtaxed brain. It was a miracle I made it to my destination.

After throwing my car down in a spot reserved for commercial parking only, I strode into Hurricane's building. For an instant I was positive I'd left the elevator key card Hannah had given me at my desk, and I nearly had a heart attack thinking I'd have to go all the way back to Brooklyn to retrieve it. But after some frantic pocket searching, I located it wedged in my commission book. Of course, after I'd gotten on the elevator and punched the floor for the Sin Bin, it occurred to me that I could've just called upstairs and asked one of the on-duty agents to come get me, thus negating the need to go anywhere. Yeah. I wasn't thinking clearly.

I shifted my weight from foot to foot and checked my BlackBerry three times for messages as I endured the endless ride upstairs. By the time I made it, I was all kinds of anxious, and I'm sure it showed in my body language as I barged into the command post.

The agents on duty all looked up from what they were doing, but none of them appeared surprised to see me. Of course, I'd been a somewhat regular fixture there in recent weeks. I didn't even bother to greet any of them.

"Is Hannah here?" I was unable to keep the panic out of my voice, and I cringed at the realization.

One of the detail guys pointed toward two small offices at the back of the room, the doors to both of which were closed. "Hers is the one on the right."

I nodded my thanks and made my way back there, still trying to figure out what I was going to say. I rapped lightly on Hannah's door, checking my phone one more time as I did.

"Come in," she called.

I opened the door just enough to slip inside and then shut it behind me. Hannah frowned at me in obvious confusion.

"Hey. Did we have plans today?"

I shook my head and chewed on the corner of my lower lip as I settled into the chair on the other side of her desk. I was spending a lot of time that day sitting on one side of a desk or another trying to deal with a problem I had no idea how to even begin solving. Somehow, it seemed wrong.

"Everything okay?"

Hannah's question pulled me out of my inane musings about chairs. When I finally looked into her eyes, the concern I saw there was both touching and heart wrenching.

"Yes. I mean, no. I mean, I need to talk to you. And Claudia. I need to talk to both of you. Is she around?" I was rambling. I took a deep breath, forcing myself to push past the panic burrowing into my chest and focus. "Something happened that you and Claudia both need to be aware of. And I'm going to need her help in order to fix it."

Hannah's expression of concern morphed back into confusion and then became tinged with fear before settling into determination. She stood and grabbed her suit jacket off the back of her chair. "Let's go talk to her, then."

I felt a trickle of fear all my own. I didn't want to go anywhere near Hurricane's apartment. But before I could even think to object or ask where our protectee was, Hannah had already popped her head into the adjacent office to let someone know she was headed upstairs and was well on her way to the elevator. I had no choice but to go after her.

Not knowing what to say, I busied myself with playing with my phone again as we took the elevator up to the floor where Hurricane's apartment was located. My nerves felt like wind chimes in a tempest: twisted and tangled and jangling discordantly. I couldn't help thinking that each second this took was one second less I'd have to save my sister. And I'd already lost almost an hour as it was.

The time between Hannah's knock on the door of the apartment next to Hurricane's that the detail used as a crash pad and Claudia's opening it felt like at least an age and a half, and I had to force myself not to fidget as we waited. If nothing else, it gave me something to concentrate on besides what special brand of hell Rory might have been enduring at that exact second. It was something, I supposed.

"Ryan, how are you?" Claudia's voice startled me, and I blinked. She looked surprised.

"SAIC Quinn. I'm sorry to bother you, as always. I'm afraid this is becoming something of a pattern for me." I shoved my hands into the pockets of my pants so she wouldn't see them shaking.

Claudia opened the door wider. "Don't be silly. You're always welcome here. Please, come in."

Hannah and I trudged inside, and I turned to face her the second she closed the door behind us. A small, distant part of me was screaming to at least let the poor woman sit down or fix herself a drink before I started bombarding her with my latest personal crisis, but the part of me that was all too keenly aware of the passage of every solitary millisecond won out over reason. I licked my dry lips and took a breath.

"Do you have a moment? Hurricane isn't scheduled to depart any time soon, is she?"

"She has an open schedule today, so we have time. Just give me a second to make a phone call. Please, make yourselves at home."

I shifted my weight back and forth between my feet as Claudia told someone she wouldn't be able to make the meeting and that he or she would have to conduct the interview by themselves. Then she holstered her phone and turned back to me. "So, what can I do for you?"

I cleared my throat. "The very first time we met, when I stopped by a few weeks ago, did Hannah brief you on why I was here?"

Claudia's face gave away nothing. Instead, she made her way

over to the living room and took a seat on the couch. She crossed her right leg over her left and laced her fingers together in her lap.

After a long moment—during which I had to force myself not to rush her—Claudia's eyes flooded with recognition. She nodded. "Yes. That PI subject. Adam Royce Walker. He'd been let out of Saint E's and was on his way here, correct?"

I was relieved she remembered. I definitely wasn't in the mood to catch her up. Not when we had only—I consulted my watch—two hours and four minutes until Walker would call back demanding to see Hurricane or else. I nodded as well.

"That's right. Walker has been fixated on Hurricane for quite some time now." I went on without giving either of them a chance to chime in. "As the years have progressed, Walker's delusions have apparently only gotten stronger. He's now under the impression that he and Hurricane are married. He also seems to believe I've been running interference and deliberately keeping her from him because I want Hurricane for myself."

Claudia and Hannah both stared at me.

"You can't be serious," Hannah said.

"That was actually his second theory. His first was that I wanted him."

Hannah smirked, clearly unable to help herself, but Claudia continued to watch me in silence.

"When we came here a few weeks ago to intercept him, he became extremely agitated and belligerent. We ended up having to commit him to Bellevue for a psych eval."

"Is he out now?" Claudia asked.

I nodded. "He is, yes."

"Do we need to be worried about him?" Claudia cast a troubled glance toward the door.

"Not in the way you're thinking, no."

I took another deep breath and willed myself to get through this next part without any discernable display of emotion. I was already more involved in this entire situation than I had any right to be. I was afraid if Claudia saw even one iota of feeling, she'd shut me out of the rest of the investigation entirely. And if I were forced out of the loop, I'd go insane.

"We received a call in NYFO a little more than an hour ago on the main PI Squad line. Walker has a hostage. He said if we don't let him see Hurricane, he's going to kill her."

Claudia didn't even try to conceal her surprise. "What did he say? I mean, exactly."

I reached into my interior suit-jacket pocket and retrieved the printed copy of the transcript of Rico and Adam's conversation, complete with my own handwritten notes regarding the things of particular interest. I unfolded it and smoothed it out before handing it over. Claudia took it without a word and started to read. She hadn't gotten very far before she stopped and pinned me with a dark look.

"He thinks he has you."

I nodded. "Yes."

"Why does he think that?"

"Because he has my identical-twin sister, Rory." I was unable to keep the tremor from my voice.

"What?" Hannah nearly shrieked.

Claudia ignored her. She kept her eyes locked on me, but for some reason, she looked almost angry now. "You could've led with that."

"I didn't think you'd see that as the most important piece of information." And I meant it. For her, it shouldn't have been. Rory wasn't her concern. She was mine. All Claudia needed to worry about was Hurricane, and on that front, she needed to know only that a hostage was in the mix. It didn't matter who it was.

Claudia narrowed her eyes, and the muscles in her jaw tensed as though she were clenching her teeth. "We'll talk about that later. But for the record, you couldn't be more wrong."

I sat squirming in silence as I waited for her to finish reading and then pass the paper to Hannah so she could peruse it as well. She fixed me with another intense stare, and I felt like she was trying to see straight into my brain. It wasn't a pleasant feeling.

"How much time is left on the clock he gave you?" Claudia asked.

I consulted my watch again. "Just about two hours."

"Not a lot of time."

I shook my head. "No. It isn't."

"How do you want to play this?"

"This isn't strictly a matter of national security, but since the president's daughter is peripherally involved, I was hoping you could pull your magical strings in the AUSA's office and get a tracking order authorized. If I can figure out where they are, maybe we can have NYPD-ESU do an extraction."

"You want the Emergency Services Unit to do it?"

"They have the most experience." I didn't say I was afraid to take any chances with Rory's safety. I didn't have to.

"Done," Claudia said without hesitation. "Give me the numbers, and I'll call right now. I assume the cell-tracking team is standing by to respond and narrow it down to a more specific area?"

"Yes. One of my colleagues is setting that up back at the office as we speak."

"What does *dearg choíche* mean?" Hannah asked.

"What?" I blinked at her, momentarily confused. *Oh. Right. The transcript.* "Loosely translated, it means 'ever red.'"

"Why would you tell her that?"

"Adam always asks me what color he's thinking of, and the answer is always red. It's something of a ritual for us at this point. I was hoping if he asked Rory what color he was thinking of, she'd remember that and answer correctly." I didn't say he'd know something was up if she answered wrong. I'd been trying very hard not to think about that for the past sixty-six minutes. I didn't even want to contemplate what such a revelation would mean for her.

Hannah nodded thoughtfully, and I thought Claudia looked a little impressed. "And *éigin, muinín, socair*? What about that?"

"I was more or less trying to tell her to be vague, project confidence, and remain calm. I never act unsure or scared around him. Not even when he's in a rage. If she does…"

"And *Laval, Asha*? What's that?"

"I was telling Rory that I love her," I whispered softly as tears welled up in my eyes.

Out of the corner of my eye, I saw Hannah and Claudia exchange helpless glances. I didn't blame them for not knowing how to react. I barely knew how, and I was the one that said it. I opened my eyes as wide as they would go in an attempt to dry the moisture gathering there and cleared my throat, feeling a little self-conscious.

Claudia rose and placed a reassuring hand on my shoulder. "We're going to get her back," she said. She held out her hand, wordlessly asking for the numbers she needed to get a tracking order for. I reached into one of my jacket pockets and pulled out a small piece of paper. Claudia took it with a sympathetic expression and, after giving me one last pat on the arm, disappeared to start making calls.

CHAPTER THIRTEEN

After the bombshell I'd just dropped, everyone and their brother needed to be informed about the situation. My dad had arrived not long after Claudia had gone to see about the tracking order, and the two of them made easily a dozen phone calls each, presumably to other bosses in the agency, although they could've been talking to anyone. I wasn't paying enough attention to be able to tell. I was pacing back and forth wringing my hands and standing at the window staring into space.

My mind during that time was busily traversing some pretty rugged terrain. I sort of heard the sounds of commotion around me as each new person arrived and was looped in on the circumstances we were attempting to navigate our way out of, but I didn't register the specifics of who was being told what. As far as I was concerned, none of that mattered. Only getting Rory back did.

But we were being forced to wait. For the judge to sign the tracking order for us. For the phone companies to give us the trace. For Walker to call us back with details on where and when he wanted to do this meet. For some information we could actually act on instead of the litany of endlessly gruesome possibilities we were staring down at present. I don't need to reiterate how waiting has never been my strong suit.

"Hey, gunner," a soft voice all but whispered almost directly into my ear.

I closed my eyes and let out a heavy sigh, recognizing that tone immediately. Without much thought, I turned and fell into Allison's arms. I rested my chin against her shoulder and took a long moment to relish the feel of her holding me.

Allison had one arm wrapped securely around my back and the other running soothing trails across my shoulder blades as she pressed kisses to my temple and cheek. We were standing in a room full of people who were likely soaking up our display with more than a passing interest, but I couldn't bring myself to care. I needed the consolation of her embrace too badly to leave it.

"We'll get her back, Ryan."

I sighed once more and buried my face in her neck, allowing myself a few more seconds of vulnerability before I reluctantly pulled back. I cleared my throat and dabbed at the tears that'd welled in my eyes. My smile felt shaky and slightly embarrassed.

Allison's answering smile was both radiant and comforting. She tangled our fingers together as she searched my face. "How're you holding up?"

"Honestly? Not as good as I could be."

"Well, that's to be expected. I can't even imagine what you're feeling right now."

I ran my thumbs across the soft skin of her hands. "I can't turn my mind off. I can't stop wondering…What if he does something to her?"

"You can't think like that. You'll drive yourself crazy."

"Too late."

"Do you want to walk me through what happened?"

I recognized the distraction technique for what it was, and gratitude burst within the already crowded confines of my chest. I shook my head. I grasped at her fingers and held on to her. "I don't think I can go through it again. I'm sorry."

"It's okay. You don't have to."

"Why don't you tell me about your day? What are you doing here, anyway?"

"I told you I was coming to New York."

"Yes, but not that you were coming *here*."

"Oh. No. I guess I didn't. That was supposed to be part of the surprise. I came up here to meet my potential new boss."

I gaped at her. "Huh?"

"I told you I planned to come back to New York permanently."

"Yeah, but I assumed that'd be when you were finished with your detail time. I didn't think it'd be now."

Transferring to Hurricane's detail was just one step shy of taking a demotion. This assignment was considered a satellite—part of PPD, but not quite—and you did that to prepare for your time on the president's detail, not the other way around. The move could have catastrophic consequences for her career. Why would she volunteer for that?

"Are you complaining?" Her tone was teasing, but her words held hints of insecurity.

Oops. Way to be an ass, Ryan. "Of course not. I just don't want you to feel like you have to take a step backward in your career for me. Your detail time is almost up. And I'm not going anywhere."

"Who said I was doing this for you? Maybe I'm doing it for me."

"Going to DC, stepping onto the fast track to promotion, those were for you. You said that yourself. This move doesn't make any sense."

Allison glanced around as though she'd just realized we were still standing in a room full of people and then took a step closer. She looked directly into my eyes. "I lost years I could've had with you because I was scared of how much I felt for you and because I put the job first. I'm not making that mistake again. And I'm not spending one more day apart from you that I don't absolutely have to."

I was touched. "That's one of the sweetest things you've ever said to me."

"Well, I meant it."

"Allison, are you sure this is what you want?" I was afraid that later, after she'd settled back in up here and some time had passed, after it finally sank in exactly what this move could mean for her, that she'd resent the decision. Resent me.

"I'm positive. And don't worry. I've already made all the necessary connections. My career will be fine. I promise."

I chuckled, unable to help myself. "Cocky."

"Confident," she retorted with a grin.

I grinned back but abruptly stopped when something occurred to me. "This doesn't have anything to do with you and Byers, does it? Is he making you do this?"

The notion that he was forcing this on her made me see scarlet. I still had no idea why he held such a grudge because she left an assignment early to come home to see me after I'd been shot, and I didn't really care. But if I found out this was his doing, I'd find some way to repay him.

Allison glanced over her shoulder, and I followed her gaze, stunned to see the man in question deep in discussion with someone I didn't know on the other side of the living room. I hadn't realized he was here, and I frowned as I attempted to figure out why.

"No. He isn't making me do this. I asked for the transfer."

"Because of him?"

"No. Although getting out from under his thumb is definitely an added perk." Allison rested the palm of one hand gently against my cheek and turned my head back so I was looking at her. "I told you, I'm coming back for me. And for you. Not for him."

"Promise?"

"Cross my heart."

"What's he doing here?"

"He insisted. Something about smoothing the transition. I wasn't really paying attention. Unless we're discussing how he wants us to handle the president's movements, I tend to tune him out."

"Who's he talking to?"

She glanced again. "Oh. That's my new boss. Donovan Ware. He's going to be the SAIC of Hurricane's detail when SAIC Quinn leaves."

"He's relatively new, isn't he?" I asked, referring to his recent promotion to the SAIC level. I'd heard the name when the transfer orders had come out a couple weeks ago, but I hadn't yet had the opportunity to meet him. I studied him with interest.

"He is."

"Do you know him?"

"We've crossed paths a handful of times. Back before I was on the detail, we worked a few foreign digs together here in New York."

"Good guy?"

Allison shrugged. "He's competent enough. And he seems to get the big picture. Only time will tell."

"Well, I'm happy for you."

Allison pinned me with an enigmatic look. "I was hoping for a little more enthusiasm."

My lips twitched in the semblance of a wry smile. "Talk to me after this is all over and we're alone. I'll see what I can do."

"You're on."

"If I could have everyone's attention." Claudia's voice cut through the low hum of activity permeating the room. "I'd like to get started."

People halted their conversations and shifted so they could see Claudia where she stood at one end of the room. I blinked in surprise at the number of people present. How the hell had I not noticed when all these suits had wandered in? And who in God's name were some of them? I'd never seen half of these people before.

It took me a second to collect myself, but when I finally fixed my own attention on Claudia, I saw she'd been joined by my dad, Allison's new boss, and her current one. All of them looked deathly serious, which served as a completely unnecessary reminder of how high the stakes were. I gripped Allison's hand tight, and she stroked the skin on my knuckles with the fingertips of her free hand.

"For those of you who might not know me, I'm Claudia Quinn, SAIC of Zoey Carmichael's detail. To my right, we have DSAIC Donovan Ware, who'll be taking over for me as SAIC when I transfer down to DC. Next to him is Beau Byers, an assistant to the special agent in charge on the Presidential Protective Division. And to my left is Ben Flannigan, special agent in charge of the New York Field Office.

"We don't have a lot of time, so I'll cut to the chase. Earlier today, agents of the New York Field Office received word that one of their Protective Intelligence subjects had abducted a woman with the intention of using her as leverage to force a meeting with Miss Carmichael."

The room was suddenly abuzz with the low drone of several voices. I wasn't interested in what anyone might have to say on the matter. An agent I'd seen around once or twice who I figured was likely on Hurricane's detail had just approached me. He leaned in to whisper in my ear as he pressed a small folded piece of paper into my hand. I nodded my thanks and set about reading it as Claudia went on.

"The subject believes he has abducted one of our agents, his one-time handler, Special Agent Ryan O'Connor, when in fact he has her twin sister, Rory. I don't think I need to tell you that under any circumstances we would proceed with caution. With this current new twist, the situation needs to be handled with the utmost care." A long pause. "I will now open the floor to any questions."

A uniformed NYPD lieutenant raised his hand to get Claudia's attention. She nodded at him. "Can you give us a little more background on this guy?"

"Absolutely. I'll turn the briefing over to Agent O'Connor." Claudia motioned for me to join her.

Allison gave my hand one last reassuring squeeze before letting go and allowing me to thread my way through the crowd. I glanced at my watch again and saw we had just over an hour of Walker's imposed time limit left. A tiny frisson racked my body, and I felt a little light-headed.

"Are you okay?" Claudia asked in a low voice.

I blinked, surprised. I hadn't realized I'd made it all the way over to her already. *What the hell's happening to me?* I nodded dumbly and tried to appear calm.

"I'm fine," I murmured back.

I searched the crowd until I saw Rico and raised my eyebrows at him questioningly. He nodded once and held up a stack of papers so I could see it. I nodded back once in thanks.

"Special Agent Rico Corazon will be passing around BOLO sheets containing our target's picture, identifiers, and other pertinent information. Please remember that this material is sensitive and is not to be disseminated outside of this room. Agent Corazon will be collecting the sheets again before we leave.

"The subject in question is Adam Royce Walker. He first came to our attention several years ago when he called 9-1-1 to report that he had information regarding a plot to assassinate President Anderson Carmichael. Subsequent investigation revealed that he suffers from paranoid schizophrenia and is generally noncompliant with his prescribed medication schedule.

"Over the years, Mr. Walker has attempted, on numerous occasions, to infiltrate several of our protected sites with the intention of obtaining a meeting with the president's daughter, Zoey Carmichael, who he now believes to be his wife. He's also made frequent phone calls to several of our offices and sent countless letters to both Miss Carmichael's residence as well as to the White House, expounding on his perceived nature of their relationship as well as detailing the level of his devotion to her.

"Mr. Walker contacted us earlier today to report that he'd kidnapped me, and during his conversation with Agent Corazon, he threatened to kill me if we didn't facilitate a meeting with Miss Carmichael. He gave us three hours from the time of that call to set it up. We have a little more than an hour of that timetable remaining."

I paused to take a deep breath and allow the murmuring to die down.

"It's important to note that while Walker has not been known to carry weapons, he can become extremely violent, and the change can come on quickly. In the past, he's become unnecessarily combative with various members of law enforcement. This appears to be his normal response, particularly when he feels as though they're either belittling him or deliberately interfering with whatever goal he's set his mind to.

"With his mental history, it doesn't take much for him to arrive at that conclusion. When we do finally encounter him, I encourage you to exercise extreme caution. I recognize that the convention is to assume that because he's mentally ill he's less of a threat than someone with all their faculties. It's easy to underestimate him, but I can tell you from personal experience that's a good way to get yourself knocked upside the head."

I held up the piece of paper Claudia's colleague had handed me earlier. "Thanks to SAIC Quinn, our tracking orders on both Walker's and Rory's cell phones are about to come through. We're just waiting for information from the telephone companies. In theory, they should be able to provide us with a rough location where they were during Walker's last call phone call, which may or may not have been the one he made to our office a little over two hours ago. We're expecting another call from him to discuss the terms of his meeting with Miss Carmichael soon. By that time, the phone companies should be on board with what we need. As soon as he does call, we'll be able to get a fix on where he is now and plan from there.

"Are there any questions?"

"I have one," a voice behind me said.

I turned. "Yes?"

"What are you doing here?" Byers asked, his face an interesting mix of condescension and arrogance.

I frowned, confused. "Excuse me?"

"Why are you here? You're too close to this situation to be involved. You should go back to your office and let us handle it."

My cheeks blazed, and the heat must've burned out all my neurons because I swear my mind was one big blank. I had no idea how to respond and was aghast that he'd chosen such a public forum to voice his concerns. I glanced helplessly into the crowd but didn't register any of the faces. Not that it mattered. I hadn't known what I'd been looking for anyway.

Claudia smoothly stepped in. "Agent O'Connor is here because no one in the agency knows Walker better than she does. We need information, and she has it. It's that simple."

"It's against protocol," Byers insisted. "She shouldn't be here."

The rest of the group continued to watch in uncomfortable silence, their glances bouncing from me to Byers to Claudia and back again as though we were engaged in some sort of high-stakes Ping-Pong match. The heat from my cheeks was rapidly spreading to engulf the rest of my body.

Byers shifted his attention to my father and renewed his attempts to plead his case. "Sir. With all due respect, Agent O'Connor cannot be expected to be impartial about this matter. And, frankly, the errors in judgment that could lead to have given me cause for concern."

Oh, boy. He'd picked the wrong ally for this battle. I wasn't one for letting people fight my skirmishes for me, but I had to admit I was curious to see how this one would play out.

Out of the corner of my eye, I saw Rico move to engage our spectators, most of whom appeared to be high-ranking members of the NYPD. The majority of the ones who weren't in uniform were wearing lapel pins I recognized as ones their detectives wear, and the remaining men were exhibiting enough familiarity with the rest of the group that I figured they must work together.

"Gentlemen, if you'd come with me, please, I'd like to start discussing what additional assets we might need and what you might be able to make available to us on such short notice."

A lot of murmuring and whispering underscored the pointed looks we received, but everyone followed Rico to the dining area of the apartment and started taking seats. It didn't completely remove them from the set, but it went a long way toward making the encounter less awkward. I shot Rico a grateful look, which he answered with a sympathetic one.

"I appreciate your opinion, AT Byers," my dad said. "Your concerns have been duly noted."

"But you're not going to remove her." Byers appeared irritated.

"No, I'm not. Agent O'Connor is a professional. She's handled the situation as well as anyone not intimately associated with the victim would have, and I have faith that she'll continue to conduct herself accordingly." Dad glanced at me then. "Right, Agent O'Connor?"

I nodded. "Of course, sir."

Byers frowned. "But, sir—"

"Beau," Claudia said a little sharply. "Ben has given you his decision. It's his call to make, not yours."

"The life of one of our protectees could potentially be endangered if she loses her objectivity for even an instant. That makes it my call."

"Actually, that makes it mine. And you're walking a very fine line just this side of insubordination," Claudia warned him. "Consider your next words carefully."

"Actually, that makes it Ethan Luke's call," Byers said, referring to the SAIC of PPD, who technically outranked Claudia since Hurricane's detail fell under the umbrella of PPD. "And I can't imagine he'd be even remotely okay with this."

I was in total disbelief. Why was Byers continuing to push this issue? Especially when two people who were higher on the proverbial food chain had already told him to let it go.

"We could ask him," Dad said. He pulled his phone out of the holster on his belt. "He and I were on the detail together back in the day, and I need to touch base with him anyway to reschedule the golf game I had to cancel last time I was in DC. Now's as good a time as any to have that conversation."

"There's no need, Ben," Claudia said. "Beau, you've received your answer. If I doubted Agent O'Connor's ability to perform or thought she lacked focus that could put Hurricane in danger in any way, I'd remove her from this operation faster than she could open her mouth. I have no such concerns. Agent O'Connor stays."

I felt a little tug around my heart, touched by her unwavering faith in me. It meant more to me than I'd ever have been able to describe.

"Thank you," I whispered softly.

Byers scowled. His lips were set in a thin line, his jaw clenched. Anger wafted off him in pungent waves that soured the air around us, which only served to confuse me. What was he so upset about? Surely his ego wasn't so fragile that he couldn't handle a little professional difference in opinion. It just didn't make any sense.

"Perhaps you'd be more comfortable if you went back to DC, Agent Byers," my dad said, his tone making it clear that he wasn't really making a suggestion. "We can take it from here. Thank you for your assistance."

Byers had been dismissed, and he knew it. Fury sparked in his eyes, and it looked like he might've considered protesting, but Ware shot him a warning glare. He bobbed his head once curtly and stalked away, physically pushing past me as he went.

I ignored the shove and let out a huge sigh of relief, grateful he wouldn't be participating in the rest of the operation. This whole thing was a giant clusterfuck as it was. The last thing I needed was somebody who would argue about every decision just for the sake of it. We couldn't afford such a waste of time.

I reached in my pocket for the piece of paper containing the information we'd received from the cell-phone companies and handed it to my dad. "Would you mind shooting this information over to the cell-tracking guys? It's the contact information for the people at the phone companies who will be helping us out. I thought they could reach out, get a jump on things, maybe help move it along faster. I wouldn't even know what to say to them if I called. I don't understand most of this cell-site stuff. It's all gibberish to me."

"Sure thing," Dad said, accepting the sheet from me. "I'll pass it along to them right now."

"Perfect. Thanks."

I started to turn back to Claudia and Allison and ended up running bodily into Byers, who'd apparently crept up on me when I wasn't paying attention. I recoiled, startled. "Jesus Christ."

The expression on Byers's face was odd. Unsettling. His countenance was wooden, and his eyes were flat, but it immediately struck me as a mask. I sensed that underneath that strange blankness was a whole host of emotions churning away, none of them pleasant. A cold sliver of dread pierced my heart.

"Yes? Did you need something?"

Byers stared at me for a long moment, saying nothing, which creeped me the hell out. I tired of it after a few beats and rolled my eyes as I moved to brush past him, but he grabbed me by the arm, forcing me to stop.

"Hey!"

"I just thought you should know," Byers said in a low voice with that disturbing non-expression. "I fucked your girlfriend."

Time ground to a halt as the chill from that sliver of dread washed outward to permeate my whole body. My ears started ringing, and I suddenly felt small inside myself. I was trying to think, but rational thought had become elusive.

"Wh—what?"

Byers shrugged and looked away, but I would've sworn I caught the faintest gleam of triumph in his eye before he dropped my gaze. "More than once, actually."

I struggled to gain traction and start thinking again, but nothing was happening. I couldn't hear anything except the echo of his earlier words. *I fucked your girlfriend.*

My face crumpled, and a tremor racked my body. I glanced to my dad and Ware, who were standing nearby, to see if they'd heard, but they appeared to be engrossed in their own conversation and not paying attention to us. I shifted my attention to Claudia, who looked as though she couldn't decide whether to hug me or punch Byers. And then I looked at Allison.

My stomach immediately collapsed in on itself, and the whole messy pile felt like it had dropped out of my body to land with a wet splat on the floor at my feet. I wanted to argue that it wasn't true, what he was saying. More to the point, I wanted to believe it. But all it took was one look at her face, at the fear and guilt splashed all over her beautiful features, and I knew.

He was telling the truth.

Byers leaned closer so he could whisper to me, but he didn't lower his voice enough to really warrant the action. Feeling his breath on my ear made me shiver in disgust.

"Gotta love foreign trips, huh?"

And having wrought all the chaos he was apparently inclined to, he turned and walked out, leaving me with about a million questions I never wanted answered.

Chapter Fourteen

Not knowing what else to do, but desperately needing some space and some fresh air, I thundered up the fire stairs toward the roof. I slammed bodily into the panic bar to fling the door open and more or less stumbled outside, ignoring the screaming alarm that accompanied my great escape. If the guys in Platform watching the cameras that monitored all the entrances and exits to the building knew what was good for them, they'd stay exactly where they were and leave me the hell alone.

I stomped to the roof's edge and dug my hands into the rough mortar ledge, reveling in the stinging pinpricks of pain. On some level, it felt right that I should hurt on the outside, as well. Lord knew my insides were causing me serious agony at the moment. Like things weren't fucked up enough already. I didn't need this new distraction.

Tears welled in my eyes, blurring the streetlamps and apartment lights that dotted the picturesque view of the New York skyline spread out in front of me. I tried to take a deep breath, but the air lodged painfully in my chest, an agonizing ache in the general area that used to be occupied by my heart arresting its easy ebb and flow.

"Ryan." Allison's soft voice broke into my pity party.

I gasped and wrapped my arms around my middle, as though I could hold myself together through physical force alone. Just knowing she'd followed me alternately made my heart soar and my rage burn hotter. I couldn't decide whether I wanted to kiss her or strangle her. I was in a tremendous amount of pain. I'd never been hurt this badly. Not even when she'd broken my heart that first time.

I shouldn't have been surprised. Allison had always had the ability to completely turn my world upside down, for better or for worse. She'd always exercised both options, too. I should've known it'd only be a matter of time before she shattered me again. She was the only woman in existence who knew how.

And, boy, was I shattered. My insides felt like they'd been shredded to ribbons and called to mind bloody images of twisted and mangled intestines that would've put even the goriest horror film to shame. I glanced down at my abdomen, needing to verify that my entrails were still inside my body.

I pressed the heel of one hand to the center of my chest and rubbed, seeking to soothe the ache steadily growing more agonizing the longer my mind's eye kept dwelling on made-up images of Allison and Byers tangled in each other's arms. Bile rose in the back of my throat then, and I staggered a few steps, clenching my jaw against my stomach's obvious intent to relieve itself of its contents. I closed my eyes and tried to banish the images from my mind. My stomach churned again, and I curled my lip into a disgusted sneer.

Was my current degree of revulsion due to how stirred up my emotions were about my sister? Probably. I'm sure that didn't help. But did the why of it even matter? Definitely not. All that mattered was getting a handle on myself and refocusing on what was important. That wouldn't be easy with the object of my wrath standing three feet away from me, but that didn't mean I wasn't going to try.

"I didn't cheat on you." Allison's voice slammed up against the sharp edges of those visions of her and Byers together, causing them to splinter and break apart.

"What?" The words sounded foreign to my ears for some unknown reason. Perhaps because they hadn't been what I'd expected her to say.

"I said I didn't cheat on you."

An irrational spark of hope ignited inside me, despite what I knew to be true. Even though her deer-in-the-headlights expression after Byers's announcement had said it all, a small part of me still desperately wanted to believe that I'd misunderstood, that Allison hadn't slept with him.

"So he was lying?" My voice wavered.

Allison's face fell, and she looked as sad and lost as I'd ever seen her. My guts rolled again, and my teeth chattered. In addition to feeling physically ill, I now felt stupid for even asking.

"I didn't cheat on you," Allison repeated again.

"But you did sleep with him."

Allison looked away. That told me everything I needed to know.

"Great," I drawled, sarcasm dripping poisonously off every letter. "That makes me feel so much better."

Allison's face scrunched up in obvious confusion. "I thought that's why you were upset. Because you thought I'd cheated on you. I know that's how he was trying to make it sound…" She raised her hands in a helpless gesture. "But I swear I haven't been with anybody else since before that first time I came to New York. I'd never do that to you."

"Lucky me."

At my venomous words, Allison frowned. "So, just to be clear, you believe I didn't cheat on you, and that's not why you're upset."

"No, Allison. That's *not* why I'm upset." Well, it had been initially, but it wasn't why I was upset now. My stomach squirmed as though searching for an escape route. My heart felt as though it were being squeezed from the inside out. The pressure would've been excruciating on a normal day. Now, piled on top of everything else, it was unbearable. "Listen, I can't do this with you right now—"

"Is it because he's a man?"

"What?" She had to be kidding.

"Is that what's bothering you? That I was with a man? Because—"

"No. I don't give a shit that you were with a man."

"Oh. Okay. Good."

I didn't respond, and the silence that settled between us was heavy and thick, pungent with the acrid taste of anger and betrayal. It landed on and coated my skin like a fine layer of soot.

Allison took a step closer and tried again. "So, if you know I didn't cheat on you, and you're not upset I was with a man, then what's the matter?"

I shook my head, unable to force out the words that were scalding inside me. They remained stuck in the back of my throat, making it tough for me to breathe.

"Ryan, what is your problem?" Allison was starting to get angry. At me. I couldn't believe it!

"What is *my* problem?" I repeated, incredulously.

"Yes. What is your problem? Why are you freaking out about this? It's not that big a deal. I didn't freak out when I found out you'd slept with Jamie."

Okay, that threw me. I hadn't been aware she'd actually known about that. Not known for sure, anyway. I'd had a feeling she'd suspected, but as far as I knew, no one had confirmed anything. I certainly hadn't told her. Had Jamie? I faltered. No, that was ridiculous. No way would Jamie have said anything about our past to anyone. Unfortunately, my instant of hesitation must've been enough to confirm Allison's suspicions, because she sneered at me in a vague sort of triumph.

"Yeah. Didn't think I knew about that, did you?"

I sketched an irritated wave in the air with one hand as I took a step back from her, needing distance and space. "That has nothing to do with this, and you know it."

"Doesn't it? Because I think the fact that my girlfriend fucked one of my subordinates is information I should be privy to."

"Oh, my God. It was forever ago. And it didn't even mean anything."

"Oh, so you're allowed to have casual, meaningless sex, but I'm not?"

"It's a completely different situation, Allison!"

"Of course. Please, queen of semantics. Enlighten me. How is this different?" Allison's tone was caustic.

"Well, for one thing, Jamie doesn't run around bragging to everybody within earshot that we've done it! She doesn't air our history in front of a whole crowd of our coworkers. She's actually mature enough to exercise some discretion."

The fury that'd welled up inside me had suddenly become all-consuming. A small part of me recognized that the rational thing to do would be to put this discussion on the back burner and concentrate on my sister, but I was too far down this rabbit hole now to just walk away. My anger and frustration for all of my recent plights—at myself for being unable to protect Rory, at Walker for actually taking her, at Byers for being a complete dick, and at Allison for any number of things—had all combined to create something of a perfect storm. I was livid at everything and everybody, and a sick, sadistic part of me was anxious for this fight, for any fight. I craved an outlet for my anguish, and a knock-down, drag-out argument seemed like the perfect way to blow off a little steam.

"Who are you kidding? Everybody knows you two used to be a thing."

"We were not a thing," I insisted. "And you know what? It doesn't matter if we were! At least she wasn't my boss!"

Allison blinked, startled. I might as well have clocked her. I doubted she would've appeared more surprised if I had. "That's why you're pissed? Because he's my boss?"

"No! I'm pissed because he's an *asshole*!" I exploded. My voice was huge and echoed off the walls of the nearby buildings. I balled my hands up into fists as I seethed. The air I was forcing in and out of my lungs was coming and going in an angry hiss, leaving faint, white puffs swirling between us. I turned my back on her in an attempt to wrangle my feelings.

And that really was the crux of my problem. I didn't care that Allison had been with somebody while we'd been split up. True, I didn't want to dwell on it too closely, but I would've been a hypocrite if I'd begrudged her attempts at happiness and companionship during our hiatus.

I didn't even care that she'd been with a man. I understood that people pinged at different spots on the sexuality scale. Guys weren't my cup of tea, and I didn't think there was enough beer in all of Ireland to get me to sleep with one, but if bedding the occasional dude while she was single did it for her, well, then she could ride it 'til the wheels fell off as far as I was concerned, no pun intended. Again, I didn't need details or to think about it too hard or for too long, but good for her for letting her freak flag fly.

No, the difficulty I was having at the moment could be attributed to her specific choice in partners. The fact that it'd been *Byers* was sticking firmly in my craw. I simply couldn't wrap my mind around any attribute that man exhibited that would possess her to take him to her bed. I also couldn't begin to fathom what sort of statement that made about her as a person.

I finally rounded on her so I could look her in the eye. "Beau Byers is a fucking douche bag."

Allison shrugged as though the issue held little interest for her, but her expression was hard. "I know. And?"

I goggled at her, flabbergasted. "But you slept with him anyway?"

"I wasn't interested in his conversational skills, Ryan."

My stomach rolled again as I caught the implications of her quip, and I made a disgusted face. I held up one hand as though trying to physically ward off a blow. "Ugh. Don't."

"So, that's it? That what's bothering you? That I slept with him even though he's a jerk?"

I huffed, annoyed with her for being deliberately obtuse. "I just don't get it, Allison. You're better than that."

"Of course I am."

"Then why? I know it wasn't to get ahead at work."

Allison's expression darkened. "Of course it wasn't," she snapped.

Her tone made my own irritation, which had just lost a small portion of its considerable steam and had started to ebb, roar furiously back to life. "I just said I knew that wasn't it. I simply can't come up with any other reason why sleeping with him would seem like a good idea. And more than once." I shuddered.

Allison crossed her arms across her chest. "Not that it's any of your business because I now know exactly what and who you were doing during that time, but I was lonely, okay? And it was nice to feel wanted. Even if it was by him."

"And there wasn't anybody else? At all?" My tone was borderline pleading as I asked, as though the intonation alone had the power to turn back time and influence the course that had already been indelibly mapped out.

Allison scowled at me, all defensive now. "Sure there was. You think I didn't try to date? I've been single for years, Ryan. Do you really believe in all that time I didn't at least attempt to establish a relationship?"

"Then what the fuck?" I shouted, furious and sick at the idea of Allison failing so miserably to have an honest-to-goodness relationship that she'd felt compelled to hook up with Byers. "I could walk into a maximum-security prison for violent offenders and point randomly at someone with my eyes closed and come up with a better human being than him. So why the fuck would you even bother? He couldn't have been that great in the sack."

Okay, that was probably a little dramatic, and it was entirely possible that I should've saved the hyperbole for any other situation except this one. Unfortunately, my mouth was running independently of my higher reasoning, and my mouth was an absolute bitch when I was hurt.

"I don't have to explain myself to you!" Allison shot back, starting to get angry again. "What I did after I broke up with you is none of your goddamn business. Besides, who are you to talk? Your last girlfriend punched you in the face in the middle of the sidewalk during a protective visit. After she cheated on you, dumped you, and then went through your phone and read your private text messages. I hardly think that brilliant choice in partners qualifies you to judge mine."

We both froze and stared at one another as the accusation continued to echo in the still evening air. I was aghast that she'd just thrown Lucia's last moments on earth in my face. I'd thought she had more class.

I fought to close the door on all the violently eddying emotions that bubbled up inside me. The small part of me not metaphorically writhing in pain and still capable of rational thought was screaming at me to restrain the words dying to burst free.

But I was fighting a losing battle. Too many horrible things had happened to me in too short a span of time. And all the frustration and angst that'd been building inside me for the past several weeks was about to rush out in a powerful torrent the way a flash flood springs up in the Grand Canyon. I don't know why I even bothered to try to rein it in. I couldn't fight nature.

"Pull it," I ground out, my voice low and hard.

"What?"

"Your transfer request. Pull it." The words were so icy they almost burned.

Allison's brow furrowed in obvious confusion. I didn't blame her. My statement probably seemed like a complete non sequitur. I smirked to myself, feeling victorious. Now she knew what it felt like for me to have a conversation with her. I could almost never follow her discussional segues.

"Ryan, what—"

I took a step forward well into her personal space, which caused whatever question she'd been about to voice to die on her lips. I wasn't positive what the expression on my face was, but it rendered her speechless. Uncertainty flickered in her eyes, and she shoved her hands into the pockets of her pants.

"Pull your transfer request. Or I will pull it for you. I don't want you up here."

The rational part of me cringed even as the words came out of my mouth, but unfortunately, the rational part of me was no longer in the driver's seat. No, it was forced to watch as the emotionally volatile, completely irrational part of me strung together sentences that I knew even now I'd regret later on. But I was exhausted and scared and still reeling from discovering in a very public forum that the love of my life had been having an affair with the biggest asshole on two legs, and I stubbornly refused to just shut the hell up.

Allison narrowed her eyes at me and set her mouth in a hard line. She took a step forward. We were now standing so close that we were almost touching. It would've taken only the barest of movements for our lips to brush. At that distance, I could feel the fury wafting off her in blistering waves.

"You can't do that."

"I can, and I will."

Allison scoffed. "You don't have the strings to pull to stop my transfer, little one."

I laughed, a dark, brittle, twisted sound. I didn't see anything amusing in any of this, and the humorless bark that'd just escaped my lips made that clear.

"Allison, I was just shot in an assassination attempt orchestrated by my boss, who'd been stealing counterfeit currency from our vaults for who knows how long and selling it to the Iranians to use to fund God knows what terrorist activity. A fact that all the higher-ups in our agency missed, and I had to catch.

"My twin sister was subsequently kidnapped because said boss failed to assign the Walker case to an agent for monitoring, and Walker's been running around unchecked for weeks plotting his revenge against me because he thinks I'm making time with his hypothetical wife.

"Short of demanding to be put in charge of PPD, I don't think there's a single thing I could ask for in this moment that headquarters wouldn't move heaven and earth to give me, if for no other reason than to keep me from making too big a fuss.

"Either you withdraw the request, or I will. The choice is yours."

And with that proclamation, I turned without giving her a chance to interject and stalked self-righteously back toward the door to the building. At least that's how I chose to see the action. Because otherwise I would've been forced to recognize it for exactly what it was: running away.

CHAPTER FIFTEEN

Once I'd made it back inside, I took a slight detour to the bathroom in the hallway off the security room to collect myself. No way would I be able to jump back into the fray of planning Rory's rescue like nothing had happened. Not after that conversation. No, I needed some time to calm the hell down so I could focus on that all-important task.

I leaned heavily on my hands on the edges of the sink and stared at my reflection in the mirror. I looked like an absolute mess. All the fear and anxiety slithering around inside me was visible on my face, underscored by new notes of anguish and fury. I sighed as I twisted the cold-water tap and then bent down to splash several handfuls against my cheeks, not caring that my makeup was about to become smeared and runny.

"That was quite a scene back there."

I started at Claudia's voice and spun around to face her, conscious of the icy droplets dripping from my skin to stain the front of my dress shirt and my suit jacket. She was scrutinizing me intently, which made me more than a little uneasy.

"Wasn't it though?" I snagged a paper towel and blotted my face and neck and then wrapped a piece of it around my index finger and ran it underneath my eyes to catch any traces of mascara or eyeliner that hadn't been able to withstand the moisture.

"You okay?"

"Absolutely. Why wouldn't I be?"

"Has anyone ever told you you're a terrible liar?"

"All the time. Doesn't stop me from trying, though, as you can see."

Claudia smiled and rested her shoulder against the wall adjacent to the door. With her thumbs hooked into her pockets and one ankle crossed over the other, she was the picture of casual. "Clearly. Do you want to talk about it?"

I shook my head. "Not even a little bit."

"Fair enough. I won't push you. But I need to know: Are you going to be able to focus?"

"I'll do what needs to be done. Don't worry about me."

"Good. Because I need you to be on your A game. You of all people know what's at stake here. We can't afford any slipups."

"That's convenient because I don't plan to make any."

"That's what I wanted to hear. How much time do we have left?"

I consulted my watch. "Not much. He should be calling within the next ten minutes or so."

"The guys at the field office know what to say to him? They'll pass all the pertinent info to us ASAP?"

"Rico's going to field the call. All the squad phones are rolled to my extension, which also rings to my cell. When he does call, I'll have Rico put the phone on speaker so we can listen in, and we can use him to manipulate the situation as best we can."

"Perfect. I'd much rather be involved on a firsthand level than to have to hear the information after the fact. When he does call, what do you need me to do?"

"I'd prefer it if you didn't speak. I don't want Walker interacting with anyone except Rico. We need to project as much of an illusion of control as we can, and that's one of the ways I want to do it. Besides, allowing him to talk to too many people will only confuse him, and it's tough enough to keep him on topic on a good day."

"Not a problem. What else?"

"I'd like to grab a laptop from the CP, so I can type to Rico as he talks. I'm going to need him to say certain things, and that's the easiest way to convey them. My handwriting is atrocious."

"Mine's upstairs. You can use that."

"Great. Thanks."

Claudia snapped back to studying me like I was some species of interesting animal that she couldn't quite figure out. I tried to force myself not to squirm. "Are you ready to go up? Or do you need another minute?"

I turned my back to her so I could check myself out in the mirror. I took another few moments to erase any remaining smudges of eye makeup from my cheeks and rinsed my mouth with cold water before fluffing my hair. Well, I looked a little better, at any rate. I'd say I'd been downgraded from train wreck to circus act. It was the best I could've hoped for under the circumstances.

"I'm good. Let's go."

Claudia hesitated for a long moment before nodding once and turning to exit the restroom. I blew out a long breath, tossed my balled-up paper towel into the trash can, and followed her. On a whim, I grabbed the crook of her elbow before she could lead us into the stairwell.

"Ma'am?"

Claudia turned to face me, clearly startled. "Yes?"

"I'm really sorry this happened. I know that doesn't change anything, but…" I shrugged and ran one hand through my hair.

"It's not your fault," she said.

I gave her a shaky smile. "Kinda feels like it is."

"You couldn't have done anything to prevent this."

"I couldn't?" My words were tart.

"You think you could?"

I lifted my hands. "I'm pretty good at the 'if only' game. I think I've held the title for six years running."

"From everything you've told me, this man has been gearing up to do something for a very long time. You've just been delaying the inevitable. And if it wasn't your sister, he probably would've grabbed someone else. Short of having powers of clairvoyance, I doubt you could've done anything."

"Why doesn't that make me feel any better?"

"Because you're a little too much like me for your own good." Claudia favored me with the tiniest smile before turning to head up the stairs. "Come on."

I nodded even though her back was to me and trudged obediently up the steps behind her. I was starting to sweat again, as the reality of what was about to transpire bore down on me like a freight train. Only

I didn't have the option of stepping off the tracks. Nope. I had to stand there, take a deep breath, and let it hit me.

The mood in the apartment upstairs was an interesting mixture of tense and subdued, laced through with hints of outrage and nervous anticipation. It did nothing to quell my own unease. In fact, it probably made it worse.

Upon entering the room, of course, I immediately looked at Allison, who was standing ramrod straight staring out the window. As soon as the door opened, she turned her head, and I faltered in my step as that gaze locked onto me. Frankly, after that debacle upstairs on the roof, I was surprised she was still there, and I didn't have the energy to try to figure out why. I took a deep breath and forced myself to move, trying to ignore my thundering heart as I softly closed the door behind me.

Claudia approached the NYPD brass still sitting at the dining-area table, and I hovered near the exit for a long moment, feeling like a complete and total idiot. Now that I'd had a few minutes to cool down, I felt pretty bad about some of the things I'd said to Allison. And judging by the faint air of misery shrouding her, I guessed she felt bad about a few things, too.

I averted my eyes and debated the merits of apologizing. I couldn't decide whether that would be a fantastic idea or an epic mistake. The mere notion of talking to her tied my stomach up in painful snarls and made me more than a little terrified. No, I couldn't do this now. I didn't have room inside me for any more emotional detours. I'd been on far too many today already. It was time to focus on Rory. I could deal with the mess I'd made with Allison later.

Claudia rested a gentle hand on my arm. "You okay?"

"Sure. Just thinking."

She nodded as though that was to be expected and handed me her laptop. "Here you go."

"Thanks." I made my way over to the chair I'd been perched in earlier today when I'd broken the news of Rory's kidnapping to Claudia, marveling at how much had happened in the short period since then. Had it really been only two hours? Wow. Somehow it felt like a lifetime.

I could feel Allison staring at me from her station at the window, and my cheeks burned. Having her attention on me when I was trying to ignore her made my skin prickle and the spot on my temple where I imagined she was staring itch. That it was also the spot where I sported a nice scar courtesy of the events that'd eventually led us here was not lost on me. I rubbed it absently with the tips of my fingers and huffed.

Rico settled himself on the arm of the chair and looked down at me, his expression one of fear-laden sympathy. I tried to smile at him but was afraid I'd failed. I handed him my cell phone, and he hesitated before accepting it. He shifted his attention to the device in his hands, and I started tapping random keys on my borrowed laptop to get it to wake back up, thankful that Claudia had already unlocked it for me.

"Any minute now," Rico murmured softly so only I could hear.

"Yup."

"You ready?"

"Are you?"

"Not even a little bit."

"That makes two of us. But we're going to have to keep it together."

He sighed and tilted his head back so he could look at the ceiling. "I know."

He was quiet, obviously thinking about something. I couldn't tell whether he was sifting through his thoughts searching for the one he wanted or whether he was trying to figure out how best to phrase the one he already had. Either way I was loath to interrupt.

I opened up a word-processing program and stared blankly at the cursor as it mocked me from the clear, white screen. I tapped my fingers against the keys of the keyboard—not firmly enough to make any letters appear, but enough to alleviate some of my pent-up nervous energy—somehow enjoying the faint clicking sounds that resulted.

"Ryan, I—"

The ringing of the phone in his hands startled him enough to make him fumble it and drop it. We both watched in horror as it clattered to the ground. Rico bent down to snag it and then resumed his position on the arm of my chair. He held the phone up so I could see the caller ID. Our eyes met, and I nodded.

The faint buzz of conversation that'd permeated the room around us tapered off, and though I shifted my attention to the screen in front of me, I could tell that people had started moving closer. I felt a light touch

KNOWN THREAT

on my other shoulder and looked up to see Claudia gazing down at me. Her expression was encouraging, and I took a deep breath.

I nodded at Rico once more, and he nodded back. I was as ready as I'd ever be. No sense in delaying the inevitable. I allowed my fingers to hover over the keyboard and tried to still their trembling as I waited.

"Adam," Rico said once he'd pushed the button to accept the call. His voice was clear and calm and projected a confidence I knew he didn't feel. "You're right on time."

"Did you set it up?" Walker asked without preamble. "Am I going to get to see my wife?"

"Did you let Agent O'Connor go?"

"Yes." The answer was immediate. He'd barely given Rico a chance to finish the question before he'd blurted out the answer.

He's lying, I typed. *Rory would've called me.* I tried hard not to think about the one way he could've been telling the truth. It was too horrifying.

Rico nodded and mouthed, "I know."

I pursed my lips. Walker didn't normally lie. Not to a direct question, at any rate. That he'd chosen to do so now only highlighted how completely out of my element with him I was at the moment. I may've known him better than anyone in the agency, but that didn't mean I knew all of him. Unfortunately, it appeared I hadn't encountered certain facets of his personality yet. Or perhaps he just hadn't had the opportunity or need to showcase them during any of our earlier interactions. I couldn't be certain, but it didn't matter. The answer wouldn't help me now.

I typed that Rico should call him on it and held my breath, praying I'd made the right decision. The feel of the blood rocketing through my veins was making me light-headed. I gripped the arm of the chair with my left hand in an effort to ground myself.

"Adam, that's not very fair of you."

"What isn't very fair of me?"

"I've been nothing but honest with you, and now you're lying to me."

"I'm not lying."

"You are, Adam. I know you are. Because Agent O'Connor would've called me if you'd set her free. So unless her release was

• 143 •

metaphorical and she's in a state that makes it impossible for her to do that, you still have her."

Walker didn't say anything, and I squeezed my eyes shut and massaged my temples with my fingertips. I needed to bring this conversation back to familiar ground so I could figure out how to navigate it, but I didn't know how to accomplish that goal.

Rico nudged me, and I looked up at him. He raised his eyebrows at me, and I let out a soft huff of exasperation. Silently hoping I was making the right move and not simply doing more harm than good, I typed out Rico's next declaration and bit my lip.

"If you're not going to be honest with me, we're done here."

I heard a few soft gasps and some shuffling, and I could feel everyone's eyes boring into me. My face was on fire. I tried to ignore the fact that I was the center of attention and just concentrate on the task at hand, but my focus had started to slip. I longed to glance at Allison for reassurance. It was a struggle not to.

Walker hesitated longer than I thought he would, and I was considering a new tack when he finally replied. "We're done."

His words were slow and thoughtful, almost a question, as though he was weighing the statement and looking for hidden meaning. I let out a shaky breath and typed again.

"Yes. We're done. If you're not going to be honest with me, I can't talk to you. Thank you for calling."

"Wait!" Walker's voice was panicked. "Wait. What about my wife?"

"What about her?"

"Do I get to see her?"

"Absolutely not."

"But—but you can't do that."

"Sure I can."

"But don't you want Agent O'Connor back?" Now he just sounded confused.

"I thought you said you let her go."

Walker didn't reply.

"See? You lied to me. I can't trust you. Which means you just lost whatever leverage you thought you had. We'll do this another way. And you have only yourself to blame. Remember that."

Walker absolutely lost his shit. He started shrieking at the top of his lungs, and between the volume and the pitch of his voice, I couldn't understand anything he was saying. He'd gone off the deep end, and we had no hope of reining him in.

"Hang up," I told Rico. Walker was too busy screaming. I wasn't at all worried he'd hear me.

"What?" His expression was incredulous.

"Hang up. Trust me."

With a slight frown, Rico did as he was told. The silence left in the wake of that phone call was ominous, and the entire room seemed to hold its breath. I tapped my foot as the seconds ticked by, each feeling infinitely longer than the one before it.

The phone rang again, and I put my hand on Rico's arm to prevent him from answering it too quickly. I didn't even bother to look at him. I didn't want to see his expression. I was already doubting myself enough as it was. I didn't need anyone else feeding my fears. After three rings, I released my grip.

"Secret Service," Rico said as though he didn't know exactly who was calling and why.

Walker picked up right where he'd left off, screeching like a car alarm in the middle of the night. A lot of loud banging sounds accompanied his yelling, which made me wonder exactly what he was hitting and how close Rory was to the chaos. For her sake, I hoped she was in another room.

I did glance at Rico then and bobbed my head once. Rico thumbed the call-end button and took a long, slow, deep breath. He ran his free hand through his hair a couple times before allowing it to rest back on the top of his thigh. With his other hand, he was holding the phone slightly aloft, waiting. He didn't have to wait too long before it rang again.

"Secret Service."

"Why do you keep hanging up on me?" Walker screamed.

I could imagine his face all too easily—the blotchy red hue of his cheeks, the bulging eyes, the spittle flying from his lips as he screeched—and the mental picture sent chills up my spine. I shivered and swallowed hard.

"Because I refuse to talk to you until you can conduct yourself like an adult. If you want to talk, you do it calmly and respectfully. If you can't, then I have nothing to say to you."

Walker took several deep breaths. If not for the length of each, I'd have said he was gasping for air, but this sounded way more deliberate. The knot inside my chest loosened slightly. I'd seen him do this before. He was trying to calm himself. I hoped this was a good sign.

"Okay," Walker said after a full minute. "Okay. Let's talk."

"Thank you," Rico said. "I appreciate that. Let's try again. Did you let Agent O'Connor go?"

A long pause. Then, so soft I almost missed it, "No."

I grimaced and closed my eyes for a moment, battling the sudden nausea that'd just hit me like a cannonball to the gut. I ran a hand across my brow, wiping away the beads of perspiration there before depositing them on the leg of my pants. I set my jaw and opened my eyes again.

"Is Agent O'Connor okay?"

Another pause. "She's fine."

He'd just lied to us again, but I didn't want to get into that at the moment, mostly because I couldn't do anything about it from here. I resolved to reopen that discussion with him after we had Rory back. In the meantime, I opted to move on.

"Okay," Rico said, shooting me a look of disbelief. "Have you given any thought to what I said earlier?"

"Yeah. I have. And I've decided not to let Agent O'Connor go. Not until you let me see my wife."

I tilted my head back as far as it would go and sighed. Damned if he wasn't determined to be a complete pain in my ass.

"That's an interesting choice," Rico said. "Are you sure you don't want to think about that some more?"

"I'm sure. And you know what else I'm sure about?"

"What's that?"

"That I'm tired of you jerking me around. I gave you more than enough time to set this up. Now you're just playing games. You're stalling."

"Not at all, Adam. I don't think you appreciate the delicacy of the situation—"

"What I don't appreciate is being played for a fool. No more tricks. You have one hour. Have my wife meet me in Prospect Park or Agent O'Connor dies. And make sure she comes alone. If I so much as see another agent, Agent O'Connor will pay the price."

"Okay, Adam. Okay. No need to get jumpy. Just tell me where in the park you want her to meet you, and I'll get it set up."

"I'll find her."

I heard a loud clattering sound, as though the phone had been dropped or thrown, and then nothing. Leaning forward, I struggled to hear anything but couldn't. He'd either hung up or broken the device.

I frowned as my mind drifted for a moment. My fears for Rory's safety were metaphorically drowning my thoughts of the operation. I choked back the bile rising in my throat with great effort and raised my eyes.

The weight of the collective gaze of everyone in the room was pressing down on me. Allison's, of course, felt heavier than anyone else's. I forced myself to look at Claudia instead, who was watching me in her infinitely patient way.

"What do you think?" she asked.

I took a deep breath before I replied. "We should get this info over to the cell-tracking guys in the office to see whether they can muster up and track Walker down before our hour deadline is up."

"I'll do it," Rico said. He vacated his position on the arm of the chair and moved toward the hallway, where it was quieter to make his call.

"And then?" Claudia wanted to know.

"Is Ivy working today?" I asked. I hadn't seen her when I'd stopped in the CP earlier, but that didn't mean anything.

Claudia looked to Hannah, who shook her head. "Not right now. She's on mids this week. She'll be in later."

"Damn. I was hoping we could use her as a Hurricane stand-in to draw Walker out in the park." I rubbed the palm of my hand across the back of my neck and tried to ignore Allison, who I could see staring at me out of the corner of my eye.

"I'll call her," Hannah said. "Maybe she can get over there in time."

"Doesn't she live up in Ossining?" I asked. "She'll never make it."

Hannah shrugged. "Perhaps we'll get lucky, and she'll be in the city for something. You never know."

I waved her on. "Sure. Doesn't hurt to ask, I guess."

"I'm on it," Hannah said, plucking her phone off her belt.

I turned back to Claudia. "I'm trying to think of who else we could use as bait if Ivy isn't available. We don't have all that many women to choose from. Ivy is the closest one to Hurricane's body type. After her, I guess we could try—"

"Me," a voice chimed in from the edge of the room.

We all turned to look, and my heart sank as I took in Hurricane standing just inside the door. Her hands were on her hips, and a defiant fire burned in her eyes. Inwardly, I groaned. She sure had picked one hell of a time to leave the confines of her apartment and start exploring. And who'd left the damn door unlocked? Seriously, I couldn't catch a break today.

"Miss Carmichael," Claudia said as she started to stride over to her. "How long have you been standing there?"

"Long enough."

Hurricane allowed her attention to float around the room as she sized up each of us in turn. Finally, her gaze landed on me. My heart picked up speed, and I swallowed. Or I tried to. My mouth was suddenly dry, which made the action difficult. I wondered exactly how long "long enough" was and how much she'd heard.

"This man, he's taken someone because he wants to meet me, right?" Hurricane asked me.

I debated lying to her, but what could I have possibly come up with? I nodded reluctantly. "Yes."

Hurricane smiled then, but it was a wicked sort of smile, and it looked altogether wrong on her face. "Well, let's give the man what he wants."

CHAPTER SIXTEEN

Claudia kept her eyes locked on Hurricane, who continued to stare insolently back at her. No one moved. No one spoke. Stagnant, awkward air filled the room. Again, I craved to seek out Allison for reassurance, and again, with much effort, I bested my compulsion.

"Excuse us for a moment," Claudia said to the rest of the group, never taking her attention off Hurricane. She then raised one eyebrow and gestured toward what I assumed was the bedroom. With a dark glare, Hurricane followed, and the door shut softly behind her.

I let out a long, slow breath, glad that was over, but my relief was short-lived. In my periphery, I saw Allison take a step toward me and then stop as though uncertain what to do. My midsection suddenly felt as though it were encased in an extremely tight corset, and my heart was hammering violently to break free of the confines.

Hannah approached me then, saving me from having to deal with Allison and the disaster that was our relationship. She was shaking her head. "Ivy's at home. There's no way she'd be able to make it in time. I'm sorry."

"Don't be. We knew it was a long shot."

"What are we going to do now? Do you think you could pass as a decoy for Hurricane? You have similar hair color and skin tone."

It was my turn to shake my head. "I considered that, but I don't think it'll work. For one thing, I'm shorter than she is. For another, I'm a little more…" I was unable to think of the term I wanted.

"Busty?" Hannah said with a tiny smirk.

"Yup. That's the word."

"A little?"

I cracked a smile. "Shut up."

Hannah allowed her eyes to drop to my chest as though sizing me up, and I shoved her playfully. She flashed me a quick grin and then was all business again. "Do you really think he'd notice? It's dark outside."

"I know, but he's been fixated on her for years now. He's watched her. He knows what she looks like and how she moves. I don't want to take the chance that he'll realize it's not her before we can take him down or get to Rory."

"So what do we do?" Hannah asked again.

I picked at my cuticles, not eager to break the news to her. "Hurricane volunteered to meet him."

"Absolutely not," Hannah said without hesitation.

"Hey, I'm with you. I'd much rather take the chance and do it myself than get her involved, but I'm not so sure I have any say in the matter." I shot a meaningful glance toward the closed door on the other side of the room.

Hannah picked up on my implication and glanced around long enough to note that Claudia was missing. She rolled her shoulders, obviously tense. "Ah. Well, if anyone can talk her out of it, it's the SAIC."

"From your lips to God's ears."

"So who do we have to use in the event that the SAIC does manage to pull off the impossible?"

"We have a new girl in the office. Her name's Anna. She's been out of the academy for a couple of months, I guess. It's way too soon for her to do this kind of work, but she's built similarly to Hurricane. Her hair's a different color, but we could always have her tuck it underneath a hat."

"Perfect. Will she be able to get there in time?"

"As long as she's not out on something, yes. She lives in Crown Heights, right by the park, actually. As soon as Rico comes back with my phone, I'll call her and see if she's available."

The door to the other room swung open then and Claudia strode out, her face an impassive mask. It was impossible to tell from her expression how the discussion had gone—until Hurricane wandered out looking pleased with herself. My heart sank, and I bit back a groan.

Claudia approached me and took my elbow, leading me toward the front door. She leaned into me a little so she'd be able to speak without being overheard. "Miss Carmichael will be accompanying us on the operation."

I frowned, not even attempting to conceal my displeasure. "Are you sure that's a good idea?"

"I'm fairly certain it isn't, actually. But she won't be deterred."

"Okay."

"I assume you have a ballistic vest in your car?"

"Of course."

Claudia's eyes were stormy. "I hate to ask you this, but would you mind letting her wear it? I'd give her mine, but I don't have it here."

"Not at all. I'll run downstairs and get it. I have to change out of this suit anyway, and my stuff is in the trunk."

"I don't like the idea of her wearing a vest and you not, but…"

"But she's the protectee. I get it. It's not a big deal. If you hadn't asked, I still would've insisted."

"Please don't think this means I value her life over and above yours. That's not what this is."

"I didn't think it was. Seriously, it's fine. Besides, I have an extra vest. A lower-profile one I purchased myself that's much more comfortable. I'll wear that, and she can have my issued one. No problem."

Claudia looked relieved. "Perfect. I really appreciate that."

"Any time. I'll go get it now."

"Thanks. I'll just chat with these guys to see what kind of tactical plan we can come up with."

I nodded. "Be right back."

I stepped out into the hallway and punched the call button for the elevator. Briefly I wondered where Rico had gotten to, but my curiosity took a backseat to my anxiety over the more pressing situation. My mind was twirling like some sort of runaway carnival ride, taking all my internal organs along with it. I tapped my foot, willing the car to hurry up already. I consulted my watch. We'd already used up five minutes of our allotted hour. Claudia needed to pull her tactical plan together fast. It'd probably take at least twenty minutes to reach Prospect Park, and that wasn't accounting for the traffic snarls commonplace in the city. We needed to get this show on the road.

The apartment door opened behind me before I got too deep into the weeds of thinking about what could happen to Rory if we were late, and Allison and Hannah stepped into the suddenly-too-small hallway with me. My heart and my stomach swapped places and then began an epic struggle to return to their rightful positions. All the while, the rest of my body was humming, and not in a pleasant way.

Allison hesitated just outside the doorway to Hurricane's apartment, but the door swung shut behind her, effectively trapping us all together. If she went back inside now, it'd look like she was avoiding me, and the expression on her face for the split second I looked at her told me she knew it. Trying to keep my nerves from forcing me to do something stupid, I turned back to the elevator and stared at the doors.

Allison lingered behind me for another beat before she took a step forward so we were standing shoulder to shoulder. At the edge of my vision, I saw her cross her arms and duck her head. Her silky, dark hair swung forward to rest against the hollow of her cheek, and my fingers itched to brush it back to its rightful place. Fuck. Even when I was upset with her, I wanted to touch her. I scowled, irritated by yet still marveling at the phenomenon.

The atmosphere in the hall continued to swell and press in on me until I felt as though I would either collapse or explode. Neither proposition appealed to me, although I did think both would effectively cut through the tension, which was something.

The sound of Hannah clearing her throat was loud, and my heart slammed violently against my rib cage as it rammed itself back into place. "The elevator doesn't usually take this long."

"Who are you kidding?" I said, my words sounding a tad sharper than I'd intended. "This elevator always takes forever."

"Yeah."

Hannah was clearly miserable, and I felt a stab of remorse. I hadn't meant for anybody to get caught up in my personal drama. And if I could've come up with a way to fix it, I would have. But my toolbox was empty. I was absolutely devoid of ideas.

A small part of me wanted to take Allison aside and talk this whole thing out. Now that I'd had a minute to reflect on the situation, I had to admit that she hadn't done anything wrong in sleeping with Byers. She hadn't even necessarily been wrong in keeping it from me. Her past was her business, not mine. I didn't need to know everyone she'd ever been with, although a little honesty on her part would've gone a long way to alleviate the way he'd just blindsided me. But it hadn't been her fault that Byers had chosen to hit me with that revelation when he had, so I wasn't all that positive that my earlier ire had been one hundred percent justified.

However, I was still hurting and had less than no interest in getting into any kind of discussion with her about anything at the moment. Childish, I know, but that didn't change the reality. I was upset, and I needed space and time.

I also needed to separate and compartmentalize my feelings so I could focus solely on Rory. Allison and I could settle whatever we might or might not have had to talk about after my sister was safe. That was the right call. So why was I still so sick and miserable?

The stupid elevator still hadn't come, and I'd about had my fill of feeling queasy and uncomfortable for one afternoon. With one last dark glare at the elevator doors, I spun around.

"Ryan—" Allison said.

"I'm taking the stairs," I said at the same time. I hadn't been aware that she'd been about to speak, but that didn't change my decision to distance myself. I knew I looked petulant, but I didn't care. I just wanted to get through the next couple of hours. Then I'd be able to begin thinking about how to reassemble the shattered pieces of our relationship.

Without glancing at either her or Hannah, I hit the panic bar to the stairwell with more force than necessary and left the awkwardness behind me.

CHAPTER SEVENTEEN

After I'd retrieved my gear bag complete with both vests and a change of clothes from the trunk of my car, I detoured to the bathroom just off the CP so I could change. Sure, I could've gone back up to the apartment to do it, but I needed a few minutes to myself before this operation shifted into drive. I allowed the terror I'd been barely containing all afternoon a few precious minutes to run free and unfettered, and then I shoved it back down to the edges of my thoughts where it belonged and resolved that it should stay there.

Once I was geared up and as mentally collected as I could be under the circumstances, I shouldered my duffel bag and headed back upstairs. When I reentered the apartment, everyone was engaged in various phone calls, truncated tactical discussions, and arguments regarding the best course of action. Everyone present who had any stake in taking Walker down debated the pros and cons of different courses of action ad nauseam as they planned this operation down to the very last degree as best they could, considering our abbreviated timetable.

I kept to one corner of the room, determined to stay quiet and out of the way. I didn't say much during any of the discussions. I didn't have much to add at that point, except for once, when someone else had the gall to question whether I should even be involved. Then I had a lot to say, most of it expletives. But I like to think I got my point across. It was the last time anyone brought up anything remotely on that topic, at any rate.

Whoever had said that had probably been right. I'd been thinking off and on all day that I really shouldn't have been there. But no way would I sit by and twiddle my thumbs while this whole thing played out. In the end, I think everyone recognized that and decided it was just easier to include me so they could at least keep an eye on me instead of let me go rogue.

Now that the discussion of my participation had been decided, the majority of the group huddled loosely around a map of Prospect Park taped to a wall and frowned as the discussion continued to rage regarding how many agents we were sending in, the merits of using snipers versus trying to talk Walker down, and whether to use deadly force, among other things.

I was only half paying attention. While I agreed that I had to understand the operational plan in its entirety, I was having trouble concentrating on the debate for more than thirty consecutive seconds at a stretch. Worry for my sister coupled with horrifying speculations on what hell she'd been forced to endure the past few hours had distracted me. So much for my determination to keep my fear confined to the edges of my thoughts.

A loud bang shot me out of my reverie and back into the world at large. It took me a second to realize that someone had slammed their hand down on the table. I blinked and glanced around to see whether I'd be able to determine what the problem was.

"This is ridiculous," one of the NYPD lieutenants was saying. "This is not how we do business. Somebody's going to get killed."

Claudia regarded him calmly for a long moment before formulating a reply. "With all due respect, Lieutenant, this isn't your operation. If you're concerned about bearing responsibility for any potential mistakes, rest assured that all fault will lie with me."

The lieutenant glowered at the map on the wall as he scrubbed at the edge of his jaw with the heel of one hand. "If it were just LEOs going in, I wouldn't be half as concerned, but I'm simply not comfortable including a civilian in our operational plan." He cast a pointed glance in Hurricane's direction as he said that, earning a dark glare in return.

Oh, boy. That wasn't good. I didn't necessarily disagree with the lieutenant. I didn't want Hurricane within a hundred nautical miles of this mess either. But I recognized in her the innate stubbornness that ran deep within me. If he pushed his point, the discussion would turn very ugly very quickly, and the last thing we needed was for an NYPD official to engage in a pointless argument with the president's daughter. No one would gain anything from it. It'd waste our precious time.

I exchanged a meaningful look with Claudia, and she nodded at me before she turned back to the men she'd been talking to. Her briefing didn't skip a beat, and for a long moment, I envied her poise. My thoughts and emotions had me feeling like a balloon that had been blown up way too big and then released to fly around the room as it emptied.

Forcing myself to focus, I laid a gentle hand on Hurricane's arm and leaned close so I could speak softly in her ear. "Miss Carmichael. If you'll come with me, please."

Hurricane was still glaring at the lieutenant, and it took her a second to register that I'd spoken to her. She blinked and shifted the full force of that glare toward me. "Excuse me?"

If she'd thought to intimidate me, well, she was about to learn a hard lesson. I'd been glowered at for longer by more volatile people than her. Her ire was hardly a blip on my radar. "I need you to come with me, please, ma'am."

"Why?" she demanded. "Where are we going?"

I extended my arm, allowing the palm of my hand to direct her. It was a tactic I used often with foreign delegations and heads of state. I wasn't positive why it worked as well as it did, and I wasn't about to argue with the phenomenon now.

Hurricane pinned Claudia with one last dirty look before exhaling noisily and stomping out of the room. Claudia spared her back a split-second glance as she disappeared through the doorway I'd indicated, but otherwise she gave no indication that Hurricane's departure fazed her in the slightest.

Taking a deep breath, I made my way after Hurricane. Nothing in this situation was working out the way I'd wanted it to, but I had no choice other than to make the best of it. Hurricane and I had that in common, I supposed.

I stepped into the next room—which had turned out to be a bedroom, I realized too late—and softly shut the door behind me. Hurricane was standing in front of the window, her arms crossed over her stomach, her body rigid.

"Spare me the lectures, Agent," Hurricane snapped without turning around. "The last thing I need right now is for you to speak to me like I'm a child."

"O'Connor," I supplied, as I unzipped the gigantic black duffel bag I'd brought in with me and began rooting around in it.

"What?" Hurricane did turn at that and eyed me suspiciously.

"That's my last name. O'Connor. I thought perhaps you were asking. Although you can call me Agent if you'd like. I'll answer."

Something about that struck Hurricane as amusing. Her countenance and stance softened, and I saw the barest hint of a smile.

"And what if I wanted to call you by your first name? What would I say then?"

I hesitated, not comfortable with that level of familiarity with one of our protectees, and that did make Hurricane smile. "Ryan."

"Ryan." Hurricane rolled the name around in her mouth, as though tasting it and trying to decide whether she liked the flavor. "I don't think I've ever met a female Ryan before."

"That's not actually my name, ma'am. Not technically."

"Ma'am? Really?"

I paused in the process of pulling things out of the bag and depositing them on the floor. "I'm sorry?"

"Do you really have to call me that? It makes me feel old, and I can't be *that* much older than you."

I tried not to chuckle. "Actually, you're several years younger than I am."

"You're kidding."

I shook my head.

Hurricane's eyebrows disappeared beneath her hair as she gaped at me. "You look barely old enough to drink."

"Good genes, I guess."

"Wow." She deliberated for another moment. Then, "So, what's Ryan short for?"

"My middle name. Aeryn."

She continued to stare at me expectantly as she presumably waited for a further explanation for my nickname. Instead of providing it, I closed my hand around the object I'd been hunting for in my bag and pulled it out. Her eyes blazed a trail down my arm to inspect it as I offered it to her.

"What's this?"

"It's a ballistic vest."

"Whose?"

"What?"

"Whose vest is it? I know how government funding works. I don't imagine you guys just have spare vests lying around. So whose is this?"

"Mine."

Hurricane frowned at me and shook her head. "No."

"This isn't up for discussion. You wear this or you don't go." When she opened her mouth, I held up my free hand. "You can threaten to call your father all you want, but it won't do any good. Claudia and I've already talked about this. She'll back me up."

I could see hurt and annoyance eddying in Hurricane's eyes, and her face crumpled for an instant before hardening again into an angry mask. She shook her head once more. "I won't wear that and leave you unprotected. It's out of the question."

"Who says I'm unprotected?" I adjusted my grip on the vest so I was holding it up by the shoulder straps. "Now, come on. Let's go. Get your shirt off."

Suspicion seeped back into Hurricane's expression. "You're not wearing a vest."

I rolled my eyes and dropped one side of the vest I was holding so I could thump the heel of my hand against the hollow of my chest. The thunk of flesh meeting Kevlar was unmistakable. I offered the vest in my hand again. "Come on. I'll help you put it on, and then I'll wire you up."

Hurricane's face now was a conglomeration of wonder and disbelief. She took a step closer and rested her own hand against my chest. Her eyes grew wide as she tested the strength of the vest I was wearing with her fingertips.

"I can't believe it. It doesn't look like you're wearing anything at all."

"I know," I told her. "This is the one I use when I'm on protection. It's designed that way, for underneath a suit."

"What's this other vest, then? Why is it bigger than the one you have on?"

"This is my raid vest. It's bigger because it provides more coverage. Which is why you're going to wear it instead of me. This will protect more of your body and internal organs."

"Won't this guy notice that I'm wearing it? Won't it freak him out?"

"It'll look more suspicious if we send you in there without anything at all. He knows us well enough to realize we'd never let you go in completely defenseless. He'll probably notice the vest, but it likely won't interest him one way or the other."

"Is that a good idea? To tip your hand like that?"

"Despite what he said, despite his insistence that you come alone, I guarantee he's expecting us to be watching. He'll be sizing up everyone in the park, trying to determine who's an agent and who isn't. If we're lucky, we'll be able to slip a couple of people past him. We just want to make sure he doesn't make everybody we have on set."

"Do you really think this will work?"

"Honestly, Miss Carmichael? I have no idea. This entire operation will be one crapshoot after the other. I'm relying on my past experiences in dealing with him to gauge his frame of mind. We've planned this operation to the best of our ability, down to the smallest detail. The only thing we can do now is follow the plan and pray that we've prepared for every contingency. That's why I need you to wear this vest."

It was a blatant attempt to drag this discussion back on topic, but I was running out of patience. I was painfully tense, ready to snap at even the slightest provocation. The last thing I needed was to lose focus on the important nuances of the operation.

"I want to wear the little vest. The one you have on."

I laughed, tickled despite myself by her endless moxie. "Sorry. No can do. If something goes wrong out there, I want you to have your best chance. And that means you wear the vest with the most coverage."

"What about your best chance?" she asked in an almost inaudible whisper.

I smiled at her, touched by her concern. I'd never met a protectee who hadn't treated me like I didn't exist. How sweet. I almost hated to burst her bubble. Almost.

"I'm there to make sure you don't get hurt. That's my only function. It's my job to worry and keep you safe. And it's your job to let me do my job."

"I hate this," Hurricane exclaimed, her outburst surprising me. "I hate that you guys have to do this day in and day out for years at a time.

And worse, it doesn't appear to bother any of you. Like you've all been brainwashed into just accepting that your only purpose in life is to be a…a…" She was obviously searching for the word she wanted.

"Bullet catcher?" I suggested. "Meat shield?"

Hurricane's glare darkened, and she pointed one finger at me. "That's not funny."

I sighed. "No, it isn't. I'm sorry. Look, I tell you what. How about you get dressed, and we can fight about this later, after this is all over. I'll let you call me by my first name and everything."

Hurricane shook her head and ripped her shirt off without saying a word. She was now standing in front of me wearing only a bra, which I'm sure wasn't comfortable for her. It wasn't for me. Her eyes were fixed on an uninteresting spot on the wall beyond my shoulder, and I tried to look anywhere but directly at her as I undid the Velcro straps that held the vest together.

Carefully, I settled it on her shoulders, adjusting the straps so it molded tight to her body. "Is that okay?" I asked as I worked.

Hurricane nodded. "It's fine, I guess. I haven't worn many of these, so I don't really know how they're supposed to feel."

"Take a deep breath. Can you breathe easily?"

Hurricane complied, inhaling long and slow. "Yeah. It's okay."

"Take a few more breaths. Do you think you'll be able to breathe all right if you have to run?"

"I think so."

"Good. Can you turn around?"

She did as asked, and I pulled a tiny wireless tracking device out of my bag. I took a second to ensure it was on before I tucked it down the back of the vest between her shoulder blades. There was a small pocket I'd made sure was on the inside of her vest, next to her skin. It usually went on the outside and was intended for an armored plate, but we were going to use it for this purpose instead.

Hurricane squirmed as though trying to become accustomed to the feeling of the device against her body. I retrieved her shirt from the floor where she'd flung it and handed it back to her.

"What's that for?"

"In case something goes wrong and he makes it out of the park with you, we'll need to be able to track you. Hopefully it'll take him a while to find it, since on an initial pat-down, he'll feel only the vest. In a perfect world, we'll be able to extract you before he even knows you're wearing it." I didn't even want to think of what he'd do if he did find the tracking device. It wouldn't be pretty.

"I thought you'd be there with me," Hurricane said, putting her shirt back on.

"The only way he's leaving with you is if I'm dead," I assured her.

Hurricane winced. "I really wish you wouldn't say things like that."

I shrugged. "Do you want me to lie to you? Or sugarcoat the truth so it sounds like something easier to swallow? I can, if you'd prefer. I don't mind painting you a picture that's all rainbows and unicorns, if you'd like to remain blissfully ignorant."

"Are you always this much of an asshole?"

"Nah. Sometimes I'm worse."

Hurricane rolled her eyes at me. "Of course you are."

"Speaking of which, I need to go over something with you real quick."

"What?"

I pursed my lips and fiddled with a lock of hair that had escaped my hair tie. "The goal of this operation is to neutralize Walker and rescue Rory. It is *not* to trade you for her."

"I don't know what you're talking about." But Hurricane averted her gaze, which told me she was lying.

"Sure you don't. It would never occur to you to offer yourself to him if he promised to let her go."

"Right."

I took a step closer and leaned in, in an effort to get her to look at me. She did, but with obvious reluctance. "I know you've done some mixed martial-arts training at your mother's insistence, and you can absolutely take care of yourself, but I need you to understand what could happen if Walker does manage to get his hands on you."

"He won't."

I smiled at her. "You've had protection long enough to know that we're a largely pessimistic bunch. We like to deal in worst-case scenarios. Humor me."

"Okay."

"Walker is a big man. Very big. He's over six foot eight. I don't even come up to his shoulders, and I don't think my hands would touch if I tried to put my arms around him, if that gives you any sort of clue."

Hurricane's eyes widened, and for the first time, she appeared vaguely uneasy.

"He is also a paranoid schizophrenic who's likely off his medication and thinks you're his wife."

"What?" She was clearly stunned.

"I guess they didn't give you the rundown on his bio."

"No," Hurricane said bitterly. "They didn't."

"Okay, well, it isn't that big a deal." It was, but I didn't think I had anything to gain from pointing that out to her. "I'm telling you now. He's been fixated on you for years."

"Years?" Hurricane now appeared almost ill.

I stopped and mulled over her reaction. It didn't seem all that strange that someone would nurse an obsession for that long, but then I supposed I'd had plenty of time to become accustomed to the concept. I doubted that Hurricane was kept informed regarding details about guys like Walker. She most likely had only a vague, abstract sort of inkling that they existed, but I imagined she didn't spend a lot of time dwelling on the specifics. And now I'd gone and rubbed her face in it. Oops.

I tried to redirect her. "Not the point."

"You've been running interference with this guy—keeping him away from me even though he thinks I'm his wife—for years?"

"Yeah. I guess. Unfortunately, he's recently come to that same realization. Only now he thinks I've been keeping him from you because I want you for myself."

Hurricane blinked at me. "Are you serious?"

"Completely. And he took my sister thinking he was taking me. He wanted to punish me for coming between you two. There's no telling what he's done to her while he's had her." The words felt too large and heavy and got stuck on the way out. I cleared my throat to make room for my next thought. "I need you to promise me something."

"What?"

"Just don't get within arm's reach of him, no matter what."

Hurricane appeared insulted. "Do you think I'm stupid?"

"No. I think you're too noble for your own good. And I think if you saw a chance to distract him, to fight him to let Rory make a run for it, you'd take it."

"Would that be such a bad thing?" Hurricane's expression was earnest.

"It'd be terrible. No good could come of it, trust me." If she did that, she'd put me in the worst position imaginable by forcing me to choose between tending to Rory and ensuring her safety. That was a losing proposition for me no matter how you looked at it.

"Just sitting idly by doesn't come naturally to me."

"I know it doesn't. But just please try."

She studied me. "Okay. I'll try."

"Thank you. There's one more thing."

"What?"

"If things progress in the absolute worst way possible and Walker does somehow manage to get his hands on you, ignore your initial gut instinct to fight him and just go limp."

Hurricane shot me a look that clearly said she thought I was insane. "You want me to go limp," she repeated.

"Yes. Don't struggle at all. Just drop to the ground."

"What's that going to accomplish?"

I took a long, slow breath. "It's going to give us room to take a clear shot."

"A clear shot?"

"Yes."

"Like with a gun?"

I refrained from rolling my eyes but just barely. "Yes."

"You're going to kill him."

"We don't shoot to kill," I clarified, parroting our training verbatim. "We shoot to neutralize the threat."

"But you might kill him."

I shrugged, disinterested. "It's possible. But let's hope it doesn't come to that."

"Wow," Hurricane breathed.

"That about sums it up."

Hurricane took her time letting that information sink in, and I didn't push her. It was a lot to handle. "Thanks," she said finally.

"For what?"

"For not trying to shield me from reality. Thank you for not handling me with kid gloves."

"Well, you're walking into an unorthodox situation. The least I can do is shoot straight with you. No pun intended. Thank you for this, by the way." I swallowed against the lump forming in my throat. "I can't tell you how much I appreciate it, you helping me get my sister back. I feel terrible that you got dragged into it at all."

"Hey," Hurricane said quietly, resting a gentle hand on my arm. "I wanted to help. I demanded it, actually, if you'll recall. And once Claudia told me exactly *who* this guy had—that it was your sister and not just some random woman off the street—well, there was no way I wasn't going to help. I mean, if one of my brothers had been taken…" She shook her head as though she couldn't even bear the thought, let alone finish it. She cleared her throat. "You guys all put your lives on the line for me every single day without expecting anything in return. This is the least I can do."

I let out a ragged breath. "Well, thank you anyway, Miss Carmichael."

"Zoey."

"I'm sorry?"

"I want you to call me Zoey."

"Oh, Miss Carmichael, I don't think that's—"

"Come on. Don't you think we at least deserve to be on a first-name basis? I mean, we've made out, for crying out loud."

I felt as though someone had thrown a huge bucket of ice water directly into my face. "What?"

Hurricane grinned at me. "I told you that day you showed up in my hallway that you looked familiar to me. Did you really think I wouldn't figure it out?"

Oh, shit. "Uh, I'm not sure I follow you," I lied. There was no way she remembered that night in the bar, and there was also no way I was going to be tricked into mentioning it.

Hurricane's smile turned mischievous. "You are one hell of a fantastic kisser, Agent O'Connor. I'll give you that. I spent several days after our little encounter lamenting the fact that Hannah showed up and I never got to bed you."

I froze and willed myself to neither blanch nor blush. Given

Hurricane's low, throaty chuckle, I didn't succeed in at least one of those endeavors.

"You turn almost as red as Hannah does. How adorable."

"Miss Carmichael." My tone was a blend of chastisement, embarrassment, and exasperation.

"Zoey."

I pondered how to respond. "She told you, didn't she? Hannah, I mean. You didn't figure anything out. You merely badgered Hannah into spilling the beans."

"I can neither confirm nor deny."

"Spoken like a true politician." I didn't know what else to say.

"You were pretty low-profile, too," Hurricane said, her expression musing. "I can usually spot you guys a mile away, and I hate to admit I had no idea you were an agent that night. Although I suppose I should've figured it out right away. I mean, you did rescue me from that overbearing guy like some sort of knight in shining armor."

"Um...thanks?" Had that been a compliment? I wasn't sure.

"Anyway, I think we're far beyond the usual formalities, don't you?"

I considered that question for a long moment. I didn't feel comfortable addressing a protectee by her first name but didn't have much to gain by arguing that point with her. Especially not now.

"I'll try. That's the best I can do."

Hurricane laughed. "Fair enough. Just out of curiosity, if Hannah hadn't shown up, would you have gone to bed with me?"

My brain shuddered and then ground to a halt. All I got was static, and even that was faint. "I'm sorry. What?"

Hurricane's eyes were dancing. "What? Did you think I kissed you just to get rid of that guy?"

"I—I, uh...Yeah. I did think that."

"Well, I mean, that didn't hurt, but that's not why I did it."

"But...but you're straight!"

"Says who?"

"Says your fiancé, for one." That was a stupid response. I mean, my own girlfriend was like the poster child for sexual fluidity. But my brain wasn't exactly working correctly. How the hell had we ended up talking about this? And how in the world did I stop it?

"Sexuality isn't a constant. Just because I prefer boys doesn't mean I don't enjoy girls every now and again."

"Oh." My head was buzzing now. I was searching for a way to change the subject and coming up empty.

"You're a very attractive woman, Agent O'Connor. Surely you know that."

My face wasn't just on fire. It burned with the heat of a thousand suns. Seriously, why were we even having this conversation? She couldn't have been sincere. In fact, something occurred to me, and I frowned. "You're messing with me, aren't you?"

Hurricane seemed amused. "Yeah. Maybe a little. I may not go out of my way to ditch you guys anymore, but a girl's still got to have a little fun. For what it's worth, I did think about it, at the time. And I did wonder what would've happened if Hannah hadn't shown up."

I gaped at her, uncertain of the appropriate response. It'd never occurred to me that she would've wanted to go to bed with me, or with any woman. I'd never followed that scenario with her through to any sort of conclusion, so I had no clue what I would've done.

A light knock on the door interrupted our little bonding session, and I breathed a sigh of relief. Hurricane shot me a wide grin and moved to answer it while I retrieved all the items I'd previously flung out of my duffel bag and stuffed them back inside. I was so focused on my task I didn't notice Hurricane's return until she was standing right in front of me.

"Okay," I said as I finished with my bag and zipped it closed, thrilled to return to familiar bounds. "You're all set. We should—" As I'd been talking, my eyes had traveled from what I'd been doing over her shoes and up her legs, and not until I looked all the way up did I realize I wasn't speaking to Hurricane.

I was speaking to Allison.

Son of a bitch.

Chapter Eighteen

The words I'd been in the process of uttering dissolved on my tongue, and my heart sputtered. I froze, too overwhelmed to speak.

"So," Allison said, letting the word hang in the air.

"So," I repeated, getting to my feet.

"Big op, huh?"

"Yup."

"You ready?"

"As I'll ever be."

"Don't worry. We'll get her back."

"Yeah."

We existed in silence for a long, uncomfortable moment, during which I determined that I really liked the color of the bedspread. And the stitching was amazing.

"We need to talk," Allison said, straight and to the point, her voice low and throaty.

"What about?"

Allison stepped closer, and it took every ounce of willpower I had to hold my ground. Did I want to get as close to her as possible or retreat? Being pulled in two opposite directions put the kibosh on my momentum altogether.

"Really?" Allison's tone dripped skepticism, and she lifted one eyebrow. "That's what you're going with?"

I shrugged and ducked my head, picking at the fraying strap of my duffel bag. "It was worth a shot."

The air between us was charged as an uneasy silence once again descended. Allison slid the fingers of her right hand beneath my chin and tipped my head back up.

"Ryan, you promised. *We* promised. We have to talk about this."

I sighed and took her hand, removing it from the far-too-intimate position of cupping my face. I couldn't handle that level of closeness. "Allison, we don't have time. And this definitely is not the place."

"Claudia promised to come get us when they finish hashing out the details. We aren't holding anything up."

"I still don't think that—"

"After you got shot, I stopped taking for granted that you'd always come home in one piece. It reminded me that no matter how mundane the assignment, things can always go wrong. I want to talk about this now, before everything starts. Please."

She didn't point out that this situation could go south at least half a dozen ways, and we might not have another chance to talk about it. But she didn't have to. I supposed she was right. However, that didn't make me any more inclined to have this discussion.

"I'm sorry. I can't. I'm just not ready."

Anger flashed in her near-black eyes like lightning crackling over a desert—there one instant, gone the next. Unspeakable sadness rushed in to fill the void, and my heart clenched.

"Not ready to talk? Or not ready to forgive me?" she asked. Her words had an edge that made me tread carefully.

"There's nothing to forgive. You didn't do anything wrong. I know that. I'm just not quite…ready to address it. That's all. Not right now. Hell, maybe it doesn't even need to be addressed. I know we said we wouldn't keep anything from one another anymore, but maybe we can break that rule just this once."

Allison's expression was part wary and part hopeful. "So, you're not breaking up with me? Because earlier you said you didn't want me up here, and—"

"I do," I whispered softly, not bothering to banish the pain or longing from my words. "I really do. I was being an asshole before. I'm sorry."

"Good. Because I don't know what I'd do without you."

The admission stole the air from my lungs and made my stomach free-fall in the most wonderful way. A small, sad smile crept over my lips.

"I don't know what I'd do without you either. It's just hard for me to…" I was unsure whether I should even finish that sentence.

"Me, too." The stillness stretched taut between us, heavy and smothering. And then, so quiet that I had to lean in to hear her, "I don't like thinking about you with anybody else, either. I can barely look at Jamie without wanting to punch her in the face. And I actually like her, so…"

"Yeah." Because that summed it up perfectly. I couldn't go a full five minutes without picturing her and Byers together, and it made me ill and furious all at the same time. Irrational, maybe, but here we were.

"It was because of you, you know."

I furrowed my brow. "What was because of me?"

"The reason I couldn't find anybody to date. That was your fault."

Anger spiked within me once again, and I narrowed my eyes. "How was that *my* fault?"

Allison sighed and favored me with a look of embarrassment shot through with amusement, underscored by a despondent sort of smile. "Every single woman I went out with reminded me of you."

My anger stalled. "What?"

"It wasn't always big things, either. I made sure to avoid blondes with blue eyes for obvious reasons. But little things about them crept up on me. Like the way one woman's eyes sparkled when she looked at me. Or the perfume another one wore. Or the way another woman memorized my coffee order right off the bat."

"Exactly how many women were there?" I tried for teasing and somehow managed to hit the target, if not the bull's-eye.

Allison smiled mysteriously. "A few."

"Great," I muttered sarcastically.

"The point is, not a single one of them could ever have hoped to eclipse you in my eyes. Or in my heart."

I flushed yet felt chilled. I hated thinking about her smiling at someone else, holding someone else, kissing someone else. But it was tough to get wrapped around the axle about those things when she'd basically just told me I'd managed to ruin all of that for her without even being there.

"Oh," I said.

"You asked me earlier why him. That's why. He was about as far away from you as I could get. Nothing about him reminded me of you. It was less painful for me that way. Easier for me to pretend I hadn't made the biggest mistake of my life when I let you go."

I grimaced, as much at the reminder as at her twisted logic. Clearly, despite my earlier plea, we were going to discuss this. My heart felt heavy, like it'd been flooded with twice the normal amount of blood and was now too full inside my chest. Its ache was making me anxious.

"For what it's worth, it wasn't even that regular a thing."

"That's not what it sounded like earlier."

Allison now looked irritated. "Yeah, well, he did that on purpose. Probably because, as you pointed out, he's a douchebag. We slept together a handful of times at most. And as soon as I found out I was coming up here for that PPD visit, I told him it would never happen again."

"You did?"

"Of course."

Okay, that threw me. "But…why?"

Allison appeared embarrassed. She suddenly became interested in studying the bedspread that'd captured my attention earlier. "Because I was going to see you."

I hesitated as I attempted to decipher her meaning. "Did you want to get back together before you came up here?"

A long pause. "The thought had crossed my mind."

"Huh." That revelation both pleased and confused me. Would she have gone back to Byers if I hadn't suddenly become single in the middle of her visit? "Wait. So you and Byers were over before that trip to Hong Kong."

"Yes. We were definitely over."

"And he knew that?"

"Trust me. I was perfectly clear."

I frowned as I mulled over her words. "But then why would he imply otherwise?" I murmured more to myself than to her. "And why would he—" A sudden flash of realization hit me. "Holy shit."

"What?"

I smacked my forehead with the heel of my hand and closed my eyes. "I can't believe I didn't see it."

"See what?"

"He wanted more. He has feelings for you."

For an instant Allison looked like she wanted to deny it—or at least pretend she hadn't already reached the same conclusion—but ended up nodding again. "I sort of suspected that. He always seemed way more into what we were doing than I was."

"Oh."

"And then when we were in Hong Kong, I guess he overheard our last conversation before you were shot. I know we didn't say anything graphic, but it was clear that whoever I was talking to wasn't just a friend."

"So, that's why he started giving you such a hard time after that. He was pissed."

"Yes." Her answer came just a little too quickly, and the fraction of a second she averted her gaze clued me in to the fact that wasn't the whole truth.

"What aren't you telling me?"

"We don't really need to get into this right now."

"You've been putting it off for weeks. And *you* were the one who wanted to do this now. So talk. What happened between you two?"

Again, I could see the impulse to lie flit beneath her eyes, but after a moment, she sighed, seemingly resigned. "He came to my room."

"What do you mean he came to your room?"

"I think the statement is pretty self-explanatory."

"Let me rephrase, then. Why did he go to your room?"

Allison shot me a meaningful look. "Why do you think?"

"I don't get it. You told him you were over before that trip, so what could he possibly have had to gain by that?"

"I guess he didn't think I meant it. Or maybe he just didn't want to accept it. I'm not sure. I didn't ask him."

"But you turned him away. You didn't sleep with him."

Allison broke eye contact with me and rubbed at the back of her neck with the palm of her hand. "Well…"

My stomach felt like a javelin had punctured it. "You *did* sleep with him?"

"What? No. No, I didn't. Of course I didn't. I told you I didn't cheat on you, and I never will." When I looked away from her, she took my face between her hands and gazed into my eyes. "I never will."

"Okay." I wasn't sure I believed her, but that was my issue, not hers. And I definitely didn't want to get into that now.

"Something else might've happened though." Allison's voice was small as she said that, and she looked away again.

A harsh, grating buzz started at the base of my skull, and I was suddenly cold once more. I had no idea what was about to come out of her mouth, but I was positive I wouldn't like it. My tongue felt like it was too big for my mouth.

Allison favored me with a very serious look then, and I felt a tremor run through her grip. "I need you to promise me you aren't going to freak out when I tell you this."

My lungs seized, and my heart constricted. I wasn't sure I could handle much more of this conversation. At least not without being sick. And if I blew chunks all over what was essentially the boss's bedroom, I'd never live it down.

"I promise." My voice sounded tinny and far away to my own ears.

"I'm serious, Ryan. You absolutely cannot react to this. At all. No yelling. No walking away. No retaliation of any kind."

Okay, and now I was definitely nauseated. "Jesus Christ! Just tell me already."

"He didn't just come to my room. He let himself in."

"What?"

"Please don't make me repeat it."

"How the hell did he get a key to your room?"

"The field-office counterpart had checked everybody in ahead of time, so we wouldn't have to waste time at the front desk. He had all our room keys for us when we arrived, but he was busy trying to schedule our various meetings and get us cleared to go into the embassy, so he handed Beau all the keys to pass out. Beau must've taken one of mine out of the little envelope before he handed it to me. That's the only thing I could come up with."

"Huh." My brow knitted as I considered that scenario.

"I want to be clear that I didn't invite him. And as soon as I realized what was happening, I told him to leave."

The ringing in my ears was almost deafening now, and I tasted bile on the back of my too-big tongue. "What do you mean 'what was happening'? Did he sexually assault you?"

Allison shook her head. "No. Not exactly."

Now my blood was boiling, and my hands shook. "I think you need to tell me what happened."

Allison took a deep breath and let it out slowly. She appeared to be gathering her nerve. "He slipped into my room while I was asleep. I awoke to an arm around my waist and him kissing my neck. I…I was still half asleep, and I thought it was you for obvious reasons, so I mumbled your name and turned to kiss him back. It didn't take long to realize it wasn't you, and I stopped him."

I glared at her. It was a good thing looks couldn't kill, because I was sure the one I was sporting could have wiped out entire armies. It was also a good thing my dad had sent Byers back to DC because I'd have had several choice words for him on the subject of how to treat a lady. "That sounds like the textbook definition of sexual assault to me. With some undertones of unlawful entry and trespassing."

Allison ignored me. "The situation blew up pretty quickly after that. A lot of yelling and arguing. I actually kept waiting for someone to call hotel security on us for being too loud. And then I threatened to do it myself when he refused to leave my room."

"I'm so sorry." I felt like an idiot for even saying that to her, but I hadn't been able to come up with anything better. I was pretty sure she didn't want to hear any more about what laws I thought he'd broken. What were the statutes in Hong Kong anyway? And did they apply to people in country for diplomatic missions? I wasn't sure.

"Don't apologize. It's not your fault. It's mine for getting involved with him in the first place. I should've realized sooner just how big a jerk he is, but who could see that sort of thing coming?"

I refused to touch that one. "Are you okay?"

"I'm fine. You wanted to know what happened in Hong Kong. Well, that was it. So now you know the whole story behind why he's always giving me such a hard time. Clearly he can't handle rejection, as evidenced even further the day Mark was arrested."

"What happened the day Mark was arrested?"

Allison appeared annoyed. "Do you remember how you came to DC because you couldn't reach me all day, and you were worried?"

"Yeah. Your phones died."

Allison shook her head. "No, they didn't. But Beau wouldn't stop calling and texting and emailing me, so I shut them off. I just got tired of dealing with him. That's part of what we were arguing about when we left the House that night."

I remembered that day well, and my heart ached for her. No one should have to go through that, especially not at their place of business. That was why people said you shouldn't get involved with someone you work with, and it made me wonder whether it was the best idea for us to be together. But we were too far down that particular path to turn back now. I pushed the notion to the back of my thoughts.

"Are you sure you don't want to report him for sexual harassment?"

Allison looked at me like I was crazy. "What good would that do?"

I shrugged. "Just because you once had a…a thing"—God, that'd been hard to say—"that was consensual doesn't mean he gets to treat you like this now that you've called it off."

"Do you really think reporting him would make any difference?"

"I don't know. But he shouldn't be allowed to get away with it."

"No, he shouldn't. But you know this agency's track record on dealing with matters like this. Or do I need to remind you about what happened with Merlier?"

I sighed, beyond frustrated but knowing she was right. The old-school guard protected one another to the bitter end, even through multiple accusations of harassment by numerous women from several separate occasions over a long period of time. It sucked royally. But it wasn't likely to change any time soon.

I swallowed. "I'm sorry you're having to put up with all of this."

"Me, too. But it's almost over now. Ware said he could get my orders cut to come home within the week, which means I could conceivably be up here for good inside of a few months. Sooner, if they allow me to move up my date." She hesitated. Her brow fluttered, and the skin around her eyes tightened. I could see she was sucking on the inside of her lower lip as she studied me.

I flushed, feeling like a moron for my earlier outburst on the roof. As if I had any business telling her where she could or couldn't live. Regardless of what happened with us now or in the future, it wasn't my place. I was such a tool. "That's…That's great. I'm glad you're finally going to be able to get away from Byers."

"Is that all you're happy about?"

I pursed my lips, trying to untangle my feelings on the situation. I shook my head. They were far too complex to even begin talking about. Maybe later, when Rory was safe and we weren't operating under time constraints, I'd be able to pinpoint precisely what I thought.

Allison looked disappointed. "I'm going to fix this," she vowed, her voice shot through with determination.

"There's nothing to fix."

"Don't say that. Please, don't say that." Allison sounded damn near defeated as she mumbled that, and it took me a second to work out why.

"Oh, baby, no. I didn't mean it like that. I just meant that we aren't broken. Not really. We just…I just need some time. That's all."

"Are you sure? Because that's not what it feels like to me. You've been avoiding making eye contact with me all evening. Even now you can barely look at me. And I can't decide whether that makes me sad or pisses me off because I didn't do anything wrong."

"Both reactions are probably appropriate," I admitted. "You don't know how much I wish that wasn't the case. You don't know what I'd give to be able to let this go. But it bothers me on a level I don't think I even understand. Like I said, I just need some time. I hope that's okay."

Allison stepped back into me again and wrapped her arms around me, pulling me close. I stiffened, but she didn't release me. She squeezed me tighter and buried her face into my neck. After a long moment, I sank into her embrace and wrapped my own arms around her waist.

"Take all the time you need," Allison whispered. "I'm not going anywhere."

I nodded but didn't reply. It was time to change the subject. We'd been over this ground already and hadn't made any progress. No sense in beating a dead horse, especially when we were so pressed for time. Best to let it go for the moment.

I shifted my attention off my relationship anguish and back to the task at hand. Pulling back slightly, I let my eyes drift over to Allison so I could look at her, really look at her. I took in her casual attire and frowned.

"What are you wearing?" I asked, suddenly suspicious.

Allison glanced down at herself, perplexed. "What?"

I took a step back so I could fully inspect her outfit, which wasn't the suit I'd seen her in earlier. I narrowed my eyes at the worn jeans and white tank top covered by a short-sleeved button-down shirt that she let hang loose over her sides. Now that I was paying attention, I could see the slight outline of her duty weapon marring the line of her overshirt toward the back of her right hip.

"When did you change?"

"The same time you did. Right after the phone call from Walker came in."

"Why?"

"Why what?"

I pointed accusingly. "Why are you dressed like that?"

"How else should I dress for an operation?"

Panic, anger, and fear roared to life inside me, overwhelming and unexpected. My mouth was suddenly dry, and a cold sweat had broken out across my brow. My fingers twitched.

"No!" I barked, my intonation harsh and grating.

"Excuse me?"

"There's no way in hell you're going out on this."

Allison put her hands on her hips, brushing the hem of her shirt back out of the way so her badge glinted wickedly at me in the lamplight. Whether the move was deliberate or inadvertent, I couldn't have said. Her countenance had darkened.

"I am absolutely going out on this."

"No," I said again, shaking my head.

"Do you really expect me to just sit here and wait to hear how things play out? Do you think I'll be able to stand doing nothing while you're out there in who knows how much danger? You're out of your mind."

"And you're out of *your* mind if you think I'm going to just sit back and let that happen. You haven't been in the field in years. You probably don't even remember how to conduct yourself on an op. I don't want you within fifty light years of this mess."

"What are you going to do? Huh? Pull some of your strings? Call headquarters and have me benched?" Her tone was caustic. "I'm a federal agent, Ryan, the same as you. I went through the same academy you did, and I've been doing this for longer. There's no reason why I shouldn't be involved. Frankly, we can use all the help we can get on this."

She was right, of course, but that didn't mean I had to like it. I decided to try a different tack: honesty. I stepped closer to her and rested my hands against her biceps. "Allison, please. I'm barely holding it together worrying about what Rory might be enduring. I can't worry about her and you at the same time. I won't be able to focus."

And just like that, her ire sputtered and died. Her countenance softened, and she placed her hands on my elbows. "And I can't stand worrying about you at all. I need to see for myself that you're okay. And if, God forbid, for some reason you aren't, well, I'll need to see that, too."

Damn. When she put it that way, how could I argue? Especially when I completely understood. I sagged as all the fight went out of me. "What do they have you doing?"

"I'll be taking a leisurely stroll along the outer roadway of the park, observing the general public for any suspicious behavior and keeping an eye out for Walker and your sister so we can tell you when they arrive on set. I'm not supposed to engage him, and I'll be far removed from all the action. I promise."

"Okay." I tilted my head so our foreheads were touching. "Just be careful."

Allison smiled. "Always."

CHAPTER NINETEEN

The plan seemed simple. Hurricane and I planned to take a nice, easy jog around the park—followed at a safe distance by the ever-vigilant Hannah—and wait until someone called out that Walker and Rory were on set. Then we'd split up, and Hurricane would break off to go meet them while I attempted to stay in the area to see if I could hustle Rory out of there. The rest of the agents and officers who'd been sent in ahead had been instructed to blend in with the general public and try to put themselves in a position to assist while remaining as inconspicuous as possible. It wasn't a phenomenal plan, but we hadn't been afforded the time to come up with anything better, so we were doing the best we could.

The irony that I'd somehow managed to land myself smack-dab in the middle of yet another running situation so soon after I'd vowed to avoid it wasn't lost on me. Fate really was a vengeful bitch. I frowned and made sure to keep my pace nice and slow, barely faster than a trot. I wanted to be sure I'd have whatever energy I needed to see this clusterfuck of a situation through to the end.

I cupped my hands together and blew on them. The night air was chilly enough that my breath produced little white puffs with each strained exhale, and I wished I'd thought to grab my coat before I'd left NYFO. My hooded sweatshirt wasn't doing all that much to combat the cold. At least running warmed me up a bit.

I listened through the earbuds I had wired to my radio as my dad conducted coms checks with the team to ensure that everybody was on the air and in place, but I wasn't paying attention too closely. I was scanning the area, sizing up each person we crossed paths with as we jogged. I could feel the change in myself as my game face snapped securely into place. I was on problem now and all business. For the time being, at least, I had something else to concentrate on besides how scared Rory might be.

"How do you guys do that?" Hurricane asked.

"Do what?" I was so focused on verifying that no one nearby was Walker, I had no idea what she was talking about.

"Turn it off like that?"

"Turn what off?"

"Your fears. Your emotions. Earlier, I could see how tired you were and how terrified you were for your sister, but now it's like neither of those even registers with you. You all do that. I can almost see the steel door clanging shut on your feelings."

I shrugged despite the fact she was barely looking at me. "I'm still scared. But now I have something else to focus on and something specific to do. It helps keep my mind off the fear. Eclipses it for a time. That's all. But I still feel it."

"I can't see it."

"You're not supposed to." I didn't point out how annoyed I was that she'd been able to before. "You're supposed to be confident that we have everything under control. And you won't if we're all basket cases."

"Do they teach you that at the academy?"

"No. You sort of pick it up along the way. Just like the acronym-speak."

"Oh." Hurricane was quiet for a long moment. "I'm scared."

"I'd be worried about you if you weren't."

"I don't want to be, but I can't help it."

"No. I would imagine you can't. And that's fine. Nothing wrong with being afraid."

"Yeah, but right now I'm afraid for me. You, you're afraid for others."

I really didn't want to go down that road. I was having enough trouble keeping my mind off that topic. Having a direct discussion wouldn't help matters any. I hummed and attempted to remain focused on my surroundings.

"Is it easier for you, dating an agent? Since you're one yourself."

"What do you mean? Is what easier?"

"Your girlfriend's here with us, isn't she? She's—how would you guys say it?—involved in the operation?"

I smiled at her attempt to use our vernacular correctly. "Yes. She's here somewhere, covering a portion of the outer-perimeter roadway."

"Yet you don't seem concerned about that, either. If Noah were out here, I'd be a wreck. Is that part of your being focused on something else? Are you scared and just not showing it? Or do you not get worried about her when she does this?"

"Allison will be fine. It's you I'm worried about."

"She could be hurt today, you know. Protecting me."

I gave her a dirty look. "Seriously?"

"Sorry."

"No one's getting hurt today. Not if I can help it."

"That's the thing, though. You can't help it. None of you can do anything to stop something like that."

She had a point, but I wasn't in the mood to argue. "You're inventing things to worry about. It's counterproductive." If anyone knew about that, it was me.

"Do you have any idea what it's like? Knowing that someone might die because of you."

I clenched my jaw against the agony building up inside me. I knew she didn't mean anything by it, that she was thinking solely about her own concerns and had no idea what'd happened to me. To Lucia. So I pushed the pain down and continued my visual sweep of the area. I cleared my throat. "I'm sorry you have to deal with that."

"I want to not be scared right now. I want to turn it off like you do. I was hoping you could teach me how."

"That's not something you can teach." I thought back to the argument Allison and I had before we'd left, about me begging her to sit this one out. "And it isn't exactly that I'm not scared for Allison. I'm just not thinking about anything happening to her. And on the rare occasions I do, I just assume she'll come out on top."

Hurricane snorted. "That's it? That's your big secret? You assume you guys will always win?"

"What can I say? We're a cocky bunch." I stopped talking to

listen to the radio traffic the rest of the guys were putting out. When Hurricane started speaking again, I held up one finger, silently asking her to hold her thought.

"Flannigan, Flannigan from Valentine."

"Go for Flannigan," Dad said.

"Flannigan, we've had negative contact at the residence. I repeat, negative contact at the residence. We have phones but no bodies. Copy?"

"Flannigan copies. Do you have a rough distance from your location to us?"

"Less than ten mikes on foot," Valentine replied. "Probably closer to seven. No way for us to know how long they've been gone, though."

"Flannigan copies direct. Relocate your team to your secondary positions. Break. Flannigan to all units at the park, be advised that the cell-tracking team was unable to locate the targets. It's likely they're already on their way to us. Keep your eyes open, and don't be afraid to speak up if you see anything."

I heard a lot of double clicks of various microphones as people acknowledged the new information. My heart fluttered. I hadn't realized just how solidly I'd pinned my hopes on the ESU team being able to extract Rory from Walker's clutches before they ever left wherever he'd been holed up with her until I heard that they hadn't. I swallowed hard.

"What's going on?" Hurricane asked.

I frowned. My examination of everything and everyone around me had ratcheted up a notch. "Huh?"

"The guys were talking?"

"Yeah."

"Well?"

"Well what?"

"I don't have a radio, remember?"

"Oh. Right. Sorry. The team tracking the cell phones just reported that when they hit the residence, Rory and Walker weren't there."

"Is that bad?"

"It isn't necessarily good or bad per se."

"But?"

"But obviously it would've been better if they'd been able to get Rory away from Walker sooner rather than later."

What I didn't bother to say—couldn't have made myself say—was that now that Walker had ditched the phones, we had no way to track them. He could be spiriting her away to Mexico right now. He probably wasn't, but I hated the complete lack of assurances.

"They're on their way here then?"

"That's the assumption, yes. But we can't be sure." I tried not to think about that. "You okay?"

She looked like she might be sick. But she nodded and tried to put on a brave face. "Yeah."

"You'll be fine. Just remember what I told you. Keep several arm's lengths between you at all times, all right?"

"Okay."

"I'm going to stop and pretend to fix my shoes so you can get a little ahead of me, okay? They should be here any second, if they're not already, and we need to look like we're not together."

"Flannigan, Flannigan from Reynolds." Allison's voice floated over the air. "Be advised that two individuals matching the subjects' descriptions just left the roadway to cut through the trees due west of the zoo. They appear to be heading in the direction of the Picnic House. The male is dressed in jeans, sneakers, and a dark hooded sweatshirt with the hood pulled up. The female is in jeans and a white button-down dress shirt. He's keeping her pretty close. Copy direct?"

"Flannigan copies direct. Break. All units in the park, be advised the subjects are on set. Everybody hold your positions and stand by for further instructions."

Shit. Hurricane and I were already circling down around the south side of the ball fields. Rory and Walker were well behind us. Considering that the house his cell phone had been traced to was on the west side of the park, it meant that he and Rory had to have been wandering around in here for a little while to have ended up all the way over by the zoo. My stomach turned as I considered the implications. He'd likely been conducting countersurveillance, trying to spot the agents. *Fuck me.*

Determined not to let that notion distract me, I grabbed the sleeve of Hurricane's puffy coat to get her to stop and changed direction, pulling her back up the roadway we'd just run.

"They're here. Keep following this path back past the softball fields toward where we came in, okay? He's dressed in jeans and a dark hoodie. My sister's in jeans and a white shirt. You should see them in the big field on your right. When you spot him, make sure he sees you and then stop. Make him come to you, okay? But not too close."

Hurricane looked almost terrified now. That was not good. I needed her to keep it together for at least another few minutes.

"Zoey." I deliberately used her first name to get her attention.

"Yeah?" She looked dazed.

"I'm not going to let anything happen to you, okay?" She nodded, and I clapped her on the shoulder. "Go on."

"Wait. Where are you going?"

"I'm going to keep following the path the other way so I can come up on the opposite side of the ball fields to try to get in between him and you. Don't worry. I'll keep you in my field of vision for as long as I can. Hannah's right behind us, and the rest of the guys will keep an eye on you even when I can't. They'll make sure I'm updated on where you are at all times, all right?"

Hurricane nodded, took a deep breath, and ran off. I watched her go for a moment before I slowly reversed direction again. Watching her out of the corner of my eye, I keyed the mike I had clipped to the strap of my sports bra under my T-shirt.

"Flannigan, Flannigan from O'Connor. Be advised Hurricane and I have just split up. She's headed north on the inner roadway just to the west of the ball fields. I'm taking the roadway around to the east so I can try to cut them off and scuttle Rory out of there while he's distracted talking to Hurricane. I'm going to need someone to call out Hurricane's locations to me, copy?"

"Valenti copies. I'm about two dozen steps behind her. I'm going to need a little help since I'm so far away, though."

Rico jumped in. "Corazon copies direct. I should be able to see her in a minute or so. I'm on a bench between the fields and the Tennis House. No sign of Walker yet, though."

"Roger," someone else interjected. "They're still in the trees just north of the Ravine. I'll call it out when they clear them."

I increased my pace, determined to at least put eyes on them before Hurricane reached them. Adrenaline was coursing through my veins, making the run slightly easier than it might otherwise have been, although I didn't think the desire to verify my sister's well-being hurt either.

I continued tooling along as fast as I could. The bellyband that held my weapon flush against my lower abdomen underneath my shirt was irritating me. It didn't sit right with the vest I had on. It'd been a bad idea to wear it. I should've just gone with the fanny pack like I'd originally wanted. I rubbed at the band as I strode.

My breathing was beginning to become labored, and my legs burned. I yearned so badly for this to be over that I ached inside. Except for the occasional glances I spared for trying to see Hurricane across the fields, I kept my eyes on the path in front of me as I strained to see the open meadow up ahead. Letting out a frustrated huff, I struggled to increase my pace.

Time seemed to both speed up and slow in the same moment. I kept my ears tuned to the earpiece I was wearing, almost willing someone—anyone—to say something. But the silence stretched on, driving me insane.

The signs dotting the path told me I was nearing the first of two small lakes on my right, and I glanced again toward the west inner roadway while I was out of the trees for a moment. I'd hoped to glimpse Hurricane before I hit the next set of faux-forest, but the trees on her side of the park still concealed her.

My heart dropped. Maybe splitting up so I could intercept Walker had been a bad idea, too. The notion that my poor decision could lead to Hurricane getting hurt made my head swim, and I tried to banish the thought. Rico and Hannah had her now. They'd keep her safe.

"They just broke through the trees and turned north," someone said. "They're now headed straight up the field in the direction of Grand Army Plaza."

I sighed in relief and pushed myself harder. Every time I swung my right arm, the area just below my elbow banged against the outline of my pistol and jammed it into my hip. I was likely to have bruises from the encounter, but it seemed like a small price to pay.

"That's a good copy," I heard someone else say. "They're headed right to us, but the woman is still too close to him. It looks like he's holding her arm. We need to get her farther away. When we do, I'll have the officer with me release the dog."

"Copy," Dad said. "Stand by for that. Does anybody have a location on Hurricane?"

"That's affirmative," Rico said. "I've got the eyeball. She passed me on the roadway a minute or so ago. She's walking now. I'm following behind at a safe distance."

"What's her ETA to the target?" Dad asked.

"Less than one mike," Rico replied.

"Corazon from Valenti, you've got her now. I have to run past you guys, so I don't look too suspicious. I'll try to double back when I can."

Someone—presumably Rico—clicked their microphone twice in acknowledgment, and the radio went silent once again. I scowled as I attempted to figure out how much farther I'd have to run in order to be able to see my sister.

I thought back to the NPC-50 the other day and how desperate I'd felt as I'd raced toward the finish line, how every cell in my body had been crying out for that goal. At the time, I'd thought I'd never again be crushed underneath the weight of the desire for something to be over. Not like that. Fuck if I didn't just hate being wrong.

Finally, after what felt like an eternity, I burst through the trees and out into the meadow. There, in the distance, I could see Rory and Walker. With a strangled cry that was a cross between despair and elation, I locked myself into an all-out sprint.

In the far corner of my vision, I saw Hurricane step off the path and onto the grass of the field Walker and Rory were slowly making their way across. Walker had been looking around the entire time he'd been walking and spotted Hurricane almost immediately. He froze, pulling Rory to a halt with him. She stumbled at the abrupt motion, and Walker yanked her arm hard.

Before Walker had seen Hurricane, I'd been at his six o'clock, and therefore he couldn't have seen me. Now, however, he'd turned so that he could face her, and I was at his eight. If he swiveled his head even a little bit to the left, he wouldn't be able to help noticing me racing across the grass. My heart stuttered, and I prayed as desperately as I'd ever prayed for anything that he'd be too focused on Hurricane's presence to bother looking at anyone but her.

I was closing in fast, but I still didn't feel like it was fast enough. And the fact that Walker still had yet to release Rory unsettled me. I didn't like the tight hold he appeared to have on her arm. I didn't like the way she seemed to be having trouble walking. I didn't like the way he continued to advance upon Hurricane. I really didn't like the way she was still creeping away from the relative safety that the distance between them afforded her and inching toward him. Actually, I didn't like a single thing about this situation.

Walker had Rory pulled tight to his right side and looked to be keeping her there with an iron grip on her bicep with his right hand. For a long time, I couldn't see his left since it was concealed from my view by his body, but when he finally brought his hand into my field of vision as he waved it to emphasize some point, I saw he was holding a knife. I felt an immediate pressure in my chest, and my body went cold.

Where the hell had the goddamn knife come from? And why the fuck hadn't somebody called it out before now? Did anybody else even realize Walker was armed? Shit, I needed to call this out over the air. I lifted my hand toward my mike.

"Flannigan, Flannigan from Ng," a voice broke in before I could pass along my own message. "Be advised, the K-9 handler reports that Rory's still too close, and now so is Hurricane. He can't release the dog until they're both clear. Copy?"

"Flannigan copies. Corazon, Corazon from Flannigan. Do you still have the eyeball?"

"Copy. I've still got it. I'm working on getting closer without alerting him. Stand by."

The chatter between the other agents on set continued, leaving me no opportunity to interject. I tuned them out. Sprinting the way I was, I'd have to engage the threat sooner rather than later. I had no time left to even make the notification. Not if I wanted to keep off Walker's radar.

I was close enough now that I could almost hear what Walker and Hurricane were saying as they talked. Or I would've been able to if not for the roar of my own heart screaming in my ears. I was trying not to panic, not to let my emotions take over, not to do anything stupid. But my entire world view had narrowed and locked onto that weapon, and that wasn't exactly aiding my thinking processes.

Secret Service policy dictates that when there is an assault on a protectee, we send the maximum number of agents to the protectee and the minimum number to the actual problem. That's what we'd all been trained to do. It was a law-of-averages thing. In theory, with a bunch of us there, one of us would end up intercepting the threat—one of *us* would take that hit—so the rest of the agents could evacuate the protectee from the situation unharmed.

My training was kicking in pretty damn hard. Rory might not have been a protectee, but to my mind, it didn't matter. She was in immediate danger, and the way I saw it, I could ensure her safety only one way.

I had to get between my sister and that knife.

CHAPTER TWENTY

Spurred on by my resolve to finish this before it somehow got even more complicated and messy, I unzipped my sweatshirt and shucked it as I ran, desperate to get my hands on my weapon. There was no end to the litany of curses I uttered at myself for allowing the guys to talk me into wearing this stupid bellyband. I'd never used it before. I was completely unpracticed on how to draw quickly and safely from it. I'd known it was a horrible idea to stray from our oft-muttered adage of "play how you train" when I'd put it on, but I'd agreed to it out of a desire to be as inconspicuous as possible. Fanny packs screamed law enforcement, and I hadn't wanted to call that kind of attention to myself. Now it looked like Rory and Hurricane might have to pay for my lack of common sense.

Frantic now, I clawed at the hem of my shirt, trying to lift it up out of the way so I could worm my hand between the butt of the gun and my vest. I needed to get a good grip. Now I was able to lament my other mistake: carrying a weapon I wasn't used to. This thing was tiny compared to my issued duty weapon, and I was having a hard time getting a secure handle on it so I could draw. I didn't think either the pressure of the situation or my attempt to do this without breaking stride were helping matters.

After several unsuccessful attempts, I gave up. Clearly the only way to draw that weapon would've been to stop running, and that wasn't going to happen. Besides, what the hell would I do with the gun once I had it drawn? Training and protocol dictated that I should call out to Walker, to identify myself as law enforcement and give him a chance to drop the knife before I shot him. Not doing so would've been tantamount to execution as far as a defense attorney was concerned, and I didn't have any desire to see him die or to be raked over the coals for killing him. But issuing the requisite verbal warning would also give him more than enough time to stab Rory, and that was out of the question.

Also out of the question was shooting anywhere other than center mass. I was too hopped up on adrenaline and nerves to trust my aim with anything smaller than his chest. A shot to the thigh or the arm would've made for great television, but I couldn't take the chance that I'd miss and hit Rory or Hurricane or anyone else.

No, my gun was definitely out. That left me no choice. If I wanted that knife, I was going to have to wrest it from him, and in order to do that, I'd need to get close to him and then take him by surprise.

I was closing in fast. When I was maybe six steps away, I shouted to my sister to run. *"Asha, rith!"*

As soon as the words were out of my mouth, I launched myself at Walker. He'd let go of Rory and started to turn at the sound of my voice, and I caught a fleeting glimpse of his eyes widening before I slammed into his chest with my shoulder. The force of the impact was jarring, and I bit my tongue hard as we tumbled to the ground in a cacophony of grunts and a tangle of limbs.

We rolled over and over together as a twisted mess of arms and legs forever before I was finally flung free. It took a second before the world righted itself and I was able to see straight. My vision was foggy from banging my head against the ground as I fell, and I shook it to clear it as I attempted to get a bead on Walker.

He appeared just as stunned as I was, and he took a moment to just lie on the ground. Then he pushed himself up onto one elbow and took stock of the situation. His eyes fell on Rory first, and he started to go after her as she fled. He got only as far as one knee before I tackled him again, only this time I landed squarely on top of him and stayed there.

My heart was working overtime, and my movements were quick and jerky with the panic I felt. Just like the last time I'd had Walker on the ground on his back, I scrambled to turn myself so I was kneeling by his head in order to grab his arm in an arm bar, effectively ending the tussle before it even began. Unlike the last time, it didn't work.

Walker recovered from his surprise more quickly than I'd anticipated, and before I had a chance to move, he snagged the back of my T-shirt just under my neck in his big, meaty fist and pinned me to his chest. With his other hand, he hauled off and decked me across the mouth. The pain was immediate, and I saw stars.

My own words to Hurricane about not letting Walker get his hands on her echoed in my mind. The irony of my own situation wasn't lost on me. I drove my knee hard into Walker's stomach, and he let out a soft "oof" and yanked on my shirt. I went with the momentum and rolled off him and onto the ground.

I turned my head in the general direction of where I thought I'd last seen Rory, but she was nowhere near. My relief was short lived, however. I barely had a second for it to register that she was out of the way before Walker was on top of me, plopping himself down to straddle my stomach and knocking the air from my lungs.

The weight of him pinning me down sparked a sharp feeling of alarm, and I started to struggle. I bucked my hips the way we were taught in training, but he didn't budge. He didn't even appear to register my attempts to free myself. His eyes were crazed and furious, and my alarm morphed into terror. I wouldn't be able to reason with him. Not this time.

Walker's eyes went wide as it finally dawned on him who he was straddling. Unfortunately for me, his surprise was fleeting. He pulled his lips back from his teeth in a snarl, and he lunged and reached out to wrap his gigantic hands around my throat. I struggled and wiggled and fought to keep him from establishing a good grip as my mind attempted to recall how long I'd have before unconsciousness should he actually get one. I couldn't remember the exact time I'd been cited, but I knew it wouldn't be long. My flailing only delayed the inevitable, and after a bit he wrapped his fingers around my throat and squeezed.

I clawed at his hands with my own but couldn't break his grip. I could see his mouth moving, see that he was screaming something, but the words weren't reaching my brain. I couldn't hear much of anything over the thud of my own heart or the sound of my mind screeching at me to get him the hell off. I opened my mouth wide, but no air was coming in or out.

My vision started to go fuzzy, and the edges of my awareness were dark. Frantically, I punched at the inside of Walker's elbow in an attempt to get him to break his grip. But my limited range of motion didn't allow me the space I needed to build up any kind of real force behind the blow. I was basically just smacking his arm, and he reacted to that the same way he'd reacted to my lame attempts to buck him off me, which is to say not at all.

Desperate now, I tried to reach up toward his face, but the angle at which he was sitting and the position of his arms made it so I couldn't quite reach. Not enough to do any kind of real damage, anyway. I'd been hoping to be able to jam my thumb into his eye socket but had to settle for jabbing ineffectually at his chin with the heel of my hand. I considered trying to fishhook him, but he kept moving his head, and I couldn't get a good hold, but all of my struggling seemed to make it impossible for him to keep his grip quite tight enough to make me pass out, so that was something.

Nope. My mistake. I'd thought that too soon. No sooner had the notion flitted through my thoughts then Walker's grip on my throat tightened even more—which I wouldn't have thought possible—and I began slipping out of consciousness. My legs flailed as I tried to knee him in the back or kick him in the back of the head, but either I simply didn't have the energy to put into the motion or he was too far gone into his rage for it to have any kind of effect on him. Probably a little of both.

In a last attempt to distract him from his clear intent to choke the life out of me, I worked my hand between our bodies. When I felt his inner thigh, I curled my fingers and grabbed as big a chunk of skin as tightly as I could. Then I twisted. Hard.

Walker let out a bellow of pain and loosened his death grip on my throat. He nearly released it altogether when I followed that up with a sharp jab to the nuts. I sucked in a huge lungful of air and sat up as much as I was able. I wrapped my hands around his head and got a good grasp on his hair. Then I jerked him toward me at the same time I surged forward. My forehead met his nose with a sickening crunch that I felt more than heard, and he roared again. I head-butted him a couple more times, deriving a sick sort of pleasure from the wet cracking sound that resulted.

My limbs felt like they weighed a ton, and I was having a hard time getting them to do what I wanted. They seemed to belong to someone else, and that someone was reluctant to follow any of my commands. The adrenaline that'd fueled me to this point had waned. I panted heavily, and my grip on Walker's hair slackened.

Walker wrapped one hand back around my throat and slammed me back into the ground, but he seemed more intent on holding me in place than throttling me. I started trying to pull my T-shirt up so I could get my gun, but his knee was keeping my shirt trapped and pressing the gun hard into my hip. He adjusted so his forearm was against my throat and leaned a little to one side.

The new position still made it tough to breathe, though not quite as tough as before, but it also allowed me to reach his face, and I resumed trying to jab my thumb into his eye socket. Walker growled and ducked so his temple was resting against my chin and his eyes were effectively out of my reach. I grabbed a handful of his hair and pulled. I could feel Walker flailing his free arm around out to his side. He was likely looking for the knife he'd dropped earlier, and the blood in my veins turned to ice.

Holy fuck.

A new surge of adrenaline flooded me, and my panic increased. Determined to end this, preferably before I felt the sharp pain of cold steel as it slipped between my ribs, I yanked on his hair again as hard as I could. He had no choice but to lift his head. It was only a couple of inches, but that was all I needed.

I wedged my other hand in between us and braced the edge of my fist against his jaw. Then I used both of my hands to twist as hard and as fast as I could. I felt a series of pops right on top of one another that reminded me of what happened when I wrung bubble wrap between my hands. And then Walker collapsed heavily down on me.

Still caught in my terror, I didn't trust his sudden stillness. He could've been playing possum. I wrenched his head back and forth as violently as I could, twisting a few more times for good measure. The action failed to produce any response from him, and I let out a huge sigh of relief, collapsing like a marionette whose strings had just been cut and lying in a heap on the ground. I gasped, unable to hear the sounds of my own breathing over the ringing in my ears.

I'm sure I could have had a million more appropriate thoughts, but all my poor, oxygen-deprived brain could come up with was, *Thank God.*

That summed things up well enough.

CHAPTER TWENTY-ONE

I lay still beneath Walker's unmoving body, staring up at the sky as I struggled to breathe. He was ridiculously heavy, and I was having a tough time making my chest rise. Each scant breath of precious air I managed to draw burned worse than the last. I coughed, wincing against the pain in my throat.

I sighed again and gave in to the temptation to close my eyes. My body ached in places I didn't know I had, and the mere idea of moving ever again was too much for me. I didn't have it in me to fight anymore: not to be out from under Walker, not to breathe, not to do anything. The adrenaline I'd been running on had finally vanished, leaving me weak and trembling.

I turned my head to the side, away from where Walker's forehead rested against my neck, and relished the prickling sensation the individual blades of grass made against my cheek. I sighed once more and allowed myself to drift. Down, down, down. Like a feather gently gliding to the ground. Away from the world. Away from everything.

"Oh, no, no, no. Ryan, come on, baby. Stay with me." Allison's voice floated to me as if from a great distance, and I wanted to smile. I may have, for all I knew. I couldn't exactly tell. I was so far removed from my body. I felt gentle hands caressing my face, brushing the hair back off my forehead.

More noise buzzed around me, but I noted it only dimly. Voices, many of them sounding alarmed, tickled the edges of my awareness. I wanted to tell them to relax, but that would've taken too much effort.

Crack!

I heard the sound of the slap more than I felt it, and my eyes shot open before I even had a chance to fully register what'd just happened. My cheek burned, and I lifted my free hand to it. It was hot to the touch.

"What the hell?"

Allison was staring down at me with wild eyes. "Ryan? Oh, thank God."

"Did you just hit me?" I couldn't believe it.

The fear in her gaze ebbed, and she rolled her eyes at me. "That's what you get for falling asleep on the job. Can you tell me where you're hurt?"

I frowned at her, momentarily confused as to what job she was talking about or why I might've been lying on the ground. My thoughts were sluggish and slow and disjointed. I licked my dry, cracked lips and winced at the sharp stab of pain the prodding of my tongue produced. My frown deepened as I tasted blood. I could hear other voices around me again, but the exact words weren't penetrating my awareness.

A collective grunt caught my attention, and I inhaled long and deep as the oppressive weight crushing me was finally lifted. Being able to breathe freely felt so good I nearly cried. I lay gasping on the ground for a bit, enjoying the sensation of not being squashed as I ignored everything and everyone around me.

After several long minutes, I rolled over onto my stomach and clambered to my hands and knees. My limbs were rubbery and heavy, and they didn't feel connected to me. I hung my head, startled to see bright red drops of blood appear on the backs of my hands. *Funny. Where did that come from? I don't feel injured. At least not the kind of injury that would result in bleeding. Weird.*

"Ryan?" Allison's voice was soft near my ear. She was rubbing gentle circles on my back.

I closed my eyes again and relished her touch, wondering at the faint sensation of déjà vu it invoked. I spat a few times, trying to get the taste of blood out of my mouth, and made a face upon realizing that hadn't done anything to help. I grappled with my sluggish thoughts in an effort to make sense of where I was and what I'd been doing. I'd been struggling with that a lot lately. I didn't think that was a good thing.

Let's see. I'm on my knees in the grass. I'm tasting blood. I'm shaking, and I feel like I've just run a marathon. Aha!

"Hmmm? Did I win?" I mumbled.

"Did you win what, sweetheart?"

I thought she sounded alarmed, and I tilted my head to the side so I could regard her with one eye. Had that not been the right question? I couldn't be sure. "The race."

Allison's expression now was pure panic, and she twisted to look at someone over my shoulder. I turned my head and tried to follow her gaze but ended up so dizzy I tumbled down again. The fall seemed to take forever, which was odd considering I wasn't all that far off the ground.

I sprawled on my side for a moment, waiting for the vertigo to pass. I sniffled and ran the back of one hand across my nose, wrinkling it in disgust when I saw the crimson smear marring my normally pale skin. I rolled onto my back and allowed my head to loll to the other side. For several heartbeats, I stared blankly at the blond-haired woman curled up in a tight ball not twenty yards from me being fussed over by a whole bunch of people.

My brain stalled. Nothing about this situation made any sense. I fought through the gray-matter sludge to put the pieces together so I could assign some meaning or purpose to the scene, but nothing was coming.

Until the woman lifted her head, until her eyes caught mine. Then, as the anguish and despair I saw there threatened to drown me, my mind caught, and time resumed its normal rate of passage. I suddenly knew exactly where I was and what'd happened. Having reality slam me that abruptly was painful.

"Rory!" My voice was hoarse, and I hissed at the pain my shout evoked. Trying to ignore it, I rolled back up to my hands and knees and scrambled across the meadow to my big sister.

Rory stared at me for a long moment with wide, frightened eyes before bursting into hysterical tears. I pulled her tight and cradled her head to my chest. Closing my eyes, I rocked her gently, murmuring to her that I was sorry, that she would be okay, that I had her now, and I'd never let anything happen to her ever again. She only cried harder and squeezed me so tight, she almost cracked my ribs.

We sat tangled up with one another for so long my feet fell asleep and my thighs and back began screaming at me to move. I ignored them. The pins and needles were unpleasant, but I gladly paid the small price for the knowledge and reassurance that Rory was safe.

Someone draped a cotton blanket over my shoulders and wrapped it around both Rory and me with great care. I didn't have to open my eyes to know that Allison was responsible. The whisper-soft kiss pressed to the top of my head confirmed it, and I smiled.

"I'm going to get you some water," she murmured in my ear. "I'll be right back."

I nodded as I tried to shift my stance, to get my legs out from under me so they could splay out on the ground beside me, but I only jostled Rory from her position tucked against me. When she pulled back to let me adjust, I caught sight of the blood on her face and in her hair, and I gasped.

"Oh, my God, Rory. Are you hurt?" I lifted the hand that wasn't wrapped around her shoulders to the vicinity of her face. I wanted to touch her, to see where she was bleeding from, but I was afraid of hurting her even more. "Did you hit your head?"

Rory's sea-foam-green eyes were as wide as monster truck tires as she stared at me, her expression one of horror. Her tears began anew as she covered her mouth with her hand and moaned, sounding despondent. She pulled the blanket off her shoulders and gently blotted my face.

"Not me. You," she whispered, her voice sounding more hoarse than I'd expected.

I wiped the pad of my thumb across the stain on her temple, relieved to discover it came off without revealing a wound underneath. I let out a shaky breath and tried to smile. Now that she'd pointed it out, I realized she hadn't had any blood on her when I'd first taken her into my arms. I felt terrible for getting her dirty.

"Ryan, you need a doctor," Rory said softly.

"Nah. I'm good." I still felt punch-drunk but figured that some time and a plate of hot wings would cure me.

"No. You're not. You're covered in blood."

"I am?" I looked down at myself. The front of my shirt was stained a dark, sickening scarlet color. "Oh. Well, that sucks."

I untangled myself from Rory's koala-bear-like grasp to remove the soiled garment and winced as I pulled it up over my head and felt the slide of the sticky, wet cloth against my skin. I probably would've just done better to cut it off but couldn't do anything about that now.

I glanced down at the front of my vest. Some of the blood had soaked through and stained my vest carrier as well. My mind flashed back to the race and how I'd been reluctant to remove my shirt for fear of having all my scars on display. Strange how my perspective could change so drastically and so quickly. I undid the Velcro straps in order to get it off me. Seemed showing my scars was preferable to keeping them covered by a dirty vest. That was good to know.

Once I was free of all blood-stained clothing, I started probing my forehead, my cheeks, my nose, wherever I could have been wounded seriously enough to produce that much blood. Aside from the slight sting of the scrape I'd earned the other day, the pain of a split lower lip, and the ache of some assorted cuts on the inside of my cheek and my bitten tongue, I couldn't find any wounds anywhere.

"I don't think any of it's mine," I told Rory.

A figure loomed over us, standing far too close for comfort. "Agent O'Connor."

I craned my head around over my shoulder and tilted my face up so I could look at the man who'd just addressed me. He wore the crisp white shirt of the NYPD brass, his eyes as cold as the glints reflecting off the double gold bars decorating his collar. I didn't recognize him, so he hadn't been at the briefing earlier, which made sense, seeing as how we were now in a different borough.

"Yes?"

"I'm Captain Urbina. I'd like to take your statement now." He held out a hand to help me up. "If you'll come with me, please."

I ignored the hand. "My statement?"

"Yes, ma'am. Your statement. We have a dead body. I need to hear from you how he got that way."

I gaped at him for a long moment, waiting for the punch line. The haughty expression on his face as he stared at me clued me in on the fact that there wasn't one. Was he freaking kidding me? I was sitting here covered in blood holding a traumatized woman in my arms, and he wanted to take my statement? He was out of his damn mind. I'd just opened my mouth to tell him so when somebody else came to my rescue.

"That actually won't be necessary, Agent O'Connor. Not at this time."

Captain Urbina's expression became even colder, and he took a step back and turned to face the man who'd spoken. "I'm sorry. And you are?"

"Forgive me," the man said, not sounding at all apologetic. "Special Agent Eli Haag, FBI."

"What is the FBI doing mucking about in my crime scene?" the captain demanded angrily. "How did you even hear about it?"

Clearly, SA Haag was unmoved. "Actually, the kidnapping of Dr. O'Connor was a violation of federal law, which makes this *my* crime scene." He refocused his attention on me. "If you could tell me where your boss is, I'd appreciate it. I'd like to inform him that we've officially assumed responsibility for the scene. The federal interim presence of the Secret Service is no longer required."

"You have got to be kidding me," Captain Urbina grumbled. "Look, Agent Haag, the NYPD is responsible for all homicide investigations in the city of New York. That makes this my crime scene. Not yours. And I'd like to question this witness."

"Well, Captain, you're going to have to wait. Agent O'Connor is injured and needs medical attention." He turned to me again and shot me a look laced with meaning. "Don't you?"

I nodded, going along with him. "Yes, sir. I do. I am experiencing some pain. I need to be checked out."

Captain Urbina narrowed his eyes at us. He knew as well as I did that I wasn't required to give a statement right away. I was perfectly within my rights to request to be taken to a hospital and treated for any injuries I might have sustained during the operation. He also knew that as soon as I checked into the ER, the doctors would give me painkillers, and once that happened, he was forbidden to talk to me until after the drugs had worn off. Clearly, he'd been hoping to bully me into talking to him before any of that could take place and was unhappy because SA Haag had thwarted his efforts.

"Captain Urbina, I'm sure Agent O'Connor will be in touch."

He'd been dismissed, and he knew it. Shaking his head, the captain spun around and stalked away.

Once he was gone, SA Haag nodded at me in that way all agents from all agencies do. "I wasn't kidding about that hospital visit. I think you both need to go."

"We will," I said. "Don't worry."

"And of course you realize that I'm going to need a statement at some point. Call me when you've touched base with your FLEOA rep and are ready to make one. I'm in no hurry." He handed me his business card.

I took it with trembling fingers. "Thanks, Agent Haag. I will."

"I'll check in on you later," he said and waved a hand at the chaotic scene sprawled all around us. "I have work to do."

"Give 'em hell."

Nodding again in parting, Agent Haag left to resume his duties as incident commander. As he walked away, I recommenced my subtle examination of my sister. Rory was watching Agent Haag thoughtfully, but a deep, soul-crushing anguish lingered behind her eyes. My stomach wrenched, and I didn't think I could attribute it solely to the metallic taste of blood clinging to the back of my tongue.

"Rory," I whispered, craving her eyes on me yet terrified of what would happen once I had them.

Rory tensed when I said her name, and her whole body froze. She remained staring in the direction Agent Haag had just gone for what felt like hours before her gaze began the long journey over to meet mine. She moved like she was encased in cement. My heart hammered the entire time.

Allison returned then with two bottles of water and handed one to each of us. I tried to smile at her in gratitude but didn't manage it very well. My lips formed more of a grimace. I went through several rounds of swish-and-spit, trying to get the taste of blood out of my mouth before I poured some of the cool water on my face. I used the back of the shirt I'd just removed to wipe some of the blood from my skin. Judging by the looks on Allison's and Rory's faces, I could only assume that just made things worse.

I struggled to get to my feet. My legs were shaky and weak, my head spinning. I stumbled into Allison, who caught me.

"Whoa," she said. "Take it easy."

"I'm okay. Where's Hurricane?"

"She's fine. She's already been evac'd. An ambulance is on its way for you."

"I don't need an ambulance. I'm fine."

My bullshit didn't reassure Allison. Concern was seared into her features, and she tightened her hold on me. "Can you please just humor me and let them check you out when they get here?"

I nodded, too tired to argue, and held a hand out to Rory. "Can you stand?"

Rory winced as she slipped her hand into mine. Allison released me to take Rory's other hand, and together we managed to help her to her feet. She winced again and clenched her jaw as though trying to bite back a groan. It wasn't until she shivered that I realized she wasn't wearing a coat. I was still overheated from all the running and the brawling, but she had to be freezing. I started to search the ground for the sweatshirt I'd discarded earlier, but Allison removed her own jacket and draped it across Rory's shoulders. Rory flinched again as she drew the material tighter around herself.

I narrowed my eyes as I examined the way Rory was standing. Something about the way she held herself bothered me, but I couldn't put my finger on why. As gently as possible, I helped her put her arms into the sleeves of Allison's coat. Once I was satisfied she was sufficiently bundled up, I took her hand and looped one of her arms across my shoulders, then threaded one of my own around her waist. Allison took up a mirroring position on the opposite side.

"We should be doing this for you," Rory murmured into my ear. She looked at least twice as exhausted as I felt.

"I'm fine," I said, focused on the way she was limping. She was obviously in some serious pain. I just couldn't figure out what her specific injuries were. She didn't appear to be favoring any particular body part, but she was definitely moving gingerly.

I glanced toward Allison. She held my eyes for only a split second before averting her gaze and staring resolutely forward. Her nostrils flared, and she set her jaw. But she looked more worried than angry, although that darker emotion was present, and I thought I'd caught the barest traces of tears welling in her eyes before she looked away. I had no idea why she would be so upset, but it sparked a tiny fire of unease inside me.

"Rory, what happened to you?" The question was soft, barely louder than a whisper, and I wasn't positive she even heard me over the wail of the siren screaming away in the distance.

The three of us continued our slow trek across the field toward the roadway. Rory hadn't answered me, hadn't even acknowledged that I'd spoken, and I faltered, unsure if I should press the issue. She'd just been through an arguably traumatic ordeal. I couldn't decide whether I thought it'd be more or less productive to try to get her to talk about it sooner rather than later.

"Rory?" My voice cracked and sounded small as I said her name, but I could tell by the way she'd stiffened in my arms that she'd heard me. "Where are you hurt?"

"Forget it, Ryan." Rory's words were flat and lacked any sort of heat or emotion. Fear, sadness, anger—those I would've understood. But this hollowness of tone reverberated loudly inside me and made me sick to my stomach.

I stopped walking without warning, causing Rory to stumble. And in my fear and impatience, I grabbed her a little harder than I meant to. She hissed in pain, and I felt an immediate and painful stab of remorse.

I slipped out of her grasp and positioned myself directly in front of her. My heart was racing again, causing my throat to throb with every beat. I swallowed hard and wiped the palms of my hands on the legs of my running pants. Rory still wouldn't look at me, preferring instead to focus on a spot on the grass just behind me and a little off to my left.

I frowned at her as I took in her appearance. The limp, messy hair that tumbled lifelessly down over her shoulders. The dark circles that sat heavily underneath her eyes. The disheveled and dirty clothing that looked like it'd seen the wrong end of a scuffle. The air of defeat she wore around her the way you'd wrap your coat around yourself on a cold, blustery winter day. The small horizontal scratches lining the front of her throat. The faint bruise I saw on her neck peeking out from beneath her collar—

My eyebrows flew up, and I gasped. I chanced a quick glance at Allison, who was staring at me with watery eyes, looking like she was trying not to cry. My brain refused to dwell on why that would be, and I reached out with trembling fingers to brush Rory's collar away from her throat so I could take a better look.

My sister winced and tried to pull back, still keeping her eyes away from mine. I used my other hand to capture the back of her neck to hold her still. Rory's jaw clenched, and the tears that'd been welling in her eyes finally spilled over and started making slow, lazy tracks down her cheeks. She sniffled and closed her eyes.

I paused in my inspection long enough to wipe the wetness away with the pad of my thumb. Then I reached for her collar again. My hand was trembling violently now, and the rest of my body joined it. I clenched my own jaw when I realized my teeth were chattering.

I pulled the collar of her shirt aside only as much as necessary so I could get a good look at Rory's wound. When I did so, I noticed several other marks below it, all of a similar size and shape. I hesitated, unwilling to admit to myself exactly what they looked like. I leaned in closer and closed my own eyes when I noticed the distinct impression of teeth marring her skin.

I took a deep, shuddering breath and forced myself to open my eyes. I couldn't tell if the world felt like it was spinning because I was light-headed or if I was light-headed because the world felt like it was spinning. I only knew it was taking a great deal of effort not to be sick.

I opened my mouth to ask the question no one should ever need the answer to, but I couldn't form the words. My mouth refused to cooperate, and my voice had suddenly dried up. I licked my lips, wincing at the faint stab of pain and grimacing at the taste of blood that still lingered before I tried again.

"Rory." A cracked, breathy whisper. "Did he—"

"Don't." Rory hissed, her face contorting into something tormented and unrecognizable.

"But I—"

"Ryan, please. Don't ask me. Please, don't ask me."

My heart felt like it was trapped inside of a car crusher. The cracking, splintering sensation I experienced after Rory's anguished plea reminded me of shattering glass. My lips twisted and trembled.

I looked back to Allison, who was watching me with a heart-wrenching expression. She'd obviously caught on to the subtle nuances of the situation long before I'd worked them out, and her countenance told me she was having just as much trouble with her feelings on the subject as I was.

I stood there, dumbfounded, feeling nothing save for the vaguest sensation of disbelief. I could hear the keening of the ambulance drawing closer, and I sort of registered the flashing red-and-blue lights that made Prospect Park feel like some sort of messed-up dance club, but both of those were at a remove.

"He—"

Allison shook her head at me in warning, her eyes telling me to shut the hell up. Her grip around Rory's shoulders tightened, and Rory leaned into her with a sigh, her eyes still closed, tears making languid tracks down her cheeks.

I frowned then as I tried to muscle my brain into working properly. I narrowed my eyes as I let them slowly drift from Rory's heartbroken expression to land on Walker's body lying on the grass in the distance. He was on his back, neck bent at an unnatural angle. The flashes of light that flickered around us allowed me to see a considerable amount of blood drying across his lips and chin, but despite that, his expression was almost peaceful.

I felt a new cracking sensation inside my chest, only this time it was more like the breaking of foot-thick ice than of glass, and a soul-searing fury overcame me. I ground my teeth together and balled my hands into tight fists as I shook. My nearly overpowering rage was looking for an outlet.

Scowling, I turned and started across the field, locking my gaze on Walker's unmoving body. If my glare could've started a fire, he wouldn't have required a funeral. He would've combusted on the spot. Not even ashes would've been left.

I clenched my right hand tight around the grip of the pistol I didn't remember drawing as I stalked ever closer. I was holding it so rigidly, I was sure I'd bear the grooved imprint of it on my palm for a long time to come. But I didn't care. It didn't matter. My entire world had narrowed down to a single point. Nothing would come between me and my vengeance.

"Rico," I heard Allison shout. She sounded panicked, but, fixated on my revenge, I didn't bother to turn around to see what the problem was. I might not have been able to undo what Walker had done to my sister, but seeing his brains splatter across the grass and his face disappear inside an unrecognizable pulp of mutilated flesh and bone would go a long way toward making me feel better about it.

"Whoa there." Rico stepped in front of me and placed his hands on my shoulders. "Slow down."

I used my free hand to knock one of his off me. "Get out of my way, Rico."

If my fury fazed Rico at all, he didn't show it. His face was the picture of calm. His fingertips encircled my biceps just above my elbows, and I glared at him murderously. He didn't appear to care. The age-old question of what happened when an unstoppable force meets an immovable object came immediately to mind.

"You can't do this, Ryan." He kept his voice low and even, shooting a quick, nervous glance around before capturing my eyes again.

His expression now was so earnest and concerned, I almost burst into tears. Now that he'd stalled my momentum, other emotions slipped between the cracks in my rage to begin the battle for dominance. Guess I wasn't as unstoppable as I'd thought.

"Rico, he...Rory..." I couldn't even bring myself to say it. I ground my teeth together in frustration.

Rico's eyebrows shot up as he took in the implication of my words. I could see the anger leech into his eyes once he'd finally worked out what I hadn't been able to tell him, but two heartbeats later, it was gone, and his face was once again a perfect mask. I would've smirked at him if I wasn't drowning in a whirlpool of emotions.

Rico slid his hands down my arms so they rested lightly on my wrists. I knew what he was doing, wanted to fight him even, but I wasn't sure I had the energy. A tremor ran through my entire body, and it took an effort to stay upright.

"Listen to me. You can't do this. I know you want to. Hell, I want to, but you need to stop and think. The momentary satisfaction you'll feel will not be worth the fallout."

I sighed, annoyed and exhausted. He was right. Of course he was. But that did nothing to quell the fire for retaliation burning a hole in the pit of my stomach. For a few long, tense moments, Rico and I just stood there and stared at one another. I was still teetering on the edge of a life-altering decision, and he appeared to be holding his breath, waiting to see what I'd do, positive I'd make the right choice.

"The squeeze isn't worth the juice?" The corners of my mouth tried to turn up as I tossed our oft-uttered adage at him.

His expression softened, and he managed a more convincing smile. "Exactly."

"Okay."

We stood there for another few moments before I felt the fingers of his left hand close around my right. He searched my eyes as though looking for permission, and when I nodded, he carefully eased the gun from my hand. Once he had it, he glanced around to see whether anyone was paying attention to us. Outside of Rory and Allison, nobody was.

"You were just coming to find me to give me your gun before you went to the hospital, understand?"

I nodded again and clenched and unclenched the fingers of my right hand a few times, trying to relieve the ache that'd settled there from holding the gun too tightly. "Of course I was. What else would I have been doing?"

"Good." He took a moment to unload the weapon before tucking it into the waistband of his pants. Then he shifted so he was standing next to me, and both of us were facing Walker. "You got your shots in. I know it wasn't quite what you wanted, but you made him bleed. That has to count for something."

"Not nearly enough," I said softly. I turned back to where Rory and Allison were watching us. Behind them, I could see the ambulance pulling off the path and onto the grass of the field. "Thanks, Rico."

"Anytime," he said.

Without looking at him, I squeezed his hand, hoping the gesture alone was enough to convey everything I couldn't say.

CHAPTER TWENTY-TWO

Rory was silent all the way to the hospital. We might have been sitting side by side on the edge of the gurney in the back of the ambulance, but between her refusal to speak and the haunted look in her eyes as she stared at the far side of the rig, I felt like she was somewhere else.

I'd thought—hoped? prayed?—that she'd snap out of it once the paramedics had escorted us into the ER and we had forms to fill out and questions to answer, but I was once again disappointed. She didn't appear invested in the check-in process, so I filled out her paperwork and answered the questions for her as best I could while trying to pretend I wasn't dying inside.

Fortunately, the agency was on a first-name basis with the head of the Trauma Department at the hospital, and someone had called ahead to let him know we were coming. He'd met us in the ER just as I was finishing our forms and had us escorted to a private room, away from prying eyes and the hustle and bustle of regular, day-to-day hospital life. I was grateful for that courtesy. I had no doubt the press would catch wind of this all too soon for my liking, and the last thing I needed was a dozen reporters asking questions.

Rory broke her self-imposed vow of silence just long enough to tell her treating physician exactly what dosage of medication she required—a request I was surprised he went along with—and then she lapsed back into it until the drugs kicked in and she drifted off to sleep.

Unable to stand being away from her after her ordeal, I crept out of my own bed and eased myself into hers. I took great care to be gentle with her as I arranged her limbs so the two of us could share the gurney as comfortably as possible. Once I had her head tucked under my chin and my arms draped protectively around her back, I slipped an earbud into my right ear and fired up the music app on my phone, hoping the songs would help lull me to sleep or would at least distract me so I wouldn't have to think too much.

No such luck. Since I had just a few cuts and some minor bruising, the doctor had given me only aspirin for my aches and pains. And aspirin wasn't strong enough to send me off to dreamland as easily as whatever cocktail Rory had prescribed herself, so I got to lie there and try to wrangle my traitorous thoughts.

My mind raced, navigating curves and corners with all the speed and precision of a spaceship going warp speed in a blockbuster sci-fi movie. The landscape of my thoughts was treacherous and seemingly without end, and I was unable to stay away from the chasm that was the litany of the ways Rory's current condition was my fault for more than a minute at a stretch. I hopped back and forth between anger and self-flagellation with all the skill and finesse of a politician flip-flopping on hot-button issues during a campaign. It was becoming something of a default setting for me now.

I allowed myself to wallow for an undetermined length of time. Recent events had taught me that fighting the impulse only led to tension and exhaustion. Better to give in and let myself splash around in the deep end of the emotional pool, even if only for a little while each day. Somehow, it seemed to speed up the healing process, if only a bit.

The key was to stop as soon as possible. Until someone somewhere perfected the science of time travel, I couldn't do anything to change the past, so floundering in guilt and self-loathing for too long was pointless. I needed to balance those periods with intervals of focusing on a solution.

Now, for example, after ruminating on everything I'd done wrong, everything I could've done better to avoid landing us here, and what a shitstorm my life was about to become because of it, I'd managed to drag myself out of the whirlpool of despair and self-reproach to deliberate on what came next. My life had been out of my own control for far too long. I needed to figure out a way to take it back.

"You're just like her." Rory's slurry voice broke into the whirlwind of my thoughts.

My heart leapt, thrilled that she'd spoken, even if I had no idea what the hell she was talking about, but I tried not to express any of my joy. I was afraid if I made a big deal about it, she'd lapse right back into her near-catatonic state. I licked my dry lips and attempted to project an air of casual confidence.

"Hey. You're awake. How are you feeling?" I winced against the pain in my throat and removed the earbud before running my fingers through her hair. After everything that'd happened, I just needed to touch her to make sure she really was safe. I suspected that'd be the case for some time to come.

"Mmm. M'okay. Hurts less."

"Yeah, well, you could've done the decent thing and had the docs give me something to knock me out, too," I croaked through the fire in my throat, my voice still scratchy.

She ignored my complaint, pulling back from her position tucked underneath my chin so she could look at me. Her gaze was glassy and unfocused. "I always wondered."

I eyed her curiously. "Always wondered what?"

"Why Mulan was your favorite. Used to think it was the gay thing. You know, because she's not your typical princess. Now I get it." She tried to smile at me, but the attempt failed. Whether that was because of the drugs she was on or a direct result of recent events, I couldn't be sure.

"What are you talking about? Where did that come from?"

"You were singing."

"I was?" Maybe that explained why the ache wasn't ebbing.

She closed her eyes and let her head flop down onto the pillow. "Mmm-hmmm. I like that song better. You were singing some '80s power-ballad stuff before." She wrinkled her nose in distaste. "Too sad."

I lifted the earbud back up so I could hear the song my phone was playing, the one I hadn't been consciously listening to. Sure enough, the last strains of "Reflections" were fading. "I'm sorry. I didn't realize I was doing it."

"'S okay. I like listening to you sing. Makes me forget. Almost." She took a deep breath and let it out in a heavy sigh.

My heart crumbled into dust, and I had to fight to contain my tears. Rory didn't need for me to break down. Of the two of us, she was the one who deserved to be allowed to disintegrate. I had to be strong enough so she'd feel like it was all right to do that. I cleared my throat as softly and gently as I could so as not to exacerbate my agony and wiped at my eyes hastily with the hand not trapped under Rory's body.

"You're just like her, you know."

"I'm just like who?" I asked, grimacing at the noticeable tremor in my voice.

Rory opened her eyes again, and even though it was evident she was having trouble focusing, she attempted to pin me with an irritated glare. "Mulan."

"I am, huh? And how's that?"

"You're tough like she is. And brave. You would've fought."

"What?" The words came out a horrified whisper, and the pile of dust that my heart had become blew away on the breath of her declaration, replaced by a cold emptiness.

Rory's eyes filled with tears now, and she looked away. Her hand came up to play with the neckline of the hospital scrub shirt I was wearing. "You would've fought him. You *did* fight him."

"Oh, Rory." I pulled her to me and tried not to lose it when she shuddered and let out a strangled sob. "It's okay."

Rory shook her head, and her hair tickled the underside of my chin. "No, it's not. It is definitely not okay."

If my heart hadn't already just broken, it would've shattered. I struggled with a response. "Maybe not right this second. But it will be."

"When?"

I closed my eyes, gave up my most recent fight, and let the tears gathering there fall. They slid down my cheeks and ended up in her hair. I wished I had an answer for her. "I don't know."

"You would've fought," she said again, her voice barely audible. "You wouldn't have let him…You would've fought."

I tightened my grip around her and struggled to keep from wailing. An all-consuming ache was replacing my cold, empty feeling. I was heavy with anguish and dread. I didn't know what I could possibly say to make her feel better. The notion that I could say nothing was making me even more miserable.

"Rory, he was bigger than you."

"So? That wouldn't have stopped you."

"Only because I'm too stubborn for my own good. The knife I saw at the park, he had that wherever he held you, right?"

Rory nodded and fisted her hand into the front of my shirt. "Held it to my throat. I was so scared."

A tremor racked my body. I'd seen the faint cuts on the skin of her neck and had already put two and two together, but to hear her actually say it... "You did the right thing, then. You did what you had to do to survive. There's no shame in that."

"Wouldn't have stopped you," she mumbled. "Knife, gun, bat. You wouldn't have cared."

"Maybe. Maybe not. In all likelihood, if it'd been me, I'd have gotten myself killed. And what's the point of that?"

Rory let out a sound that was half laugh, half sob. It was a painful, strangled sort of sound, and it almost killed me to hear it. "At least you would have died fighting instead of just taking it."

"You can't beat yourself up over this." But even before the words were out of my mouth, I knew how foolish they sounded, how devoid of any sort of comfort.

Rory ignored me. "How am I supposed to live with myself? How can I ever look at myself in the mirror again knowing that I just lay there, shaking like a leaf as he...over and over and over..."

I clenched my jaw to stop the sobs clamoring up the back of my throat, dying to burst free. They were clawing and scraping, but I held them back because I knew that once I started crying, I wouldn't be able to stop. And I was afraid if I lost it now, it would somehow, in Rory's mind, reaffirm for her that everything she was obviously convinced of was true.

"So fight now," I said, flashing back to the thoughts I'd been mired in before she'd woken up and drawing all the expected parallels between her situation and mine.

Rory stilled, and she said nothing for a long moment. "What?"

"Fight now."

"How? He's dead. Nothing can undo what he did to me. How can I possibly fight now?"

I deliberated how to phrase this. "You went through a terrible ordeal that I can't even begin to understand. Walker took something from you when he...when he did that to you." Somehow I couldn't say the actual words, and I hoped my inability wasn't undermining my entire point. "He took something precious and valuable, but it's up to you now. Do you want to let him keep it, or do you want to take it back?"

Rory was quiet for a bit. I wasn't sure whether she was thinking about what I'd said or had drifted back to sleep. Finally, after an impossibly long time, she spoke. "I don't know how."

I buried my face in her hair and dropped a gentle kiss onto the crown of her head. "You don't have to figure that part out right now. We can make it up as we go. You just have to decide that you want to. Someday."

Rory nodded. "See? Just like Mulan."

I smiled sadly. It must have escaped her notice that Mulan had been the hero in her tale, whereas I was just a total failure in mine. I'd failed to protect her. I'd let her down. The lump in my throat felt both suffocating and painful. "Sure."

"You'll help me?" She sounded exhausted, and a jaw-cracking yawn punctuated her question.

"Of course."

"Good." She snuggled further into my embrace, and I held her as she drifted back to sleep.

My lips quivered, and I sniffled as I slipped the earbud back into my ear. I closed my eyes, too, hoping to drift off to sleep as well. Instead, I spent the next who knows how long trying to avoid being sucked back into my earlier unpleasant thoughts. I'd already used my allotted wallowing time for the moment and wanted to focus on something a little more empowering. Unfortunately, that was easier to say than to do. The skirmish between what I wanted to dwell on and what I actually was dwelling on was long and bloody, and I appeared to be on the losing end.

The why of the whole thing overwhelmed me, and the *why* questions never ended. Why had Walker snapped? Why had Bellevue let him out in the first place? Why hadn't we been notified that he'd been released? Why hadn't we assigned someone to monitor him? Why hadn't I seen this coming? All of those *why* questions tempted me to start playing the "if only" game, and that would only be counterproductive. I sighed.

"How's she doing?" Allison's soft voice jostled my awareness.

I allowed my eyes to drift open and pulled the earbud back out of my ear so I could concentrate on the conversation. I was glad for the distraction. Struggling not to play the "if only" game had just made me edgy. I could use a break from all my introspection.

"As well as can be expected, I suppose." I tried to duck my head so I could look into Rory's sleeping face, but with her nestled against me, I couldn't see anything. Disappointed, I shifted my gaze so I could meet Allison's eyes.

She, too, was looking at Rory, her expression such a mixture of sadness and frustration it pained me to see it. "She'll be okay."

"Eventually, yeah. She will be."

"You, on the other hand—"

"Me, what?"

"You just had to go and prove me wrong, didn't you?" Allison's voice was low, but that did nothing to disguise her annoyance.

"Prove you wrong about what?"

"The last time we were in this position, after you got shot, do you remember what I told you?" She pulled up a chair on the opposite side of the bed, facing me, and sat down. Her eyes took in Rory's still form cradled in my arms, and her expression softened, if only slightly.

"Refresh my memory. You said a lot of things, but even with a hundred guesses, I bet I still can't come up with whichever one you're talking about."

The skin around Allison's eyes tightened for an instant. "I told you I'd never been as terrified as I was the instant I heard you'd been shot."

"Oh. That. Okay." I still wasn't sure where she was going with this.

Allison obviously picked up on my cluelessness and rolled her eyes in fond exasperation. "And then you had to get into an all-out brawl with a man twice your size. Tell me. Do you enjoy testing my limits, or do you just have a death wish?"

I frowned. "Neither. What the hell was I supposed to do?"

"Shoot him." Her answer was immediate and sure. The cold gleam in her eyes told me she would've had no qualms if she'd been in my position.

"You know I couldn't have done that. Not without warning him first. That's what we're taught. And I couldn't take the chance that Rory would end up hurt because I gave him that warning."

"You could've shot him without the warning. You could have articulated it."

"Maybe. Maybe not. It doesn't really matter now, does it?"

"Definitely. There's no question."

"Definitely it matters? Or I definitely could have articulated it?"

"Either. Both. Pick one."

"If I'd shot him without warning, an attorney would've hammered me."

Allison shrugged. "So what?"

"So, I didn't want to be on the receiving end of an inquisition. Besides, I don't know if I would've been able to live with myself." Our conversation had been soft to begin with so as not to wake Rory, but my voice dropped even lower with that admission.

Allison appeared angry, though at what exactly, I wasn't sure. "And if you'd known what he'd done to her? If you'd known that he forced himself on her, would you have done it then? Would you have been able to live with yourself?"

I sighed, then froze as Rory stirred, shifted, and then nestled herself further into my arms. Once her breathing had evened back out, I gave Allison's question some thought. Fat lot of good that did. I had no idea what the correct answer was. Most of me wanted to say yes, but a tiny part of me wasn't positive.

"I don't know. I likely would've done it, yes. Whether I'd have been able to live with myself after is another matter. I'm glad I don't have to find out."

"Yes. It's fantastic." Allison's words were caustic enough to burn.

I winced. "What's wrong? You seem upset."

"I do, huh? Well, look at you, using your investigative skills to crack the case."

Now I frowned. I tried to keep my words soft, but it was tough. "What's that supposed to mean?"

Allison's countenance was dark, and she was clearly struggling with something. Something big. I tried to ignore the anxiety pooling in the pit of my stomach as I watched the emotions swim beneath her eyes.

"I am so furious with you," she said, her words low and even. Apparently it'd taken a great deal of effort to make them that way. But also a definite amount of affection colored her expression and took some of the sting out of the words.

"You're what?"

"You could've been killed, Ryan. You reacted instead of acted. You didn't think."

"No, actually, I did think. I thought about how whatever else Walker had done, he was mentally ill and therefore not completely responsible for his actions. I thought about how someone in the grip of paranoid schizophrenia deserved treatment, not to be shot in the back. And I thought about getting sued later if I did shoot him. Believe it or not, a lot of things went on inside my head."

"You didn't have to shoot to kill. You could've hit him in the leg or something. It would've stopped him, surprised him long enough for you to get the upper hand."

I shook my head. "I couldn't have made that shot."

Allison huffed, exasperated. "I've seen you shoot, remember? The day we met, you put twenty-five rounds into a space the size of a golf ball at twenty-five yards in a span of less than twenty seconds, including a reload. And that must have been an off day for you because I've seen you put up much smaller groupings. You're amazing on the line. I've never seen anything like it. You could've made that shot with your eyes closed."

"Yes, I'm good *on the line*. I couldn't have made shots like that today."

Allison sat back in her chair, crossed her legs, and folded her arms across her chest. She pinned me with a dark glare. "Yes, you could have."

"Allison, you've seen me shoot under range conditions. It's slow and controlled, with no stress. That makes it easy to aim, easy to hit the target where I want to hit it. But today...Today, too much else was going on, too many other factors to consider. I'd been running, and I was edgy about my sister. Then I saw the knife, and Rory and Hurricane were right there. Plus, we were in the middle of a park. Other people were around. If I'd tried for that shot and missed, I could've hit any one of them, could've killed them. Rory, Hurricane, some mother out for a jog. God, some kid playing Frisbee. I just…I couldn't take that chance."

Allison's ire faltered. "You really thought about all that?"

I nodded and realized I did have an answer to her earlier question. "Yes. And knowing everything that happened afterward, I still would've done exactly what I did."

Allison pursed her lips and stared off into space as she obviously considered my point. I continued to draw light patterns on Rory's back with my fingertips and play with the ends of her hair while I waited for Allison to decide what to say next.

"Do you know how long your fight with him went on?" she asked me.

I shrugged, once again confused by her abrupt conversational segue. "I dunno. Ten years? It sure as hell felt like forever."

"A little over a minute."

"Huh. Seemed like a lot longer."

Allison regarded me solemnly. "From the time he got on top of you to the time you put an end to it, it was a little over a minute."

"How do you know that? Was someone counting?"

"Your mike was keyed the entire time, so we could hear everything. And the radio transmissions are time-stamped at the duty desk. You know that."

"And you called them to ask?"

Allison nodded. "I did. Because I wanted to be able to tell you exactly how close you came to dying."

Guilt burst inside my chest the way a chocolate-covered cherry spurts in your mouth when you bite into it, only the taste lingering on my tongue now was dark and rancid, like spoiled meat. "I'm sorry I put you through that. You have to know I didn't intend to."

Allison inclined her head in a gesture that could've meant I was forgiven, or it could've meant absolutely nothing. She was silent for a time.

"It wasn't completely your fault," she said eventually. Her voice was hard, her tone bitter.

"What do you mean?"

Her expression was once again dark. I could tell she was still angry. I just wasn't sure at whom. "Since I was so far away, I was one of the last agents to reach you. Or should I say to get to where you were."

"Okay."

"But I shouldn't have been the first one to move to help you."

"Sweetheart, I have no idea what you're talking about."

"You know our motto: minimum to the problem, maximum to the protectee."

I nodded. Of course I knew it. I'd thought about it earlier today in the middle of everything. "That's how it should be."

Allison made a face. "That's what happened today, Ryan. That's why you almost died. Everyone else had moved to either Hurricane or to Rory. No one else on set moved to help you. No one was even looking at you. No one. It took me almost a full minute to even reach a point where I could see you, let alone get to you, and I was the only one who even thought about helping you."

Ah. Now I understood why she was so upset. I might've even understood why she was taking her frustration out on me instead of blasting the other guys who'd been there. Because how would it have looked if she'd gone off on them for doing their job and letting me do mine? But she obviously needed to yell at someone. I tried not to smile at her protectiveness, but it did such wonderful things to my insides, it was hard not to let it show.

"Allison, they did what they had to do to keep Rory and Hurricane safe."

"Someone should've kept *you* safe." She looked down at her hands, and her voice dropped to a whisper. "*I* should've kept you safe."

Now I did smile. "Come here."

Allison shook her head. She was adorable when she was petulant. My smile grew wider.

"Allison, please."

After a long moment of hesitation and much obvious reluctance on her part, Allison rose and made her way around the hospital gurney so she stood behind me. As carefully as possible, I lifted my arm off my sleeping sister and rolled onto my back so I could look my girlfriend in the eye. Or try to anyway. She wasn't making it easy, what with her fixating on the railing that framed the bed.

I reached out to her, wordlessly asking for her hand. She took a moment before granting my request. I ran the pad of my thumb over the back of her hand, allowing myself a few seconds to marvel at its softness.

"Allison, you have to let it go."

Allison's head snapped up, and her eyes locked onto me. "You almost died, and not one of your coworkers moved to stop it. How the hell can you be so calm?"

"Maybe I'm used to it by this time," I joked.

"That's not funny."

"No. You're right. It isn't. But you have to cut them some slack. It wasn't their fault. With everything else going on, can you blame them for focusing on Hurricane and Rory?"

"Yes."

I laughed and tried not to wince, not to let her see how much I was hurting. "Do you remember the first operation you and I went on together? Right before you left, when I was still in Credit Cards?"

Allison cocked her head to the side and favored me with an expression two parts curious, one part wary. "Vaguely."

"It was a counterfeit buy-bust. You and I were there only to provide additional manpower support."

"I remember."

"Do you remember how when it came time to do the takedown, everyone ran to arrest the suspects?"

Allison's eyes flooded with realization. "And you were the only one of us who even thought to go to the undercover."

I nodded. "Yes. And only because I remembered them making that particular point to us in training because we'd botched it on one of our practice scenarios. If no one had gone to the UC, it would've looked really bad. He would've gotten burned, and with that group, he could've been killed."

"This isn't the same thing." Allison tried to argue her point, but we both knew her protests were weak.

"It's exactly the same thing. Everyone gets tunnel vision during these types of operations. It sucks sometimes, but it happens." I squeezed her hand. "And I'm fine."

"This time," Allison muttered bitterly.

I tugged on her hand to pull her closer, and when she complied,

I crooked my finger at her to get her to lean down. She rolled her eyes and let out an exaggerated sigh but did as I asked. When she was within reach, I stretched up so I could rest my palm against her cheek.

A soft knock on the door to the room interrupted our moment, and Allison and I both looked to it as though that action alone would clue us in as to who was on the other side. When it didn't, I glanced back at Allison. "Can you get that?"

"Sure." Allison opened the door and then stepped out of the way so someone could enter. It was Dr. Wexler, the head of the Trauma Department. He appeared a bit tired but otherwise okay. What was he even doing here so late?

"Agent O'Connor." His eyes darted from me to Allison and back again. "May I have a word with you in private?"

The question made me nervous, and I swallowed. "Uh, that's not necessary. We can talk here."

Dr. Wexler hesitated, looking like he was trying to decide whether to push the issue. "I wanted to talk to you about getting an HIV test."

I squinted at him as I tried to figure out where he was going with this. "Okay."

"You have a split lip, some cuts on the insides of your cheeks, and several other small abrasions on other parts of your body, and you came in here with a fair amount of blood on you that I assume wasn't yours."

"Yeah. I did."

"You need to make sure you get tested."

"Okay. I will."

"I'm absolutely serious about this. I know how you agents are when it comes to medical advice, and this isn't something you can blow off. You have to get this done."

My heart sank and hardened into an icy ball that was melting in the vicinity of my stomach. "Are...Are you saying Walker was HIV positive?"

Dr. Wexler took a step closer to me and fixed with a pointed stare. "I should have no way of knowing that. Besides, HIPAA laws would prevent me from disclosing that information even if I had somehow managed to get it."

I bit my lower lip and shifted my attention to the floor in the corner of the room so I could work this out. His words echoed in my head over and over again as the feelings they stirred up sloshed around inside me like water inside a bucket when you're running. They played through several times before I caught on. He'd said he *should* have no way of knowing, not that he didn't know. I inhaled sharply. My eyes snapped back up to meet his.

"You need to make sure you get tested," he said again. "You *both* need to get tested. Do you understand what I'm saying?"

I nodded, which appeared to be the only way I could convey to him that I comprehended. Dear God. Was he serious? As if the nightmare of what Walker did to Rory weren't enough, now she might have to live with a constant reminder? My stomach shuddered, and I glanced around for the bedpan in case I got sick.

"Do you want me to tell her when she wakes up?"

"Huh?" I shifted my attention to Rory then and watched her for a long moment, my mind a sea of turbulent thoughts. How was I going to break this to her? She really should hear it from me. Shit. How would she react? My chest was so heavy.

After a moment, I realized the doctor was waiting for an answer. I blinked, cleared my throat, and looked back at him, shaking my head. "No," I said, my voice barely louder than a whisper. "I'll tell her."

His expression softened, and he reached into the pocket of his white lab coat and retrieved a card. He handed it to me, and I took it with trembling fingers.

"My direct contact info is on there. Call me when you're ready. I'll do the test myself."

My ears were ringing. "Thanks," I whispered.

Dr. Wexler favored me with one last sympathetic look before he turned and left. Allison and I drifted in silence for a while.

"Did you know?" Allison asked.

I shook my head. "No. I didn't. I mean, he told me he did drugs, and we talked about which ones he used, but I never thought…It— it didn't really impact us because we almost never touched him and certainly not when he was bleeding, so why would it even occur to me to…" I looked to her helplessly as it hit me that not realizing he had the capacity for such calculated violence wasn't my only colossal failure today. "I should've asked."

"Don't beat yourself up. It obviously didn't occur to anyone else to ask either."

I shook my head again and allowed my eyes to drift around the room. "I should've asked."

"Would you have done anything different tonight if you'd known?"

That was the second time since her arrival that she'd asked me that, and I had the same response as before. "Probably not."

"Then does it really make a difference?"

"I don't know," I said. "But somehow it feels like it does."

CHAPTER TWENTY-THREE

Since I wasn't really all that hurt, and the doctors couldn't do much to treat my injuries except give me some Tylenol, I was released from the hospital only a few hours after I arrived. The doctors had planned to keep Rory overnight for observation—though whether that'd been their idea or hers, I wasn't certain—and I'd just decided I'd stay with her when Allison informed me of an after-action meeting at NYFO. As annoyed as I was that they were planning to do this at midnight, there didn't appear to be anything I could do about it.

The ride over to the field office was eerily quiet. Although Allison looked at me several times and opened her mouth as though she were about to speak, she appeared to be having trouble coming up with the right words. I, on the other hand, simply didn't feel like talking.

I knew that nowadays people with HIV lived full, normal lives, and I could do the same. I also knew perhaps I hadn't even contracted the virus, and all my fretting would be for nothing. That logic didn't stop the emotional NASCAR race I was engaged in, though.

We arrived last, and every head in the room turned to stare at us as we walked into the room. It was like something out of an old 80s movie. I almost wished a record scratch had announced our arrival. That, at least, would've explained the unusual amount of interest we'd garnered.

I took a deep breath and pressed my hands together over my abdomen, trying—and failing—to quiet the angry swirling in there. I looked for an empty seat. During my search, my gaze fell on Meaghan, and I blinked, surprised. I had no idea what she was doing there.

Meaghan caught sight of me about a second after I'd noticed her, and she looked relieved to see me, but once she spied Allison entering the conference room after me, her expression grew cold. Meaghan still hadn't forgiven Allison for the way she'd broken my heart years ago, and she clearly didn't intend to even pretend to hide her grudge. She flashed me a tight smile, gave Allison what we regular field agents had dubbed "the PPD nod," and turned to head toward the front of the room where the podium held an open laptop. I would've smiled at her overprotectiveness if I weren't so wrapped up in my own head space.

Allison and I chose seats on the edge of the room and sat down. She reached over to take my hand in hers, and I involuntarily flinched. She shot me a wounded look before she clenched her hands into fists on the tops of her thighs.

I let out a tiny huff and closed my eyes. I hadn't meant to hurt her. I just wasn't comfortable with her touching me. Not when the HIV virus might be ravaging the cells of my body even as we sat here. That was a foolish thought. She could hold my hand, whether I had it or not, but I was still having a hard time convincing myself that it really was okay.

My dad's voice broke into my musings. "Okay. Let's get started."

The low hum of voices that'd permeated the room tapered off. I opened my eyes and focused all my attention on the front of the room. Dad was standing next to Meaghan looking tired. Had he had a chance to call Mom to let her know that Rory was okay? Maybe Mom could go to the hospital to keep her company. I was reaching for my phone to text her when Dad spoke again.

"This is a preliminary meeting to disseminate some additional information necessary to complete the follow-up investigation. The actual after-action review of the operation itself will take place sometime next week. I'll contact everyone via email with the specifics once I have something scheduled.

"In the meantime, Special Agent Meaghan Bates from the Protective Intelligence Squad will bring everyone up to speed on what's been going on here at the office. Agent Bates."

Dad stepped aside and took a seat at the head of the table, swiveling his chair so his back was to the rest of us and his attention was fixed on Meaghan. She nodded at him politely.

"Thank you, SAIC Flannigan. I want to thank all of you for coming on such short notice. I promise this will be brief. We've all had a long day, and the sooner we can get this over with and leave, the better for everyone."

Meaghan looked to the other end of the room. The lights in the room dimmed, and a PowerPoint presentation lit up the screen that covered the majority of the front wall. I tried to suppress a groan of frustration, but I must not have been very successful because several people turned to look at me, and Allison slapped my arm with the back of her hand. I grumbled and folded my arms across my chest like a scolded child.

Meaghan stepped closer to the screen so she was standing just to one side of it. Her expression was difficult to read in the semidarkness. I slouched in my chair so I could rest the edge of my jaw against the heel of my right hand and allowed my eyes to glaze over.

"While you were all out conducting the operation, several of us were back here tying up some loose ends.

"According to interviews agents of this office had with his doctors, Adam Royce Walker was released from the hospital six days ago. They had no explanation for why we weren't notified, although examination of his intake file at the psych ward did reveal that Agent O'Connor submitted the necessary paperwork to request that we would be. They admitted that they dropped the ball on that score."

Meaghan pushed the button on the remote she held, and the slide changed from the usual PowerPoint presentation cover slide. Now we were all looking at several columns of numbers that were way too small for me to be able to read from where I was sitting.

"This is the cell-site history for Walker's phone for the past six days." Meaghan clicked her remote again, and a map covered with dozens of red dots replaced the columns. The dots marked a route of some kind, but with that much of a concentration, it was tough to tell exactly where it led. The path between a few main points was obvious enough, but I just couldn't decipher what those points were. Another click and the majority of the extraneous dots disappeared, leaving spots centered around two main areas. The slide changed again and this time was zoomed in to one of the two locations.

"This is a map of the area immediately surrounding the field office," Meaghan said. After her words, the office's exact location was circled. "As you can see, Walker spent a great deal of time in the vicinity over the past few days. We believe he was here trying to locate Agent

O'Connor. This is a logical explanation. He would've been unaware that, due to her assignment to the JTTF, she didn't normally work out of this office. He also would've been unaware that she was on light duty until yesterday and technically should not have been reporting to the office at all."

The map blinked off, replaced by a grainy still photo of a street. I squinted at it as I tried to figure out exactly where it was in relation to the office. It looked familiar, but I still couldn't put my finger on it. I relaxed my gaze and sat back in the chair, tiredly rubbing my eyes.

"Once we realized Walker had been casing the office," Meaghan said, "we canvased area businesses to determine if any of them had video footage that would help us figure out exactly what happened with Walker and Dr. O'Connor."

Meaghan gave the remote in her hand a series of clicks to display several still shots of the streets around the office. When she finally reached the one she wanted, she stopped. A little red dot appeared on the screen, indicating an area of particular interest.

"This is Red Hook Place, right around the corner from the office. It's tough to see clearly in this picture, but here"—the red dot moved in a circular motion—"parked across the front of this loading dock is a nondescript white panel van. According to the guys who work in this building, it had been sitting there for the majority of the day. They assumed it was there for some sort of delivery and didn't pay any attention to it."

The screen changed again to display a different angle of the same street. The van was a little easier to spot in this one. It was sitting facing the flow of traffic, half tucked into the loading-dock alcove. I could see why someone would assume the van was there for a delivery. It looked exactly like the sort of van that did pickups and drop-offs. I wondered whether Walker had done that on purpose or if it'd been a coincidence. I was put out that I wouldn't get to ask him. I didn't like not knowing things.

"The van was a rental. We tracked down the rental company and confirmed that Walker rented it himself and paid for it with his own credit card. He didn't take any steps to conceal his identity from the rental company, and the employee who handled the transaction didn't recall anything off about him."

The slide changed again to show a slightly different angle of the same street. A visible time stamp was shown in the lower right hand corner of the frame. I leaned forward to rest my forearms on my knees and squinted at the picture.

"This is video footage from the camera at the bank located on the corner of the block." Meaghan took a deep breath, and for a moment it looked like she wanted to say something else, but she opted for clicking the remote and starting the video instead. I might've been more curious about what she wasn't saying if my attention hadn't been so thoroughly captured.

The video showed several long moments of people walking back and forth across the end of the street while the panel van sat ominously in the foreground. My heart fluttered, and I knew what was coming next. I sat back up and wrapped my hands around the arms of the chair and squeezed.

Sure enough, after another minute, Rory came into view. Only instead of walking across the street and taking the adjacent sidewalk to continue down Boerum Place with everybody else, she followed Red Hook Place into the faux alley where almost no one ever walks because there really isn't anything down there except a couple of loading docks. She ducked her head as she searched through her purse for something, meaning she wasn't in tune with her surroundings.

My stomach rolled, and I drew in a hitching breath as she came up alongside the back bumper of the panel van. I even started a little when Walker jumped out of the driver's seat, though I'd suspected he would. After that, it was over pretty quickly. Rory hadn't even looked up when Walker leapt out of the vehicle. It wasn't until he'd gotten behind her and put his hand over her mouth that she'd even noticed him.

The tape was too grainy for me to see her expression very well, but I could tell she struggled for just a few seconds before Walker wrenched open the side door to the van and shoved her in, only to disappear right behind her. The van rocked back and forth several times before becoming still. I put my hand over my mouth and clenched my jaw so tight my molars ached. I had to keep telling myself that it was okay, that Rory was safe now, and that Walker was dead, but that still didn't do as much to dampen my burgeoning fury as I'd hoped.

The tape continued to run for several agonizingly long seconds before Walker hopped out of the side of the van, shut the door behind him, looked around a bit, and then got back into the driver's seat. Then the van lurched forward and took off down the street. We were able to watch it until it made a right on Willoughby. The video paused on a shot of the taillight of the van disappearing around the corner, and the lights in the room came back on. I blinked and shifted in my seat, restless and angry and miserable all at once.

Meaghan cleared her throat and clicked the remote in her hand so the PowerPoint presentation went off. The screen behind her was now dark, and she took her time setting the remote on the edge of the podium. I knew her well enough to know that she was stalling.

"As you can see, Dr. O'Connor was taken off the street in broad daylight so quickly that no one in the area appeared to notice her abduction. We have a team of agents searching the contents of the apartment Walker held her in as we speak. At this time, and unless we find evidence to the contrary, we have to treat the abduction as a spur-of-the-moment impulse on Walker's part—a crime of opportunity, if you will—and not something he planned beforehand."

Meaghan met my eyes as she said that, her expression apologetic. I scowled and looked away, irate and a little sick to my stomach. What she was saying made sense, I supposed. Even though it'd been obvious Walker had been casing the office, we didn't have a concrete explanation as to why. And did it even matter at this point whether his actions were premeditated? We wouldn't be able to prosecute him for them. But I was still having a hard time wrapping my head around what I perceived to be the agency's laissez-faire attitude regarding the whole thing or really everything when it came to me of late. The sting of betrayal was sharp enough to draw blood.

"Also, after reviewing Walker's case file and examining his history, we found no evidence that Walker was capable of such acts as he committed today, and this agency concurs that we could have done nothing to prevent this. We're trying to keep this out of the news, but should the press call looking for a statement, everyone should remember that the Secret Service has a one-voice policy, and that voice is not yours. You can refer them to the front office, to SAIC Flannigan, who will explain our findings."

Ouch. Talk about a slap to the face. It was too much, I decided suddenly, and I was tired of it. No one had made any sort of condemning statement regarding Lucia's death or Mark's involvement in the events that'd led us there. Even when the press had called headquarters looking for an explanation, all they'd gotten was "no comment." And now no one seemed inclined to entertain the notion that what'd happened to Rory might've somehow been our fault because we hadn't been doing our jobs thoroughly enough in the past few weeks to have seen this coming. The attitude of the entire agency felt like a big game of deny, minimize, counter-accuse to me, and I was done. My patience had snapped.

Meaghan was saying something else to the group, but I wasn't listening anymore. Whatever it was, I doubted I wanted to know. It'd very likely only make me even more upset, and I wasn't in the mood to shoulder one more emotional burden. Not tonight. I just needed some time to regain my footing, to get back onto even ground. Then, maybe, I'd be able to brush off all the agency's official findings and dodging of responsibility as if it didn't bother me.

The room suddenly filled with bright light and the scraping, shuffling sounds of people moving around, and I looked up, surprised to see that everyone was filing out into the hallway. Apparently we were done. I remained in my chair, not moving as everyone made their way to the door. Meaghan tried to catch my eye as she went but dropped her head at my dark glare. It took a few more minutes, but eventually the conference room was empty save for me, Allison, and my father.

I shifted my attention to my dad, who'd swiveled his chair around so he could face me, and we engaged in a little standoff. A part of me knew this wasn't his fault. He got his marching orders from headquarters, and he couldn't do anything about them. But in this moment, he wasn't the man who'd raised me since I was a toddler. He wasn't the man who'd given my mother a reason to live after my father and older sister had died. He was simply a company man, and I was furious with him. Somehow it felt like he'd chosen between the agency and us, and I didn't like the choice he'd made.

Allison slowly rose and stood next to me for a long moment. From what I could see of her out of the corner of my eye, she appeared uncertain what to do next. After a moment of hesitation, she gave my shoulder a gentle squeeze and left the room, quietly closing the door behind her.

The atmosphere in the room was thick and suffocating. I was having a hard time drawing breath, and I was so angry, I was shaking. That my father was the epitome of calm only served to make me angrier. I didn't know how he could appear so unaffected, but I longed to provoke a reaction out of him, even if it was only to ensure that someone else was as miserable as I was.

"You're upset," Dad said finally. He laced his fingers together on the top of the table and watched me placidly. This was a departure from the man who'd watched Mark's interrogation with me a few weeks ago. Then, I'd been the calm one, and he'd been incredulous at my attitude. Funny how things could change so quickly.

"Little bit."

"Rory's going to be fine."

Perhaps he didn't know about everything she'd endured while she'd been in Walker's clutches. I couldn't imagine him being this collected if he did, and a part of me yearned to tell him. I wanted to see the look on his face when he confronted the atrocities Walker had committed, but I couldn't bring myself to utter the words. More for Rory than for him. She might not have wanted him to know, and it was her story to tell, not mine. I bit the inside of my cheek so hard I tasted blood. Then I scolded myself for adding to my superficial injuries and eased off.

"That's hardly the point," I said.

"Then what is the point?"

"Do you really not know?"

"Enlighten me."

"How the hell can you stand it?" I blurted out. "How can you be so calm? Doesn't it bother you that they're acting like none of this matters? Don't you care that they're trying to avoid acknowledging that anything even happened?"

Dad raised his eyebrows. "What's to be gained by them acknowledging it?"

"What's to be gained by them not?"

"You know the climate we're operating in right now. The Service has endured far too many scandals of late. We can't afford another one. Especially not one of this magnitude. The American people have almost completely lost faith in our abilities to accomplish our mission. We'd never recover if we acknowledged this one."

I felt like my internal organs were being squeezed and yet trying to force their way out of my body by way of my skin at the same time. My fury was crushing and seemed to literally be gathering in every single cell of my body. I couldn't clench my muscles hard enough. "I never realized you cared so much about the reputation of the agency."

Dad frowned. "I think you're taking this far too personally."

My anger spiked, and I got to my feet and approached the table. "And I don't think you're taking it personally enough."

"Ryan, the agency has a reputation to maintain and interests that are far wider reaching than the experiences of one agent."

I was floored. "One agent? Oh, you mean me. Because all of a sudden none of this counts as your experience, apparently."

"Not to headquarters it doesn't, no."

"And you've clearly never bothered to tell them, have you?"

For a moment, Dad appeared uncomfortable. But then he composed himself, and his expression was impassive once more. "We agreed when you took this job that no one could know about our relationship, and no one does. How would it look if I told everyone now? Do you have any idea the repercussions that could have? You need to think, Ryan. Act instead of react."

That was the second time in the space of a few hours someone had said that to me, and I don't think he could've made a worse word choice unless he'd found a way to blame my current mood on my period. "Would it make a difference, do you think? If they knew how recent events had impacted a SAIC instead of an agent, do you think they'd acknowledge their culpability then?"

"What's that supposed to mean?"

"It means that when you make a mistake you should admit it. They drilled that into us from day one. 'If you mess up, 'fess up.' Only that doesn't apply to them, apparently." The words came out sounding as bitter as they tasted.

"I don't know what you want from me, Ryan."

"I want you to act like you care! I want you to act like this bothers you. I don't understand how you could be so pissed off at Mark when you found out what he did, but you can be so disinterested in the agency pretending it never even happened. I don't understand how you can just be okay with them acting like everything is business as usual."

"What the hell should they do?"

"Apologize, for one thing. They could express some sympathy for Lucia's family's loss at the hands of one of their agents. That would be the polite thing to do."

"Apologize for what? It isn't the agency's fault Mark did what he did."

"I'm not saying it was their fault. I'm saying he was in a position of power and responsibility, and he abused it. They could at least admit it happened instead of not commenting on it."

"I don't see the point. It wouldn't change anything. You'd still have bullet holes in you—"

"And Lucia would still be dead," I finished for him, my tone hard and rancorous.

"Ryan, I—"

I held up a hand. Every single neuron and nerve ending inside me suddenly felt fried. I was done. Done with this conversation. Done with being angry. Done with this agency. Done with everything.

"No, you know what? You're right. It doesn't matter. None of it matters. Lucia didn't matter. Rory doesn't matter. And I don't matter. So, here. I can go *not* matter somewhere else. Somewhere where at least people who are close to me won't die or get—" I stopped myself just shy of blurting out what'd happened to Rory and shook my head.

My badge was hanging on a thin chain around my neck. I looped it up over my head and slid it across the table to him. He caught it in his palm and looked at it for a second, obviously confused, before tipping his head back up to meet my eyes. "What the hell are you doing?"

"What does it look like I'm doing? I'm quitting. It's not worth it. Not anymore."

I didn't give him time to respond. I wasn't the least bit interested in what he might've had to say. Not then. Maybe not ever. I simply turned and walked out, leaving him to call after me as I left.

Inanely, after my impromptu declaration, I felt lighter than I had in weeks. I smiled at Allison as I approached her in the lobby and kept walking toward the elevator. She tossed the magazine she'd been thumbing through back onto the coffee table in the waiting area and jumped up out of her chair so she could follow me. I pushed the elevator call button and hooked my thumbs into the pockets of my purloined scrub pants as I waited.

Allison eyed me warily. Her eyes dropped to my chest, which was now noticeably badge-less, and her eyebrows flew up. "What happened?"

I took a long, slow, deep breath, reveling in my feeling of elation.

My lips started to pull up in another smile. My decision may have been impulsive, but in that moment, it felt right. The elevator dinged, and I stepped on. I leaned against the back wall and waited for her to join me, marveling that it was likely the last time I'd be here.

"What happened?" she asked again as she settled next to me in the car.

I wasn't altogether sure how to go about explaining everything that'd led me to this moment or whether I even had to. Maybe that didn't matter either. Maybe all that mattered was me and her and what I was feeling right now, which was unbelievably free.

I grinned at her and pushed my hair back out of my eyes, enjoying the tingling feeling spreading throughout my body. A laugh was bubbling up inside me, and for a split second, I thought about holding it back but couldn't come up with a good justification for keeping it in. So I let it roll out. After so much anger and pain, it felt fantastic to laugh like that, even if it was for no reason I could articulate.

During the entire ride down to the ground level I laughed, and the entire ride down Allison looked at me like I'd lost my mind. Tears welled up in my eyes, and my sides started to hurt, but still I laughed, and still she watched.

When we reached the lobby, my guffaws subsided until they were tiny chuckles as we made our way out onto the street together. Allison didn't say anything until our feet hit the sidewalk. Then she put a hand on my arm to stop me before I could hail a taxi.

I turned to face her and studied her serious expression, smiling at how beautiful she was. I really wanted to kiss her, but the fear that I might soon register as HIV positive made me pause. I might've been ready to upend my own life on a whim, but I wasn't prepared to do it to somebody else. I settled for smiling at her.

"What?" I asked when she didn't speak.

"Are you okay?"

There was more to her question than her words suggested, but I wasn't in the mood to get into a conversation at the moment. I needed to get back to the hospital, and I needed to call my mom. Later, we could delve into everything her tone suggested she wanted to know. For now, I went with the simplest and most accurate answer I could think of.

"I'm perfect."

About the Author

Kara A. McLeod is a badass by day and a smart-ass by night. Or maybe it's the other way around. Or quite possibly neither. A Jersey girl at heart, "Mac" is an intrepid wanderer who goes wherever the wind takes her. A former Secret Service agent who decided she wanted more out of life than standing in a stairwell and losing an entire month every year to the United Nations General Assembly, she currently resides in Colorado and is still searching hither and yon for the meaning of life, the nearest Comic Con, and the best deal on a flight to London.

If anyone has any leads on any of the above, she can be contacted at kara.a.mcleod@gmail.com.

Books Available From Bold Strokes Books

Between Sand and Stardust by Tina Michele. Are the lifelong bonds of love strong enough to conquer time, distance, and heartache when Haven Thorne and Willa Bennette are given another chance at forever? (978-1-62639-940-2)

Charming the Vicar by Jenny Frame. When magician and atheist Finn Kane seeks refuge in an English village after a spiritual crisis, can local vicar Bridget Claremont restore her faith in life and love? (978-1-63555-029-0)

Data Capture by Jesse J. Thoma. Lola Walker is undercover on the hunt for cybercriminals while trying not to notice the woman who might be perfectly wrong for her for all the right reasons. (978-1-62639-985-3)

Epicurean Delights by Renee Roman. Ariana Marks had no idea a leisure swim would lead to being rescued, in more ways than one, by the charismatic Hudson Frost. (978-1-63555-100-6)

Heart of the Devil by Ali Vali. We know most of Cain and Emma Casey's story, but Heart of the Devil will take you back to where it began one fateful night with a tray loaded with beer. (978-1-63555-045-0)

Known Threat by Kara A. McLeod. When Special Agent Ryan O'Connor reluctantly questions who protects the Secret Service, she learns courage truly is found in unlikely places. Agent O'Connor Series #3 (978-1-63555-132-7)

Seer and the Shield by D. Jackson Leigh. Time is running out for the Dragon Horse Army while two unlikely heroines struggle to put aside their attraction and find a way to stop a deadly cult. Dragon Horse War, Book 3 (978-1-63555-170-9)

The Universe Between Us by Jane C. Esther. Ana Mitchell must make the hardest choice of her life: the promise of new love Jolie Dann on Earth, or a humanity-saving mission to colonize Mars. (978-1-63555-106-8)

Touch by Kris Bryant. Can one touch heal a heart? (978-1-63555-084-9)

A More Perfect Union by Carsen Taite. Major Zoey Granger and DC fixer Rook Daniels risk their reputations for a chance at true love while dealing with a scandal that threatens to rock the military. (978-1-62639-754-5)

Arrival by Gun Brooke. The spaceship *Pathfinder* reaches its passengers' new homeworld where danger lurks in the shadows while Pamas Seclan disembarks and finds unexpected love in young science genius Darmiya Do Voy. (978-1-62639-859-7)

Captain's Choice by VK Powell. Architect Kerstin Anthony's life is going to plan until Bennett Carlyle, the first girl she ever kissed, is assigned to her latest and most important project, a police district substation. (978-1-62639-997-6)

Falling Into Her by Erin Zak. Pam Phillips, widow at the age of forty, meets Kathryn Hawthorne, local Chicago celebrity, and it changes her life forever—in ways she hadn't even considered possible. (978-1-63555-092-4)

Hookin' Up by MJ Williamz. Will Leah get what she needs from casual hookups or will she see the love she desires right in front of her? (978-1-63555-051-1)

King of Thieves by Shea Godfrey. When art thief Casey Marinos meets bounty hunter Finnegan Starkweather, the crimes of the past just might set the stage for a payoff worth more than she ever dreamed possible. (978-1-63555-007-8)

Lucy's Chance by Jackie D. As a serial killer haunts the streets, Lucy tries to stitch up old wounds with her first love in the wake of a small town's rapid descent into chaos. (978-1-63555-027-6)

Right Here, Right Now by Georgia Beers. When Alicia Wright moves into the office next door to Lacey Chamberlain's accounting firm, Lacey is about to find out that sometimes the last person you want is exactly the person you need. (978-1-63555-154-9)

Strictly Need to Know by MB Austin. Covert operator Maji Rios will do whatever she must to complete her mission, but saving a gorgeous stranger from Russian mobsters was not in her plans. (978-1-63555-114-3)

Tailor-Made by Yolanda Wallace. Tailor Grace Henderson doesn't date clients, but when she meets gender-bending model Dakota Lane, she's tempted to throw all the rules out the window. (978-1-63555-081-8)

Time Will Tell by M. Ullrich. With the ability to time travel, Eva Caldwell will have to decide between having it all and erasing it all. (978-1-63555-088-7)

Change in Time by Robyn Nyx. Working in the past is hell on your future. The Extractor series: Book Two. (978-1-62639-880-1)

Love After Hours by Radclyffe. When Gina Antonelli agrees to renovate Carrie Longmire's new house, she doesn't welcome Carrie's overtures at friendship or her own unexpected attraction. A Rivers Community Novel. (978-1-63555-090-0)

Nantucket Rose by CF Frizzell. Maggie Jordan can't wait to convert a historic Nantucket home into a B&B, but doesn't expect to fall for mariner Ellis Chilton, who has more claim to the house than Maggie realizes. (978-1-63555-056-6)

Picture Perfect by Lisa Moreau. Falling in love wasn't supposed to be part of the stakes for Olive and Gabby, rival photographers in the competition of a lifetime. (978-1-62639-975-4)

Set the Stage by Karis Walsh. Actress Emilie Danvers takes the stage again in Ashland, Oregon, little realizing that landscaper Arden Philips is about to offer her a very personal romantic lead role. (978-1-63555-087-0)

Strike a Match by Fiona Riley. When their attempts at matchmaking fizzle out, firefighter Sasha and reluctant millionairess Abby find themselves turning to each other to strike a perfect match. (978-1-62639-999-0)

The Price of Cash by Ashley Bartlett. Cash Braddock is doing her best to keep her business afloat, stay out of jail, and avoid Detective Kallen. It's not working. (978-1-62639-708-8)

Captured Soul by Laydin Michaels. Can Kadence Munroe save the woman she loves from a twisted killer, or will she lose her to a collector of souls? (978-1-62639-915-0)

Under Her Wing by Ronica Black. At Angel's Wings Rescue, dogs are usually the ones saved, but when quiet Kassandra Haden meets outspoken owner Jayden Beaumont, the two stubborn women just might end up saving each other. (978-1-63555-077-1)

Underwater Vibes by Mickey Brent. When Hélène, a translator in Brussels, Belgium, meets Sylvie, a young Greek photographer and swim coach, unsettling feelings hijack Hélène's mind and body—even her poems. (978-1-63555-002-3)

A Date to Die by Anne Laughlin. Someone is killing people close to Detective Kay Adler, who must look to her own troubled past for a suspect. There she finds more than one person seeking revenge against her. (978-1-63555-023-8)

Dawn's New Day by TJ Thomas. Can Dawn Oliver and Cam Cooper, two women who have loved and lost, open their hearts to love again? (978-1-63555-072-6)

Definite Possibility by Maggie Cummings. Sam Miller is just out for good times, but Lucy Weston makes her realize happily ever after is a definite possibility. (978-1-62639-909-9)

Eyes Like Those by Melissa Brayden. Isabel Chase and Taylor Andrews struggle between love and ambition from the writers' room on one of Hollywood's hottest TV shows. (978-1-63555-012-2)

Heart's Orders by Jaycie Morrison. Helen Tucker and Tee Owens escape hardscrabble lives to careers in the Women's Army Corps, but more than their hearts are at risk as friendship blossoms into love. (978-1-63555-073-3)

Hiding Out by Kay Bigelow. Treat Dandridge is unaware that her life is in danger from the murderer who is hunting the woman she's falling in love with, Mickey Heiden. (978-1-62639-983-9)

Omnipotence Enough by Sophia Kell Hagin. Can the tiny tool that abducted war veteran Jamie Gwynmorgan accidentally acquires help her escape an unknown enemy to reclaim her stolen life and the woman she deeply loves? (978-1-63555-037-5)